JOHN HARRIS

THE OLD TRADE
OF KILLING

HOUSE OF
STRATUS

This edition published in 2001 by House of Stratus, an imprint of
House of Stratus Ltd, Thirsk Industrial Park, York Road, Thirsk,
North Yorkshire, YO7 3BX, UK.
Also at: House of Stratus Inc., 2 Neptune Road, Poughkeepsie, NY 12601, USA.

www.houseofstratus.com

Typeset, printed and bound by House of Stratus.

A catalogue record for this book is available from the British Library
and the Library of Congress.

ISBN 0-7551-0229-0

You are learning, between willing and unwilling,
The trade of fighting, the old trade of killing.
Arundell Esdaile

PROLOGUE

Summer 1942

We'd known for weeks that something was coming. We were all old hands by that time and after two years in the desert you developed a sharper ear than most for desert sounds and a keener feeling for military moods; and somehow, in spite of the briefings we'd had to be ready to move on into Libya, we'd all long since guessed that things weren't as they ought to be and that before long the route was going to change to east again towards Egypt and not further west as we'd been told.

We were waiting in a neat little hollow scooped out by the wind, with high sides where you could post a sentry and where you could remain unseen and even light a fire to boil tea. We'd stopped there several nights before, with the heat like an oven and the wind whipping up the surface of the desert in clouds so that we'd bad to do everything with our eyes half closed and our backs to the sand as it had piled in drifts against the wheels of the vehicles.

The land stretched away from us under the full blue of the sky. The coarse gravelly surface beyond the few ridges of dunes where we waited was hard and looked like brown sugar, with clumps of camel-thorn and rock here and there. It was tawny-yellow and dead, though the dunes were sculptured into fabulously beautiful shapes by the wind, and

1

the camel-thorn made a tremulous shadow pattern of sorts where the land was flat.

We'd sat there for what seemed weeks now, tending our weapons and measuring our water in precise drops so that there was always some to spare for the radiators, never once letting up in our vigil, straining our gaze against the glittering light of the desert, watching not only towards our front but also towards our rear as we waited for the tanks to come up and relieve us. We'd laid down beside our vehicles at night in the cooling sand, our ears full of the mutter and rumble of guns to the north, our eyes, prickling for want of sleep, seeing the flicker and flash of distant artillery along the coast and alert all the time for the unexpected geometric shapes against the sky that meant enemy vehicles.

We knew nothing, of course. We'd been told to wait there and it was nobody's job to tell us why. The only news we picked up was from the BBC on the receiver.

Near the coast road, hundreds and hundreds of vehicles had been bumping across the sand for days as the Eighth Army had got itself into motion towards Libya. Nobody had come near us, however, except for a few stray British fighters from the north. Rommel had been taken by surprise. We all knew that. He hadn't even been near his headquarters when the first blows had fallen on his startled troops.

Up there, young men from the Rhine and the Black Forest and the Harz Mountains and the great cities of Hamburg and Berlin and the marshy plains of Prussia waited with jaws clenched and the tense look of agonised concentration, their eyes ringed with exhaustion and lack of sleep, knowing their lives depended on the attention they'd paid to detail. As we'd done more than once, they were watching the approaching line of shell-flashes and ducking at the whirring stones and shell-splinters, biting their lips and clenching their fingers until their nails dug into their palms, praying all the time that the next lump of shattered flesh wouldn't be their own.

'Think Tobruk's been relieved, sir?' the wireless operator asked, looking up at me.

I shrugged and he went on, wishfully, voicing the thoughts of us all. 'It's about time,' he said. 'If they've done it right, it ought to be a piece of cake.'

I nodded, saying nothing, but missing nothing either. I was still hardly more than a boy at the time, desperately young to be leading a group of men like these with their deadly weapons and the dust-covered vehicles in which they had learned to live. But, like so many more of my age, I'd acquired a precise consideration for every precaution, a care that belonged to someone older in years than I was, that must have made them somehow trust me, so although they called me 'Pat' or even 'Son' to my face, they showed a surprising respect for the two pips on the shoulder of my oil-stained bush-jacket.

I had all the bad hats of the Group with me, I knew, and I sometimes stopped to wonder why I was stuck with them. The Colonel had once encouraged me by saying, 'It's the bad hats who fight best when things are sticky,' and to a certain extent he was right, but it didn't make life any easier between the fighting.

I'd always assumed it was because I was the youngest officer in the outfit and that nobody else would have them, but, curiously, in spite of barely having got rid of the down on my cheeks, I'd never had much trouble with them.

In my sentimental moods I liked to think it was because I was a good officer, because I considered their comfort and took care of their safety, but in my heart of hearts I knew it was less of my doing than that of Morena, my sergeant mechanic, a hard, square-faced regular with a tough, lean body, who never smiled much and had been in the habit of mothering me ever since I'd first arrived as a dewy-eyed second lieutenant just out from England.

I'd learned a lot since then, but Morena still managed to drop his hints on what I should do, just as he always had in the first days, saving me from embarrassment or disaster, his tips always arriving just when I was most doubtful. It was Morena who'd chosen our present position in the hollow, discovering it with the instinct of an old desert fighter and dropping his suggestion that we halt in such a way that for a time I'd almost believed I'd found it myself. Morena would have been a good officer if he hadn't been such a good sergeant. Though I'd learned how to run my little party, I still knew where its strength lay and who it was that held it together, because they were a tough enough crew to require someone just that little bit harder than *they* were.

Nimmo, for instance, my corporal: none of us knew much about Nimmo apart from the fact that he'd been at one of the great public schools and that he could have been a captain or even a major if he hadn't been such a trouble-maker, because he'd got twice the flair for it most of the time than I had. He had the background and the instincts, and with that flaming red hair and those handsome features of his, all it required to make a leader. As it was, however, he couldn't even keep the stripes on his arm for more than six months at a time. He was a lot older than I was and had a faintly contemptuous attitude towards me, because in spite of the pips on my shoulder, I was still the youngster of the party.

He was always on his own, the only one among us, even including me, who didn't have a nickname. Even Morena, with his black hair and dark Spanish eyes, was 'Wop', a term that covered all Latin races in the same way that 'Wog' covered all coloured races, but in spite of being an artist of sorts, a fact that would have got anyone else called 'Raphael' or 'Rembrandt' or something like that, Nimmo had always been just 'Jimmy' – Jimmy Nimmo, an odd clownish name that went so incongruously with his background and accent. Perhaps it was because somehow he never showed much affection towards any of the others and never asked it for himself. His was a sardonic manner and it was one of his jokes to carry a cheque-book around with him wherever he went and get people to cash dud cheques for him. He regarded it as rather a game, and there were always plenty of strangers around in the desert who could be impressed with a cheque-book handled with confidence.

Then there was Leach, six-foot-four and sixteen stone, an arch-scrounger who was inevitably known as 'Tiny', an uncertain figure of sudden moods, sullen tempers and rocky steadiness in battle, a man whose greatest delight was to slave all day with a shovel or lift heavy equipment that normally took two men to handle, showing off his strength and willing to dig anyone's slit trench just for the pleasure of using his muscles. And Houston, with the clipped accents of Carlisle, whose chief interests at all times were women and seeing that the tea was brewing; and pipe-smoking Gester, who'd been a Pole when there'd been a Poland and whose one joy in life was to kill Germans; and Bummer Ward, who got his name from the fact that he was always short of money and was constantly trying to wheedle it out of others; and Morris, who liked to read poetry in his spare time – and was tough enough to get away with it; and Smollett and Pike and a few more.

It was still a matter of wonder to me that such men would accept directions without question from me, Patrick Alan Doyle, until recently only a prefect at school. Usually, I put it down to the fact that I was simply part of the Group, and they'd been in the desert long enough to cherish their own kind.

They were all tough old-timers, a special breed of men with sun-dried, desert-wise faces who could remain shirtless and capless even under the burnished sun. They were burnt an Arab brown and marked with months of desert sores. Their rations and cigarettes and their hot sweet tea were all that mattered to them, and they were contemptuous of anyone whose base was nearer to Cairo than theirs.

There were a few beards among them and one or two Arab head-dresses – the most gorgeous of all inevitably that of Houston, who was a great man for the girls – worn mostly out of open and undiluted affection, because they looked good when they got among more conventional troops. They had learned to live easily in the desert and were untouched by the changing fortunes of war. England had long since been forgotten, because none of them from the first day they'd left it had ever expected to see it again, and even Cairo and Alex were only somewhere to go for a break. One of the deserted beaches to the north served them just as well for a weekend off.

They always had one eye squinting cynically at the brassy bowl of the sky for the sudden gleam of wings and one ear always cocked for the thud-thud of guns or the clatter of tank tracks in the silence. They had learned to ignore all shooting unless it was immediately dangerous, but when it was they leapt unhesitatingly and instinctively for the right kind of cover. They cursed constantly, using the same monotonous word for everything – at the enemy, the vehicles and me, but curiously always with a strange sort of warmth, because they were all – the enemy, the vehicles and me – sharing their lot. That was the point. We were all in it together, and it bred a strange sort of oneness that completely overrode rank. Nobody appeared to show anybody else any respect at all, but underlying all the chaffing there was an immense regard for each other, bred of interdependence and the knowledge that their companions were all experts in their own way.

In spite of the harsh comments in the 'Conduct' column of their files, I thought the world of them and I'd fought tooth and nail more than once against the Provost people when one of them had been in trouble.

The muttering that had been going on for days swelled up again that night and there were those bright flickerings in the north once more, and the sullen rumble of guns, with the occasional thud-thud-thud of nearer firing. Then the next day it seemed to die away to nothing again and for a while there was a lull, and with our sharp sense of desert fighting we knew that this was the crucial moment, after which the battle would begin to move swiftly – east or west. Always it had followed the same pattern – first, the thin rods of wireless antennae coming over the horizon and then the tanks, jinking and swaying as they cut between the patches of camel-thorn, and men running as the bullets and cannon shells traced pathways across the stony floor of the desert, whining and whistling and tumbling end-over-end as they came to the limit of their flight. It was always the heavy blow, followed by confused fighting, then a frantic haring across the desert, with one side or the other in hot pursuit.

It was anybody's guess which way we'd go this time, but we all had our private views as we found ourselves waiting with our nerves on edge for what was going to happen next. From what we could pick up from the radio receiver, it seemed that both sides had had a pretty severe mauling, but the British attack had not been as successful as had been expected, and it stuck out a mile that something else was going to happen before long, so that we hung on tensely, not speaking much, going about our work silently. Then we noticed that the German R/T traffic, picked up by the worried wireless operator with his head down over his set, had begun to grow, and we could hear the fire of the 88s beginning to build up in the west, and the following night we heard the far-distant growling of heavy engines in low gear that spoke of large numbers of tanks on the move.

'Hope to Christ it's our lot,' Leach said.

Houston looked up from the book of strip-pictures that he'd acquired in Alex and grinned. 'It's ours all right,' he reassured him. 'It's a move the General thought up in his bath.'

There'd been a lot of confident talk, of course, in the days before we'd left base, especially from the briskly moustachioed and laundered gentry who came up from headquarters to brief us. 'It'll be a walk-over this time,' they'd told us. 'There's nothing to it.'

But the people who lived at headquarters were always more optimistic than the men who lived in the desert – especially people like us who were the antennae of the army, the listening posts, the long-range groups way ahead of the main body – the men who lived all the time in slit trenches and bivouac tents and in the backs of lorries and jeeps out in the baking sand, covered with dust, the lines on their faces deepening more with every day they stared at the setting sun. And it was too quiet suddenly, and we were all nervous.

Houston was talking to Nimmo and Leach now, his voice a little louder than it should have been, and I could hear it plainly from where I sat with my maps.

'...that belly dancer in that bar where we had the kus-kus,' he was saying. 'The one who used to pick up pennies between her tits. Remember when Gester heated up half a dollar for her on the top of his pipe. Jesus, that made her jump!'

The laughter came a little too readily and a little too loudly and died a little too quickly, and very soon they were all silent again, waiting, watching, listening. They had begun to guess what was happening up in the north and they didn't like it very much. We were too isolated, too much out on a limb.

While the army probed beyond the 'boxes' and the dumps, seeking a gap through the suddenly stiffening ranks of the enemy, we were on our own, unsupported, our position unknown to the RAF who might have kept an eye on us, watching the end of the wire the Italians had erected from

Siwa to Sollum to keep the Senussi out of Libya, with the dunes of the Great Sand Sea on our left, the dust blowing off the crests like smoke from a set of factory chimneys. There'd been a little muttering over the mugs of tea at the thought of it, and they'd kept their eyes on my face, looking for signs one way or the other, but, young as I was I'd learned long since to keep my feelings hidden.

To the men around the lorries, our stay there seemed pointless, an isolated post out in the desert, but I knew we'd been sent there because Intelligence had it that any counter-attack by the Germans would come along the coast while the Italians would make a breakthrough in the south. 'Winforce' was to the north of us, with Grant tanks, then the armoured cars on our right watching towards the west; and finally us – three jeeps and a couple of three-tonners – spot-ball, right on the end of the line, on the lookout for hit-and-run Mark IVs.

When I'd lagered the vehicles in the hollow and watched them being immobilised I'd known that, to all intents and purposes, I was safe from all but air attack. So long as we remained alert we were well able to withdraw in good time before the enemy could come down on us. Morena had chosen his spot well and it was just a matter of remaining wide-awake.

But on my right flank was Qalam, a flea-bitten Arab village we'd passed through some days before – full of flies and grunting camels and surly obsequious men and women outside the tumbledown houses – and on my left was the Qalam Depression. It was a great empty hollow in the desert, running roughly from north-west to south-east, a bare sandy bowl below the floor of the desert, surrounded by high limestone cliffs and littered with rocks, and broken up here and there by rock falls or small wadis. One of the wadis led off to the ruined village of Qatu and at the other end of the track that ran through the Depression was Qahait, where several hundred Arab fighting men were waiting with

9

machine guns and mortars and a few lorries handed over by the High Command. Any big movement round the end of the wire would have to pass by the Depression, and someone in Intelligence, trying to do a Lawrence of Arabia, had persuaded Sheikh Ghad of the Qalami to come in against the Axis with the promise of further support from a couple of cousins and all their followers, too. They'd been trained up by the Australians and, on paper, looked useful, but it was an unexpected arrangement, because, for the most part, the war in North Africa was a private affair between the Allies and the Axis, with the Arabs lifting anything that was not locked up or pegged down. But Ghad had been educated in England and he didn't like the Italians, and he was still young enough to enjoy a bit of fun. To all intents and purposes, the set-up was sound, but to me it was an uneasy situation because I wasn't sure how much I could trust Sheikh Ghad. I'd been far less impressed with him than the man who'd come up from headquarters in the Delta to swear to his trustworthiness.

But there wasn't much I could do about it. I'd been told to wait there and that I'd receive my instructions when it was time for them to be sent. There were others behind me, it seemed, doing the same thing.

Trying hard to look unconcerned, I walked across to where the wireless operator was listening to the muted bleep-bleep of the set.

'Traffic's still growing,' he said in answer to my raised eyebrows. 'It's getting bloody crowded, in fact.'

'I hope it won't get so crowded they can't contact us,' I commented.

Almost as I spoke, the set began to bleep louder and the operator dropped the paper-backed novel he'd been browsing through, dog-eared from weeks of being kicked around inside a jeep, and reached for his pencil.

'Us,' he said shortly.

From time to time he tapped his key in response, then his hand flickered as he sent off the letters that indicated the signal had been received and understood.

We decoded the message together in the shade of the little shelter we'd rigged up, and the wireless operator looked round at me, puzzled. I said nothing, though, and, picking up the sheet of buff paper, I stepped into the glare of the sun.

Morena was standing alongside a sand-coloured jeep with 'Daisy' painted on the radiator. 'Daisy' was Morena's wife and it was something of a joke that he should carry her name about with him wherever he went. He had his head in the bonnet, tinkering with the petrol pump, and as he heard the shuffle of my feet in the sand, he looked up, lifted his head and slammed the bonnet down.

'Trouble?' I asked.

Morena shook his head, his face expressionless. 'No,' he said shortly. 'Just making sure we don't get any. That's all.'

I flicked the message in my hand. 'Visitors,' I said. 'We're expecting visitors.'

A flicker of concern crossed Morena's face. 'Jerry?' he asked.

I shook my head. 'No. Our lot.'

He raised his eyes. 'When?' he asked.

'He's nearly here.'

'Is that why we've been waiting here?' he asked, and I nodded.

'End of the line,' I said. 'He's been passed on from one group to the next. We're the last.'

'Must be someone important. Who is it? Churchill?'

The bleeping from the wireless had died away now and it had become quiet again, so quiet we both seemed to hold our breath at the silence. The shadows were lengthening beyond the dunes as the sun sank lower, and the brilliant whites and silvers of midday were taking on a golden glow now; and

11

over the whole wide desert beyond the hollow there was no hint of movement.

Morena made an awkward, half-embarrassed gesture towards it. 'Gets you, doesn't it?' he said.

'I'll miss it when it's all over,' I agreed.

'Often thought I'd like to come back. Have a look round. Appreciate it without worrying whether a Stuka'll be up in the sun.'

I nodded. 'It'll be nice to sleep at nights,' I said, 'without having one ear open all the time for tank tracks.'

After two years we were all beginning to grow weary of the desert, with the sucked-in cheeks and dark rings under the eyes that you got from too many nights of half-sleep or sitting up watching the north for lights or the hum of engines.

Morena offered me a cigarette and we leaned against the jeep, idly studying a map I'd produced – something we'd got into the habit of doing in our spare moments, so that it was firmly imprinted on the mind for the times when we might not have the chance to get it out and look at it. Behind us were the trucks, surrounded by mines that could take care of any intruders. In the hollow, Leach, absurd in Ward's shorts which he'd 'borrowed' and forgotten to give back, was lifting the mortar about as though it were a featherweight, bulky as a brewery horse as he bent over it. Once, for a joke, in the 'Build' column of his identity form I'd written 'Colossal' – a touch of humour authority had never appreciated, and which had been promptly changed to 'Large'. He was slow and awkward, with stiff, humourless jokes that nobody laughed at, which could change in a moment to surly ill temper.

Houston, his bootlaces trailing, handed him a cup of tea – a ragbag sparrow of a soldier whose socks always needed darning or whose shirt was always torn, a dry little man with a sharp humour who was completely unaware of his sloppiness.

It was always Houston who was first out of the lorry and filling the two halves of the old petrol-tin stove we carried – one half containing the sand on to which he poured petrol, the other half the water for the tea. Always it seemed to be Houston's job to provide the tea, and, though he regularly lost his equipment and even other people's, the one thing he never lost track of was the tea. He was a thin, slightly built little man with a big nose that stuck out from under the Arab head-dress he wore.

'Have a glass of aphrodisiac,' he said as he passed over the mug. 'Vintage, 'forty-two. Chilled, but not iced.'

Leach stared at him, uncomprehending, his mind heaving over slowly.

'You being funny?' he asked.

'For Christ's sake, yes!' Houston said waspishly, edgy with waiting. 'But don't strain your brain, mate, I'll write it down and you can get out your Child's Guide To Funny Bits and look it up.'

'One of these days I'll flatten you,' Leach growled, but Houston merely grinned and skipped away, conscious of his own superiority in spite of Leach's strength.

I watched them moving around among the other men going about their business, and I was still staring at them when I saw the sentry we'd posted suddenly retreat from the lip of the dune above and come down towards us, his feet kicking up puffs of sand as he scrambled down to the hollow. Immediately everyone stopped what he was doing and hands began to reach out towards weapons.

The sentry stopped in front of me, cocking a thumb towards the east. 'Jeep, it looks like,' he said shortly, and I turned and followed him up the slope.

As I went, I saw Ward climb into the truck behind the Bren and move the cocking handle, and Houston bending quickly to lace up his boots. Morena moved among the others, not speaking, simply indicating things with little flicks of his fingers. Everyone knew what he meant. They'd all done everything before. Houston stood ready to kick sand over the fire, and Leach bent over the mortar, his heavy face set, ready to grab it up and run with it if it were needed. The wireless operator looked up as Nimmo tapped his shoulder, and kept his eyes on me, waiting for any signal that might spell danger and the need to send out an urgent message to the north.

But the dust-cloud that the sentry had seen *was* a jeep and I could see the Pay Corps sign on it through my binoculars. The man driving it was a captain with the sort of guardee moustache all officers in the desert liked to cultivate in those days. There was an Arab wearing khaki trousers and an Arab head-dress and cloak in the front of the vehicle with him, and in the rear two Military Policemen.

I gave the washout sign to Morena and he turned and gestured with the flat of his hand. Leach's straining muscles relaxed and Houston bent and poured the dregs of the tea into his mug. Nimmo lit a cigarette and the wireless operator's tense expression vanished as he picked up his paper-backed book again and started thumbing through it.

The Pay Corps captain was a Welshman with a high voice, and I sent out Nimmo to guide him through the mines. There were a few jeers at the Redcaps because all soldiers jeer at Military Police on principle, and the men with me had been in the desert too long to have much love for anybody but their own friends.

'Oh, Mother, look!' Houston indicated the smart uniforms. 'Soldiers! Real ones! Is it right, mate,' he asked one of the Redcaps, 'that you lot take a bath once a month whether you need it or not?'

There was a guffaw, and one of the Redcaps, a young sergeant who looked as though he'd just left school, blushed and made an embarrassed hostile gesture.

'You want to watch out, chum,' he said. 'I know you. I've seen you before, back at base.'

'Not me,' Houston said innocently. 'I don't know you from a bar of soap.'

The moustached captain was staring round him with narrowed eyes, obviously disapproving of the banter, frowning at the dusty men in the hollow, all of them bleached to the colour of the fine sand.

'Christ, it's like a bloody fortress in here,' he said.

'We need a lot of guns,' Nimmo said coolly, his eyes glowing with the instinctive dislike of the front-line soldier for the base operator. 'We do a lot of fighting.'

The captain stared at him for a second as though he weren't in the habit of talking casually to corporals, then he turned to me.

'They told me I'd find you here,' he said. 'They said you'd see me before I saw you.' He glanced at Nimmo. 'You did,' he added. 'It's a good job we weren't Jerries.'

'It's a knack,' Nimmo said insolently. 'You learn it when you live out here all the time.'

The captain checked his map references with me and gestured towards the south.

'How long to Qahait?' he asked.

'Best part of a day,' I said.

'Christ, as much as that?'

'Straight on and through the Depression. It's a village at the other end to the south. Bit of a dump, but you'll find it all right. The road leads straight through to it.'

The captain grinned. 'Sheikh Ghad's going to be glad to see me,' he said. 'I've got their pay. In coin.'

'In coin?'

'Pound notes wouldn't be much good to Sheikh Ghad, would they? It's in sovereigns. Ten thousand of 'em, each worth three quid a time – silver dollars, napoleons and maria theresas, to say nothing of a bloody great bagful of diamonds.'

15

I saw Nimmo's eyes flicker, glowing quickly and full of evil, then he caught the captain's stare on him and turned away and lit a cigarette.

'Nice and portable,' the captain went on. 'And legal tender anywhere. Ghad's promised a lot more men later, so there had to be plenty of it. Fraser fixed it. You've met Fraser?'

I nodded. Yes, I'd met Fraser, a spare-looking New Zealander who'd been an archaeologist like Lawrence and had spent all the war so far doing intelligence work.

'There's enough to buy all the Arabs in Libya and Cyrenaica,' the Pay Corps captain went on. 'They drove a hard bargain. I just hope it does some good. Rumour has it that Ghad'll just bolt for the south as soon as he's got it. They're saying in Cairo that Fraser's pulled a boner this time and picked a wrong 'un. Still' – he shrugged – 'that's not my affair. My job's just to see that we deliver it intact to him.'

He patted the iron box in the back of the jeep between the MPs.

'Glad to get rid of it,' he said. 'Bit of a responsibility. That's why we're travelling light. So nobody'll notice us. Hope to meet Ghad tomorrow.'

'Hope you're lucky,' I said.

'Why shouldn't I be?'

I jerked my head towards the north. 'That lot,' I said. 'The chances are it'll move down here before long.'

The Welsh captain grinned. 'Don't let *that* worry you,' he said. 'They're moving *west*. They say in Cairo that this time it's for keeps.'

'I hope they're right.'

'Don't you think they are?'

'Doesn't feel right. We shouldn't be here.'

He slapped me on the shoulder. 'You've got the heebie-jeebies, son,' he said. 'Been out in the desert too long.'

I didn't reply. I had my own way of feeling things, just as the men around me had, and it came as no surprise to hear that the frailer flowers in Cairo felt differently.

The Welshman didn't stay long, just long enough to share some of the greasy bully beef and tepid peaches we lived on, just long enough for the Military Policemen to have their legs pulled unmercifully by the hardened set of villains round the fire, then they climbed back into the jeep, watched by the half-circle of dusty, sun-bleached men.

'Qalam, here we come,' the Welshman said, with a forced attempt at good humour.

His smile wasn't reflected in the bearded faces around him.

'Hope you enjoy it,' Houston muttered. 'Send a signal, operator. Here come the soldiers, weary and footsore from doing nothing by numbers.'

The captain heard him and his face went taut, but he had realised by now that he wasn't talking to base soldiers and, embarrassed by the silence after Houston's remark, he made a valiant effort to be one of them, going on with dogged cheerfulness that was so artificial it was painful.

'They reckon the Lost City's down in the Depression somewhere,' he said.

'Which lost city?' I asked.

'You know – the one they always talk about. People have seen it. But only people who were lost themselves. They were always coming back to look for it but they never found it.'

'How'd they know it was lost, then?' Nimmo asked disconcertingly.

The captain frowned, but went on gamely. 'They say it's got white walls and a door shaped like a bird. They say it's full of sleeping people.'

Nobody showed any enthusiasm for the story and, his voice trailing away lamely, he let in the clutch hurriedly and set off through the mines, guided by Nimmo.

'He's got it wrong,' Houston said in a solemn voice, staring after them. 'He's thinking of Sleeping Beauty.'

We stood on top of the dune watching the jeep move away, then, as the Welshman waved and began to accelerate, Nimmo turned and came back.

'Hope they enjoy the trip,' he said.

Nobody moved for a long time, all eyes watching the disappearing jeep as though it were the last frail link with civilisation. Nimmo lit a cigarette with that slow deliberate manner of his, his eyes squinting towards the west and the disappearing cloud of dust. Houston, his face shaded by the linen folds of the head-dress he wore, sipped a mug of cold tea. Leach stood like a great rock between them, his craggy face expressionless, two great hands like shovels hanging down by his sides.

The jeep had been gone some time when we heard the Messerschmitts go over. We saw them first high in the brassy blue of the sky like tiny silver fishes, then the glint of the sun on them as they banked and came down.

'They've seen something,' Nimmo said in a flat unhurried voice, staring upwards, the sun glinting on the red-gold of his hair.

Nobody said anything. We'd taken all the precautions of camouflage, even to tying clumps of scrub to the vehicles and smearing the windscreens with oil and scattering dust across them to stop them reflecting the sun, and nobody moved. Nobody ever moved until we were certain.

Then we saw the Messerschmitts were going overhead, slightly towards the south, towards some point beyond us, and we all drew breath again as they disappeared beyond the curve of the ground.

Morena's face was hard, a set of square, flat planes in the sunshine.

'What are *they* after?' he asked, in that unemotional stolid way he had.

'Looking for the ice-cream man,' Houston said. 'They heard his bell.'

Leach stared at him, his eyes puzzled, and he started to say something. But then he changed his mind and stared up with the others at the disappearing aircraft.

'Haven't seen Messerschmitts prowling about like that down here for some time,' Nimmo commented. 'Something's in the wind.'

'Probably after some soft-skinned stuff down there,' I said. 'We've probably been using Qahait as a dump. Perhaps they've seen 'em. Perhaps they've seen Sheikh Ghad.'

The Messerschmitts were out of sight when we heard the faint rattle of guns and the thump-thump-thump of bombs and felt the echo of the blast in the air, as though someone kept slamming a door.

'Somebody's bought it,' Morena grunted.

That evening we got the expected messages from the north. At first they were only rumours, springing from the wireless operator, with his secret knowledge of the private means of wireless operators all the world over, of sending messages that headquarters never learned of. Somebody had made the mistake of splitting up the armour, it seemed, so that the superior numbers of the British had been cancelled out, and it had been found that the fifty- and seventy-five-millimetre guns of the Germans had a greater range, and suddenly, instead of being on the defensive, Rommel was attacking and the retreat was on.

'Oh, well,' Houston said, with the philosophical disgust of the private for the staff. 'That'll be another general they'll have to pull the plug on. Bang goes my leave and all that beer and skittles and all those white silken bodies on black silken sheets I was dreaming of dallying with.'

JOHN HARRIS

Sollum was choked with vehicles, we heard, as the frightened men headed hot-foot for Egypt. The German attack on the British line had cut off 150 Brigade 'box' and the German transports were streaming through the gaps to replenish their tanks, and what Houston called 'The Gazala Gallop' was in full swing. Tobruk was cut off again and there was black smoke billowing from the blazing oil tanks and spreading like a pall across the sky. The Eighth Army was pulling back again.

The armoured brigades had taken a terrific punishment from the German 88s and all over the desert there were circles of burnt-out vehicles and broken weapons and littered bodies half covered with sand, and long columns of exhausted prisoners streaming towards the west. Petrol and oil and ammunition were going up in flames and, back towards the Delta, they were burning code-books and maps; and the dusty sand, criss-crossed everywhere by tracks, was smeared with blood.

The messages we received, however, were short and told us none of this, but we all knew what they meant. We'd seen it all before – the men crouched in ditches, their mouths open and yelling as they stared up at the sheen of silver wings above them and the bombs coming down like bunches of grapes out of the sky; and the transport pulled off the road in long straggles, tanks canted sideways, the crews staring with strained eyes towards the west; and the Military Police trying to sort some order out of the chaos to keep the vehicles moving so that they couldn't be caught by the dive bombers and smashed while they were huddled in great groups, perfect targets for the enemy.

'That's it, then,' Morena said, apparently unmoved by the news of the disaster.

' 'Ere's to the next time,' Leach said with heavy humour. 'They know about as much about war in Cairo as my backside.'

' "What did you do in the war, Daddy?" ' Houston said with a wry grin. ' "I picked up the clangers, son, that the general dropped. They didn't know the difference between a bear's arse and the Taj Mahal." '

There were a few more jeers as they began to collect their belongings and a few more uncomplimentary things said about the staff. But there was no panic. We all knew the drill. It was hell-for-leather for Cairo again now, until the army could find somewhere to make a stand. We'd been doing it on and off, backwards and forwards, for two years, and nobody was very alarmed. We didn't foresee any difficulties.

The word was going round rapidly, and I saw Houston kick the sand over the fire and empty the contents of the home-made stove and pick up his beloved hot-water container. Leach grasped the mortar and prepared to heave it back into the lorry, brushing aside Gester as he moved forward to help.

'When do we leave?' Morena asked.

I flicked the message paper. 'We don't,' I said. 'We stay here. We have to wait for the Paymaster to come back.'

Morena lifted his eyebrows but said nothing, and I cocked a thumb towards the north.

'With things going wrong,' I said, 'he might not make it. He might have to come back. We've got to see that he does.'

Morena nodded.

'He's got a lot of money with him,' I explained.

He nodded again and walked across to the others. His hands jerked once or twice, because Morena never wasted words, and I saw Houston look round at him and put down the little stove, and Leach, his thick legs apart, slowly lower the mortar to the ground, staring at Gester as he did so. Nimmo, who had climbed into the driving seat of his jeep, slowly climbed out again and reached for a cigarette.

Then Houston's voice came across the silence as he straightened up. 'Don't look so bloody egg-bound, Tiny,' he said to Leach. 'It should be an honour to die for England, home and beauty.'

Leach stared, uncomprehending.

For a moment Houston stared back at him, then he scowled, the nervousness showing in his manner. 'Oh, up your kilt, Leach,' he growled sourly, and shuffled off with dragging feet to replenish the tea container.

We sat there until dark, smoking in the shadow of the trucks and talking in undertones. Someone was singing softly – 'I've Got Spurs That Jingle-Jangle-Jingle' – then Morena interrupted softly on his mouth-organ with 'The Strawberry Blonde' and 'Waltzing Matilda', songs we'd been singing for months because we never managed to hear many others. The singer stopped and they all listened to Morena. A typical regular, his mouth-organ was part of his equipment, and, sergeant or no sergeant, he'd played it up and down the desert ever since 1939.

After a while I walked to the top of the dunes. Houston, who was supposed to be on lookout, was crouching in a hollow looking for his cigarettes, and angrily I tore a strip off him.

'What the bloody hell's the point of being up here if you don't use your eyes?' I snapped.

Houston didn't seem to mind the reprimand. 'Don't worry,' he said. 'I can hit a man at a mile.' He patted his rifle.

'That's a lot of bloody good if you don't see him before he sees you.'

Houston shrugged and we stared together over the empty desert. I was still simmering with rage.

'Expect Jerry's out there looking this way,' Houston said unexpectedly. 'Just like us. Doesn't matter whether you've got a desert rat or a broken palm on your lorry. You're all in the same boat.'

I looked at him quickly. Houston was a crafty little man skilled at drawing attention away from his own failings, and I got to my feet quickly, and walked back down the slope.

They were all beginning to fish blankets out of the vehicles now, all except Leach, who took pleasure in living hard. He had scraped a hole for his hip and had laid down uncovered, his head near the wheel of his vehicle.

I stretched out on the sand, thinking, half asleep but with my brain still alert for the clatter of tank tracks. My mind refused to leave the problem of the Paymaster and, as the stars began to prick the sky, cold and clear and aloof, I began to suspect that something had gone wrong somewhere and, with the knowledge, the old edgy feeling of the desert began to creep over me.

I'd waited for daylight many a time like this, staring at the eastern horizon until it took on the pale greenish-yellow tinge of dawn, watching for the blurred contours of low hills to emerge against the brightening heavens, while the imperceptible increase in the light and then the advancing sun gave the country form and colour, breaking it into humps and ridges and grass-crested dunes. I'd held my breath many a time in the utter silence, aware of the absence of any sound or movement, always startled and surprised by its immensity, until it was broken in the first hint of daylight by a drowsy bird-call from a grass tuft in a valley somewhere, a sleepy query piped from a patch of camel-thorn, and the fluttering of movement in the stillness as some tiny creature stirred in the sheltering twigs.

I'd half expected the Paymaster's jeep to appear over the horizon soon after sun-up the next morning, but the desert remained empty and bare and glaringly white, its colour reflecting in the flat planes on the rocky face of Leach who was crouched on top of the dunes staring to the west. There was a muttering round the fire among the lorries and Nimmo's voice raised in protest against Houston's cooking –

'You've burnt the bloody bacon again!' – and a brief argument as someone accused him of swiping his washing water.

Nobody said anything to me, however, and I said nothing to anyone else, but by mid-morning I was beginning to grow worried.

Morena seemed to sense what was in my mind.

'Thinking of sending off a jeep?' he asked. 'Just for a look?'

It was phrased like a question, but I knew it was Morena's tactful way of suggesting that what I had in mind was a sound idea, and I nodded, grateful for the tip.

'Think we'd better send two?' Morena went on. 'To cover the tracks.'

'Nimmo,' I said. 'He's a good corporal. He can take Houston and Leach and Ward.'

Morena hitched up his shorts and half turned.

'You'd better go with the other jeep, Wop,' I said. 'I'll stay behind here.'

Morena nodded. 'OK,' he said.

They began to throw the gear into the jeeps and they were ready quickly, though, as usual, Houston held them up when he couldn't find his gear.

'Jump to it, you bloody idler,' Morena snapped, and Houston nodded, grabbed his kit and, with his book of strip-pictures sticking from his pocket, scuttled for the jeep, his head-dress cock-eyed and flapping in his face.

'That's it,' he said as he climbed aboard. 'If you've got anything unpleasant to say, say it unpleasantly.' He flailed with his arms to make room for himself. 'Leach, you bastard,' he ended. 'You've got my belt on!'

They disappeared over the horizon, trailing a cloud of dust, and the rest of us made tea and waited, all of us uneasy and expecting the Mark IVs to appear over the rise to the west at any moment.

By mid-afternoon, with the hollow breathless in the heat, I began to be worried that I'd lost Morena, too, and I was beginning to wonder how it would look in my report – eight men gone, and two jeeps, to say nothing of the Paymaster. I moved uneasily round the hollow, making sure that everything was ready for a quick getaway, nervous and unhappy and weighing up the chances, certain that something had gone sadly wrong. Food was growing short now and water was only for the radiators, and everyone had begun to suspect that the staff had boobed again.

'The bastards have forgotten us,' I heard one of the men mutter by the fire. 'I bet nobody knows we're still here.'

Privately, I was inclined to agree with him. All my instincts told me he was right. The whole business seemed to have gone haywire, and now, with two jeeps missing, I was wondering how much longer I dared hang on. Then, with the desert turning to beaten gold as the heat began to go out of the day, I saw them returning, one behind the other, coming out of the sun; two jeeps only, covered with dust, their passengers wearied, the sweat on their faces coated in a grey-yellow mask of muddy dust that cracked as they grinned wearily at us.

They came to a stop alongside us, the heat from the engines striking at my face as I walked forward.

'Where's the Paymaster?' I asked.

'The silly bastard got himself clobbered,' Nimmo said. 'Trust the Pay Corps. We found them all right – right on track for Qahait. In the Depression. Morena found a place to hole up at the top where he could watch the desert and he sent the rest of us down to look for 'em while he prepared to take on Rommel if he came. We found 'em.'

'Where?'

'Just at the bottom of the Depression. They were dead.'

'All of 'em?'

'Every last one of 'em. The Paymaster, two Redcaps and one Arab. It must have been those Messerschmitts. They'd hit the petrol tank and it had brewed up.'

The death of the Paymaster didn't mean much to me. I'd grown too used to finding burned-out wrecks with untidy bundles hanging half out of the seats or lying in a huddle alongside to have any sentiment about death. The face of the man you found was never the face of the man you'd swapped yarns with or shared a mug of tea with. You just did what you could to bury him, putting him as far down as the rocky earth would allow and piling stones on top to keep out the wild dogs. After that it was just a question of 'Do you remember old So-and-so?' over a beer when some anecdote brought up the dead man's memory.

'You brought their – equipment back?' I chose the word carefully because not many of the men with me had over- heard the Paymaster's enthusiastic and indiscreet remarks about the bullion he'd been carrying for Sheikh Ghad.

Nimmo gave me a sharp look. *He'd* heard and he knew what I was talking about.

'There wasn't any,' he said. 'It had gone.'

'What about the till? Didn't you bring the till?'

'There wasn't any till.'

'Christ, it filled the back of the jeep!'

'Well, it had gone. Ask anybody.'

I saw Houston nodding, and Leach and Ward just behind solemnly agreeing, their faces blank. Morena stood to one side, listening, his face expressionless.

'Must have been those black bastards from Qahait,' Nimmo went on. 'They must have moved up the Depression and they must have got there before we did.'

'Did you see 'em?'

'Not a sign.'

I glanced towards the north. Up there the desert was a scrap-heap of burned-out wreckage and there was a steady stream of traffic flowing back under a hanging dust-haze towards Egypt. The Naafis were going up in orange flowers of flame and the field cashiers and the padres and the correspondents and all those other assorted hangers-on who could please themselves when to leave had long since vanished. The tents were coming down and the desert was littered with drifting scraps of torn and charred paper; and the thin-skinned vehicles were moving back beyond the check-point, hiss-hissing as they passed, lurching and rolling, gleaming ghostly in the moonlight as the endless procession went on day and night, dim faces staring ahead; while the Grants drew off the road, ready to cover the retreat with those big guns of theirs that would only traverse fifteen degrees so that they had to travel in reverse at five miles an hour to get them to bear at all – all there was between Rommel's Mark IVs and Cairo.

'You were a bloody long time,' I said. I was worried sick now and growing more and more nervous, but Nimmo only shrugged.

'We buried them,' he said. 'It wasn't easy. It was rock. Here!' He held out a fistful of identification discs. 'I searched around a bit in case we found the box lying about. Even up the Depression, in case some of those black bastards were still around. We didn't find the box, but we found some pictures. In a cave.'

I looked up angrily. 'You weren't looking for bloody pictures,' I said sharply, still with one eye over my shoulder looking for the Mark IVs. I'd been there too long and I was anxious to get back to the safety of our own lines.

Nimmo grinned at me, untroubled by my anger. 'Take it easy,' he advised. 'We found a place where the bombs had disturbed the rocks. There were a lot of old drawings in there. We might have made an archaeological discovery of some sort. I took some bearings just for safety, then we piled

27

the rocks back and shovelled a lot of sand over 'em. I thought somebody might like to know.'

I stared at him for a long time. Not far away the desert was being pulverised to dust under the thousands of moving wheels and the tramp of thousands of boots, until it was deep and floury and coated the hair and the clothes and caked in crusts on the lips of exhausted men. All the way back to Alex there were bodies lying under blankets and the smell of death and wounds, and the bewildered look of driven animals was on the faces of all the living as they struggled back through the wreckage of an army to where they could form some sort of defence and make a stand. The very thought of it made me jumpy.

My own little party had packed up everything long since and there was nothing left in the hollow now except the empty tins and the ashes of the fire and the churned-up sand. But there was a long way to go and half of Rommel's army was between us and safety.

I half turned, gesturing wearily. Somehow, I felt I hadn't the stomach for it.

'Let's make tracks,' I said. 'We're not playing kiss-in-the-ring. We should have gone three days ago.'

Within ten minutes we were heading east, passing through the derelicts of earlier skirmishes, scouting carefully towards the Delta, one jeep far to the rear watching behind us all the time, another well in front and to the north, on the lookout for Germans.

Sometimes birds flew overhead, part of the great migratory flocks, and occasionally we saw gazelle – small animals which did not drink but sucked up the dew and the moisture from chance shrubs – and once a jerboa from which the Eighth Army had taken its name, a long-legged desert rat that preyed on the exhausted birds that fell to the sand.

But for two days no other living thing, except the humps of vehicles to the north just below the horizon, miraged until they looked like battleships, so that we crept quietly along behind the dunes, uncertain whether they were German or not, and not in the least anxious to find out. We were miles behind the army and, thanks to the orders that had kept us waiting for the Paymaster, in a hopeless position. There was no one to see us home, not even anyone to direct us or tell us how the retreat was going.

When we stopped we crouched exhausted over our mugs of tea, one man sprawled on a ridge of sand staring northwards, the others not talking, their faces drawn and strained, Gester's mouth twisted bitterly at the thought of yet another defeat, Houston moving nervously, not much to offer now in the way of humour. Morena grew more silent by the hour and Leach's heavy face grew more grim. I kept seeing their eyes on me as they muttered, not questioning now, but as though they were praying quietly that I was good enough to get them out of it.

Wondering whose were the half-baked orders that had kept us waiting longer than we ought to have waited, I was half-sick with worry but curiously never afraid, though occasionally we heard firing and at night we saw green and red Very lights. Then, at last, we almost ran flat out into a large group of Italian scout cars – the ones we'd seen beyond the horizon. Fortunately, they seemed more nervous then we were and I decided to bluff it out and we roared down on them, yelling and firing with all we'd got, and trying to kid them there were dozens more vehicles behind us below the horizon.

There was some scattered shooting from them and one of the men in the lorries was hit, then, by the Grace of God, it worked and they shot off in a cloud of dust to the north, while we swung away to the south again for safety, hoping against hope they wouldn't use their radio to set the armour on us.

Finally, we began to get among the wreckage and the dead men and the little crosses with their sad simple messages scrawled in pencil – 'Corporal John Brown, died in action' – and then the date and the regiment, hurriedly set down for the Graves Registration people. After that it was tanks, still smouldering and smelling evilly, their interior fittings dragged out like the entrails of some wounded animal, with mess boxes, toothbrushes and the blankets of the crews scattered about with their little packets of biscuits, water bottles, webbing, mirrors, broken weapons and the photographs of their families.

The one thing I remember about it all was that none of us had much to say. We were all beginning to feel the strain as we bumped and rattled over the rutted ground, knowing the retreat had become a rout and that we'd been left behind – far behind. Then we came across a tank that was still burning, fuming and spluttering with interior explosions, while every now and then Very lights burst through the overhanging coils of black smoke. Even as we passed, its petrol tank crashed open in a sheet of flame.

'Anybody need a light?' Houston asked uneasily.

Morena was a tower of strength. He seemed to be everywhere, supervising everything, advising, correcting, helping, backing me up in everything I decided. One of the jeeps began to conk and he was at it every time we stopped, apparently never eating or pausing for breath. Nimmo, too, didn't let me down, working like a madman with the sand-mats every time a lorry stuck, throwing the gear out as though he were crazy, shouting at the slow-moving Leach and the nervous Houston, whose eyes were always on the north, chivvying Gester and Morris, bullying, cursing, not letting up on any of them for a minute.

All the time, as we went, sometimes swiftly, sometimes laboriously slowly according to the country and the whims of the trailing jeep, we experienced all the spasms of despair, hope and exhilaration that we'd felt a dozen times before as we'd jogged up and down the bare acres of the desert. And all the time, as we went, my mind was nagged with worry over the loss of the Paymaster.

I felt I'd boobed badly, though I knew I'd done all that could have been expected of me. I'd risked my little command to do what I'd been told to do. I'd sent a responsible corporal and a responsible sergeant to find him, while I hung on in the north, waiting to be jumped every minute. But, though they'd found the Paymaster, they'd failed to find what he was carrying with him, which at headquarters would probably be rated more valuable, and therefore I'd failed too, because, in the end, I was the one who was going to carry the can.

Even in my exhaustion, as we lay down at night, watching the sparkling horizon and the moving glows in the sky and listening to the flat thud-thud of guns, it worried me, and during the day, blinded by the glare and squinting at the horizon, it continued to worry me. I was young enough, in spite of my experience, to imagine that it was the end of the road for me. I worried as I posted the sentries and stared at the dusty maps on which I'd marked all the minefields and dumps with laborious care, and as I crouched at night over the glim of a cigarette with Morena, discussing the route in meticulous detail, and the food and the water and the condition of the engines, determined to get everybody back in one piece – just to show the bastards who'd left us behind to stew! – and terrified that I wouldn't.

Once Houston came up to us with a wry face. 'Fixing up the route into the bag?' he asked, and we both jumped on him for his defeatism and gloom, because Morena had by no means given up hope and, in spite of my worry, I certainly hadn't. We'd spent the whole day and the previous night picking our way through Rommel's scattered units, creeping past in the dark, not daring to breathe, or sidling along under the sun, behind the ridges of sand, ready to bolt for the south at the first hostile sign.

'Shut your bloody rattle,' Morena had snapped, and Houston went off, shrugging, outwardly indifferent but inwardly as uneasy as all of us.

Failure still continued to nag at me. I was worried by the desert and by the limping jeep and by the responsibility for the lives of everyone with me. And because there were still times when I felt like an overgrown schoolboy, it was still nagging me when the lone, low-flying Messerschmitt caught us and hit the tank of one of the lorries so that it went up in a flare of orange flame.

Two men were hit, but not badly, and we made tracks away from the place as fast as we could go before the black plume of smoke brought other aircraft to the scene and, dropping with exhaustion, our water gone so that we were as dried-out as old prunes, we ran into the rear of the army at last, where the defence was finally beginning to stiffen. We knew the Italian scout cars were back just to the north again because we'd been dodging them all the time, and when, reinforced and with their courage up again, they found us at last not far east of a battery of guns whose barrels had been smashed by their own gunners as they'd abandoned them, and a column of lorries all with shattered engines and split tyres, we had to run like hell.

We were still eating breakfast when we first saw them over the horizon. Houston, of course, wasn't there when he was wanted and they nearly got me as I waited with one of the jeeps for him to appear from the sand dunes where he'd gone to relieve himself. Then the dud jeep failed and there was a frantic minute of shouting as its occupants scrambled out and ran for the waiting lorry, and for a long time it was touch and go whether they caught us or not.

But we made it, short of one lorry and one conked jeep, but with every man in the party still alive and reasonably fit. As we went bounding over the desert in our overloaded vehicles we heard the guns stuttering behind us and thought that it was the end of us, but then – blessed sight! – we saw a South African field battery just beyond the dunes and we went into them like a charge of cavalry just as their guns opened up, and the scout cars came to a halt behind us among the exploding shells, jinking and rolling on the uneven ground, and swung off jerkily to head back the way they'd come.

We fell out of the vehicles as though we'd all been shot, gasping for a drink, and as the South Africans crowded round, lifting down our wounded and handing out bully beef and biscuits and water canteens, Nimmo and Morena stumbled up to me. They both looked gaunt and exhausted, their faces black with muddy dust, their eyes staring out of a mask of dirt, their mouths pale pink where they'd licked their lips.

'We made it,' I croaked.

Morena nodded. 'We made it,' he said, his voice heavy with relief.

'And now,' I said, 'I'd better contact the Colonel. He's going to be bloody pleased, I'm sure.'

Amazingly, our own major was just behind the battery, waiting for us, and he came up in a jeep and pulled to a halt.

'I thought we'd lost you,' he said. 'We'd written you off.'

'Not me.' I managed a grin. 'I don't write off as easily as all that.'

He scowled. 'The bastards forgot you,' he said savagely. 'The whole bloody thing was called off and you should have been called in. The lot of you. But the sod who was responsible bunked off with the lorries and didn't think to tell anybody.'

Same as always, I thought. Same as always. Some toffee-nosed staff wallah from base! Some smooth bastard in pressed khaki and smart desert boots! I wanted to say something vicious and bitter, but I was too tired to care.

Nimmo lit a cigarette, probably his last, and handed it to me to drag at. Leach was already humping equipment with the stolidity of a mule under Morena's gaze, and I could hear Houston's voice, high-pitched with excitement and relief.

'Christ, we knocked 'em from here to Kingdom Come,' he was saying. 'They never knew what hit 'em.'

Nimmo glanced at him and gave me a derisive grin, and as I stared at him with dazed eyes, conscious for the first time of buckling knees and a blinding headache, I remembered the story of his paintings in caves down in the lonely Depression. It all came flooding back, now that the tension had gone, now that I had time to feel other emotions than nervousness and sullen determination and edginess, and I realised we couldn't just ignore them.

'You'd better make a report for the Colonel when we get back,' I said.

Soon afterwards the group began to split up. Bummer Ward was killed in the push from Alamein and Gester's jeep went up on a mine near the Mareth Line. Smollett lost a leg and Morris died of wounds, then Morena was caught by shrapnel in Italy and we lost him, too, for a while, and when he returned both he and Nimmo were posted off to different companies to nurse new officers just out from England, just as they'd nursed me, while I was promoted and landed with a whole batch of newcomers who were still wet behind the ears and had to be taught everything I'd ever learned from Morena.

By that time, of course, everyone knew the invasion was near and, in addition to all the working-up we had to do as a group, we all had other things on our minds. Those of us who were left were ordered back to England for the second front and, with the Germans in retreat everywhere, from then on the only thing that filled my brain was the thought of peace. There were a whole lot of new things to learn about fighting in Europe and the only thing that seriously concerned me just then was learning them quickly so that I might have a chance of being alive to see the lights go on again. I wasn't sure by this time that I was glad to leave the desert. I don't think anyone was. In spite of all the cursing and the complaints, we'd grown used to it and understood it – but there was still a long hard road to travel before we'd finished and by this time I was determined that I was going to be there when we reached the end of it.

It was really only when I'd lost touch with them all that I remembered the pictures Nimmo claimed to have found. We were pushing up to Germany by then, through acres of ruined fields and charred houses and splintered forests, with the muddy ground carved up by tank tracks and trampled by the boots of thousands of marching men. It was bitterly cold, with the frost-rime on every hedgerow, and all the grassland seemed to be flooded and every puddle was starred by new ice, and I was trying to keep warm over a fire that some Americans had started in a broken-down barn.

It was as I thought longingly of the warmth of Africa that I remembered the Qalam Depression and the long wait there, and the boob I'd made over the Paymaster, and then, suddenly I began to think of the pictures Nimmo had found and wondered if anything had ever been done about them.

I was still thinking about them, wondering if they'd been lost again, when someone came to tell me the Colonel was looking for me and that there was a new job to do, and I promptly pushed Nimmo and his pictures to the back of my mind. After all, I decided as I thrust between the steaming, half-frozen men, it was all over and done with now. Whatever had or had not been done, there was no reason to worry my head about them. I'd never hear of them again.

At least, that was what I thought.

But I was wrong. Dead wrong.

PART ONE

Off to See the Wizard

one

In the confusion of peace it seemed I lost touch with every-body I'd known. After demob I tried for a while to do some writing, but nothing came of it, and in the end I went back to newspapers and ended up in Fleet Street.

Perhaps because I'd done a lot of unwilling travelling during the war they decided I might know something about it, and they gave me a page and told me to write about holidays abroad, which were just then becoming popular. I stuck it for a while and then moved on to something else, but nothing ever seemed to come to anything and I could see myself ending up like all the rest of the galley slaves, written out and indifferent, unable to work up any enthusiasm for anything.

My contract had just finished, and I was wondering whether to make a change into something else entirely, when a letter from Nimmo found me, curiously warming as it came across the years. It was addressed to 'Captain P A Doyle' and asked me to meet him in a pub near the London Docks, and, when I went there, smart as hell in my shiny exploited journalist's suit, I was surprised to find Jock Houston and Tiny Leach and Wop Morena there as well. The old nicknames came back immediately we met.

It startled me a bit to see them after so long – because they'd all changed so much. Nimmo had lost that great mop of red hair he'd had and his face was deeply lined, as though he'd spent some time abroad. Tiny Leach looked enormous,

because his waist had disappeared entirely now, and
Houston, who'd always been small and spare, had developed
into a thin, desiccated, dry little man. Morena was the least
changed of the lot. His hair was thinning but he still seemed
square and solid as teak, though the old grim unsmiling look
that had always been in his eye had gone and he looked a lot
more human than I'd ever remembered him. He'd served in
Kenya and Korea and there were little white marks round his
eyes where he'd been wounded by a grenade on the Imjin.

They all of them came forward to greet me with a lot of
back-slapping and drink-offering, because, rank or no rank,
I'd been one of them and put up with everything they'd put
up with.

'You've put weight on,' Nimmo said. 'You're a big boy
now.'

It was only when they started producing photographs and
I looked at myself in the mirror over Nimmo's head that I
realised how much I *had* changed. The old dewy look had
gone and a few more years of responsibility had put lines on
my face that I'd never really noticed before.

It had been quite an evening, but it hadn't taken me long
to discover we hadn't come together merely for a celebration.

After a while, Nimmo produced a small round bowl from
a briefcase and put it on the table in front of us, and I'd
noticed immediately how Houston and Leach had leaned
forward and how their faces had grown tense.

'Ever seen one of those before?' Nimmo asked.

'Where did you get that?' I asked.

'Qalam, 1942.'

'From the Depression,' I said immediately. 'The time you
went out to bring in the Paymaster.'

'That's it.'

'Is this what you were doing while I was sweating on the
top line waiting for the Germans? Digging it up?'

He grinned. 'I didn't think much about it at the time,' he explained. 'In fact, I forgot all about it until I turned it up a year or two ago. You remember I told you we'd found a cave and some pictures?'

'That's right.'

'There were a few old plates and bowls in there, too.'

I looked up at Leach and Houston and they both nodded eagerly.

'I didn't think much about 'em then,' Nimmo continued. 'They seemed so battered, I just thought they were cooking pots left behind by some tribe who'd been passing through the Depression and had had to do a bunk quickly because the war was coming too close, and I just picked this one up as a souvenir. But I've had it identified at the British Museum since. It's Mycaenean, they think. And it's gold!'

I stared at him, and saw the others all watching me carefully. 'Gold, for God's sake!'

'Gold. When I found it, it was so dirty, it looked like brass.' He smiled and tapped the bowl. 'If that's gold,' he said, 'so might all the other things be gold, too.'

'Good God!'

'We decided we'd like to go back and find out. If they *are* gold, they must be worth quite a bit. Whether the law of treasure trove applies to Libya or not, I don't know, but there must be *some* sort of market value for these things – even if only to a museum.'

I stared at him again, caught by the implications behind the discovery. 'Did you ever make that report out for the Colonel?' I asked.

He shook his head and I noticed for the first time that there were streaks of grey in his hair. 'Never had time,' he said. 'If you remember, we were busy just then with Rommel, and after that we never stopped.'

'We went through 'em like a dose of salts,' Leach said with a swift rush of pride, like a small boy recalling a fist fight.

'When I did think about it again,' Nimmo went on, ignoring him, 'it seemed to be too late. We'd long since bypassed Qalam, and we were rather occupied with winning the war. Italy and then D-Day remember? I never thought of it again until some time ago, and when I got it identified as gold I remembered I'd found it with a few others in the cave where we saw the wall paintings, and that I'd been so impressed by the pictures I'd taken the precaution of taking bearings and making a few drawings of the outside in case we'd made some archaeological discovery. I nearly stripped the attic to find them.'

He opened a file and on a sheet of faded paper I caught a glimpse of neat professional sketches of what looked like cliffs and rock formations and groups of numbers.

'So that's why you took so bloody long,' I said. 'Drawing a lot of pictures. You told me all you did was take bearings.'

He grinned. 'Well, you know how it is,' he said. He paused, smiling, then went on quickly, indicating the bowl. 'Ever since I got this identified as gold,' he said, ' – and it wasn't until about nine years after the war – I've been thinking of going back. I never did, of course. First of all I found that the bloody area was under the authority of the Libyan Army and you couldn't get in, then I – well, I hadn't the cash. A bit of trouble. You know how it is.' He grinned and behind his smile I saw a hint of the old sly evil Nimmo and wondered what he'd been up to and who else had lost money besides. He seemed to guess what I was thinking and winked before going on.

'Every time I thought about it there was something in the way,' he said. 'I thought I'd never make it. Then I met Jock Houston here one night a month or two back. In a pub in the West End.'

'I was chasing a bit of stuff,' Houston said quickly, and as his eyes shone he didn't seem to have changed much in spite of the extra years. 'Met her in a bar the night before. Square legs and a bust like buns bursting out of a bag. Good job I didn't catch her. Instead I walked into Jimmy and here we are.'

Nimmo cut across his chatter quickly, as though he were impatient. 'We got talking,' he said, 'and decided the two of us couldn't do it alone. We thought of Tiny.'

'What about the rest of them?' I asked, and he shrugged.

'Married,' he said shortly. 'Well married. Kids. Business. Are *you* married?'

I had been, but it had been a short-lived happiness and was none of Nimmo's business.

'No,' I said.

He nodded and began to toy with the drawings, but, as I leaned over to have a second look, he closed the file. His eyes were bright and wary.

'Even with Tiny and Jock, I knew we still couldn't do it,' he said. 'We needed a mechanic. One who knew the desert, not some spanner-pusher from a London garage. You know what the desert's like with vehicles.' He nodded at Morena. 'We found Wop. But even then we hadn't the maps, and I'd found out there are still mines lying around loose down there, some of 'em the ones we laid, some of 'em Italian. Even with Morena we couldn't find our way back.' He paused and grinned. 'But *you* might,' he ended. 'You had all the maps, and I knew you were a newspaperman and might have a few contacts who could help us.'

I made my decision at once, almost without thinking really.

'Better than that,' I said. 'I've still got my *original* map. I kept it all through the war. It's still unmarked. I've got it in a drawer somewhere with my gongs and the bit of shrapnel they took out of my backside in Normandy.'

'Then we can go?'

'I should think so,' I said. 'Shouldn't be any difficulties. What about funds?'

'We can raise them between us.'

'What happens to the stuff if we find it?'

'Surely we'll get something out of it. The British Museum's been breathing down my neck ever since I showed the bowl to them. Apart from that, though, I've always had a yen to have another look at the desert.'

So had I. Many times. After the war was over it had taken years to get it out of my system, to shuffle off the memory of the silences, the cleanness and the brilliant nights that had made all the hardship worth while. After the desert, France and Germany had seemed as crowded as a Tube station and there'd never seemed to be enough elbow-room for honest-to-God fighting, with all the houses and the civilians and the things King's Regulations and the Provost Marshal didn't allow you to do.

Nimmo had seen the look in my eye and he was grinning. 'Houston's a teacher but he says the school can go hang for a couple of months,' he said. 'Morena's brother's taken over his garage.'

'And Tiny?'

Leach guffawed. 'I'm all right,' he said. 'Except for cash. I just got fired.'

I studied all the eager faces round me, then I nodded.

'Let's have another drink on it,' I suggested.

It seemed so simple then. But it didn't work out quite like that. We fixed our date and all the major details, but when we turned up a month later for the meeting at which we intended to finalise things, it wasn't Nimmo who appeared, but his son.

Nimmo was dead.

t w o

Young Jimmy Nimmo looked exactly like his father as he was on all those nostalgic photographs we brought out which we'd had made in Cairo and Alex during the war, and all those snapshots that had been taken with illicit cameras at Kufra and Siwa, where we'd been based between runs.

He was tall, slender and red-haired, good-looking as hell and oozing the same sort of wicked charm. He hadn't known us long before he started to produce the same outrageous stories of eager girls and frantic husbands as his father, who'd often kept us laughing even while we'd made the mental reservation not to lend him a pound the next time he asked, because he hadn't yet paid back the last one he'd borrowed.

He told us his father had been in a car crash on the M1 and that, just before he died, he'd sent for his son. His wife, apparently, had been out in the cold ever since the war and had long since gone back to living on her own money, but Nimmo had somehow kept in touch with his son and had felt the need to pass on to him the only thing of value he still possessed, the knowledge of where to find the treasure of the Qalam Depression.

It was enough in all conscience for anybody, and if we found what I for one was beginning to hope we'd find, young Nimmo would be more than repaid for any filial love he'd felt for his father. By this time, I'd begun to think in terms of treasure-stuffed tombs and pharaohs' curses and gold-encased sarcophagi behind dark embossed doors flanked by obsidian blocks that were set like sentinels into the faces of the cliffs of the Depression. But this wasn't all. Whatever the intrinsic worth of what Nimmo said he'd found in the Qalam Depression, there was value in it for me as a story that might well bring in as much as the Kon-Tiki had brought in for Thor Heyerdahl.

Nimmo had caught my imagination and I'd done all the work in London, even to getting visas for everybody and the correct permission from the Libyan Government to make the journey. We'd given ourselves a name just to obscure the object of our trip from inquisitive busybodies, and I'd also got my editor interested, and he'd agreed not to sign anyone on in my place until I returned to take up a renewed contract. He was offering no wages mind you, but in return for the story he was offering all the help he could give us in the way of contacts, even to the assistance of our man in Tripoli.

Migliorini, who'd represented the paper in North Africa for years, was an Italian with a rather rococo way of writing English that sometimes stumped the subs, but he turned up trumps when it came to advice over routes and equipment. He sent me lists as long as your arm of things we might need, and information of all the new comforts and aids to living in the desert that had appeared since I'd left Africa. Half of them I'd never heard of, but Migliorini recommended them and, as he spent most of his life on the fringe of the desert, we accepted his suggestions.

Morena, who shared a garage with his brother at Reading and knew all there was to know about lorries, had fixed us up with a Land Rover and a thirty-horsepower six-cylinder Austin lorry, with an engine like a lion, and the name 'Daisy' painted on the bonnet, just as he'd had during the war. The Austin looked a good vehicle, but, of course, we were all the time concerned with the amount of money we had at our disposal and we had to take it on trust a little. Even Morena couldn't tell what damage it might have suffered before we'd seen it, or how long it might have been standing in a Service Corps park waiting for a buyer, but we had to take a chance on that. He'd fixed two hooks under the canopy frame for hammocks and air mattresses, because we remembered the ambulances during the war and what a joy it was to sleep on a bunk occasionally as a change from the hot sand, and we'd got a small transmitter-receiver in case of emergency, stored up against the cab with all our equipment.

The Land Rover was an afterthought in a way, and had been bought on Morena's advice because any penetration of the desert was always so inherently chancy a second vehicle was really essential in case of breakdown, and this vehicle we left reasonably clear to be used as a maid of all work.

We all met in a pub at Harwich where we'd waited for D-Day and young Nimmo arrived with a square leather case on a sling over his shoulder.

'What's that?' Houston demanded. 'Mine detector?'

Nimmo grinned. 'Radio,' he said. 'Might come in useful. Cheer us up a bit.'

'Oh!' Like the rest of us, Houston didn't belong to the generation that wore wireless sets as easily as clothes. 'Looks like a coffin for a cat,' he said.

Like Leach, he'd been a little uncertain at first about young Nimmo and had made a great deal of having to share any of the profits of the expedition with someone who hadn't even been in the desert when the treasure we were after had been found, but young Nimmo, of course, had the drawings his father had made and the bearings he'd taken and without them none of us could do anything. In the end, Houston's muttering died away as he faced up to the fact and, as young Nimmo had the same ability as his father to win people over, it wasn't long before we all of us, Houston and Leach included, accepted him as a full member of the expedition.

He had, in fact, a lot to offer that was helpful. He'd been for a time in Africa, though he didn't tell us where or why, and he'd spent some of his short life working there, so he wasn't entirely a stranger to the place, though Houston enjoyed telling him in the rich phrases of the Eighth Army that he needed to get some service in and ought to hurry up and get his knees brown. Nimmo grinned pleasantly enough and accepted the chaffing without resentment, though there were times when Houston's assumption of superior knowledge grew a little wearing – even to me.

He was in a gay – almost light-headed – mood and full of anecdotes about the war.

'Remember that time…?' he kept saying. 'Remember the way it went?'

Like Leach, he didn't seem to have made much of his life after the war. He'd never once had a job of any responsibility, it seemed, and somehow it showed even in his clothes. Unlike Morena's neat, well-cared-for equipment, his belongings were shabby and frayed, and, somehow, behind his humour he seemed a little forlorn. His gaiety seemed to spring from excitement at getting out of his rut for a while, and he was eager to celebrate on board during the crossing.

'Let's show 'em how to drink,' he said. 'Me and Chalky White drank all the way to Africa last time.'

But it turned out that Morena and I didn't drink much these days and in the end only Houston and young Nimmo really settled down to it, because, in addition, Leach was afraid of being seasick and the celebration turned out to be a bit of an anticlimax.

'Well, Christ, you are a wet lot,' Houston complained. 'I thought it'd be like Corporal Curtis always used to say – with the corks going off right and left like file-firing.'

It was a long drive through France and we used the tent instead of hotels because we wanted to save money. In Marseille we began to pick up the shrill overtones of the East and stood on the heights looking towards the sea between the Cathedral and the fantastic pinnacled Notre Dame de la Garde, knowing we were looking directly back at Africa.

On the ship there was no awning against the sun and we panted against the ventilators, already aware of the heat.

'Feel it?' Houston said gaily. 'The old oven. It was the same when we first came out. Jimmy Fidler said it was like his father's bakery. Remember Jimmy Fidler?'

Leach nodded in that slow fashion of his that seemed slower than ever after twenty years. 'What 'appened to 'im?' he asked.

'Bought it on the first run up to Bardia,' Morena said. 'He was acting batman to Paddick, that major with the ginger moustache who went off his nut as a colonel.'

Houston chuckled. 'I remember him. The Brigadier got him posted – that little chap who looked like Monty. Maugham he was called. You never knew whether it was Muffam or Moom. He was caught by the Ities the first time we retreated and stood up in his car wearing all his tabs and medals and bawled 'em out in German until they let him go. He got 'em so they didn't know whether they were sitting on pos or piano stools.'

Nimmo laughed abruptly and his laughter had a derisive ring to it so that Houston looked round, his thin Scots face suddenly sharp-edged.

'What's wrong with you?' he demanded angrily.

'God,' Nimmo asked good-humouredly. 'Don't you ever forget?'

'Don't we ever forget *what*?'

Nimmo moved his hand in a helpless gesture. 'Anything,' he said. 'You've got the names off so pat. Every single one of 'em. Even after twenty years.'

Houston's eyes glittered, but Morena laughed before he could reply, and the awkward moment was turned aside. But Nimmo's words had jarred Houston and damped our enthusiasm as though someone had thrown cold water over us. We'd all been looking forward to renewing the comradeship we'd felt in the desert, and his youthful realism was sinking it before it had even started to swim. That elusive something we were all reaching back to and trying to get hold of again had vanished at once, untouched.

'Christ, man,' Houston said, his face full of disappointment and indignation, 'that brigadier became one of the *big* boys in the desert. Like Monty. I suppose even *you*'ve heard of bloody Monty?'

'Oh, I've heard of Monty.' Nimmo grinned, his face full of malicious glee now. 'He's that old bloke who keeps getting up on his hind legs and telling everybody how to run the show.'

Houston gaped '*That old bloke*,' he said. 'If it weren't for Monty – and me, and these lot – you'd have been a slave of Hitler's Reich. You know what they were like rampaging round the Continent before the war.'

Nimmo laughed. 'I wasn't *born* before the war,' he pointed out.

I looked at Morena with a feeling of shock. Surely all *that* many years hadn't passed since the day we'd joined the army, surely all *that* much water hadn't flowed under the bridge?

I think it was then that I realised for the first time that Leach was not just 'colossal' any more. He'd become a fat man, and Houston was gaunt and dusty-looking and his thin lips were as cheerless as a railway track. Even Morena had the comfortable look of prosperity about him, and I began to wonder uneasily how different *I* looked.

'You might show a bit of gratitude, all the same.' Houston was speaking slowly, as though at a loss for something crushing to say in reply.

'To listen to you blokes,' Nimmo said cheerfully, 'you'd think you'd saved the world from falling to pieces.'

'Well, we did, didn't we?'

'Well, if you did, you didn't make a very good job of it, because it's in a nice mess again now.

Leach and Houston were staring at Nimmo as though he were a foreigner. Suddenly, for all the link he had with us, he might have been a man from Outer Space.

We stayed on deck all night in spite of the dew that soaked us through. We'd decided against cabins, thinking with nostalgia of the good old days when we'd slept out of doors for months at a time, but long before we were tired Houston was complaining about the cold. The decks were sodden and the rigging dripping and the only alternative was an evil-smelling lounge where people were snoring in ranks. On deck there was a bunch of Arabs singing in harsh unmusical voices.

'They don't change much, do they?' Morena said.

The sea wind had dropped as we winched alongside at Tripoli next morning, and the heat was already oppressive as the rising sun took all the moisture out of the air. But the town was up and about and teeming like a football crowd as we drove away from the great concrete quays that shone like old bones in the sun beside the flat dark water. The children came round us in shrieking hordes, shouting for alms, and Houston emptied his pockets of coins and flung them in a shower into the road, so that the yelling became a shrill baying as the children dived in the dust for them, dodging in and out of the traffic that was picking its way into the town.

The Italians had made an effort to clean the place up and turn it into a modern city, but they'd never quite succeeded. They'd paved the native quarter and disinfected everything within reach and driven fine arcaded boulevards to east and west to make thoroughfares. But the narrow streets of the old city were still spanned by wooden poles covered with ancient vines that gave shade to the shop fronts and, underneath them, behind the colonnades, fountains played in hidden courtyards paved with mosaic and full of plants, and small shops displayed vivid carpets and leathers, the craftsmen cross-legged on the floor or sweating over their work – bakers with their charcoal ovens open to the pavement, smiths hammering copper, barbers with their rows of what looked like sheeted dead.

And there were still beggars on every street, and starving children and flies and disease. Round the corner, where the new stores were, wealthy Arab women in fashionable hats were wearing the veil only as a formal strip of gauze across their mouths, but on the pavements among the arches the quacks still dispensed medicine like crown-and-anchor players on a plan of the human body, and yelling boys sold magazines of strip girls and half-naked he-men. There were still the rows of stalls covered by sticky sweetmeats and congealed dates, the gulls still shrieked over the garbage along the shore, and the youngsters still fought and yelled in the dust, as they were doing now, for the coins that were flung down for them.

'Hasn't changed much,' Houston observed gaily, his thin face alight with nostalgic pleasure. 'Flies. Beggars. Jig-jig. It was just the same in Alex when we came out in 1940.'

It was the aperitif hour and the pavements were full of people: Arab sheikhs; Italian girls so beautiful they took your breath away; hawkers selling shoe-laces, nuts, live puppies, cages of budgerigars; gharries drawn by plumed horses with mixed cargoes of veiled Moslem women, European tourists, bespectacled typists from the embassies and spring-jawed, long-legged American colonels from the airfield just inland. The street was noisy with voices and blaring klaxons and the screaming engines of buses charging like wounded buffaloes, down towards the Arab quarter, their horns going in two notes, up and down in a maniac duotone.

We had got our vehicles ashore without much difficulty and Migliorini was waiting for us at his office, small and dapper and eager to please. He greeted me like a long-lost brother. He'd been in London at one point and because we both knew the Western Desert we'd got on well at once.

'Everythink's ready,' he said. 'All you must do is take on the foods and pay the bill, then Bob's your ankle. Up the Ayghth Army.'

Nimmo stared at him. 'Oh God,' he said. 'Not another one.'

We'd planned our route via the oases because we could remember only too well having to live on a pint or two of water a day, and none of us fancied trying it again. We paid for everything we bought out of the cash we kept in a tin box in the Land Rover and that evening we all went for a swim in the creamy surf of the Mediterranean just for old times' sake.

But the beach we remembered was no longer deserted. There were umbrellas there now and English girls in bikinis who somehow made it not quite the same, and in the end we went to a bar. But even that was full of tourists, and the belly dancer looked as old as we did, with arms like thighs, and thighs like a brewery horse's back, and the kus-kus we ate tasted sour in spite of the peppers.

We went back early to the little hotel Migliorini had found for us, faintly deflated, and began to dig into our cases and kitbags – Houston's, I noticed, the original one, still with names like Alamein, Sicily and D-Day marked on it to impress the newcomers we'd met in Germany.

My own wartime shorts had long since worn out chasing the girls round the beaches of the Costa Brava, but Morena, who was sharing my room, had managed to dig out an old khaki jacket with two rows of faded ribbons still on the left breast, at least two of them more than merely campaign stars.

'Where the devil did you get that?' I demanded.

'It's my old blouse,' he said with a slow shy smile. 'I've kept it ever since. Sort of good-luck charm. You know how you do.'

It was bad enough seeing Morena in his old blouse, but it was a far worse shock when Houston appeared in the Arab head-dress he'd been in the habit of wearing to impress the Wrens in Alex, a little frayed and faded round the edges now and marked with the folds of years of lying in moth-balls at the bottom of a drawer.

He'd had a disappointing day. The girls in bikinis hadn't been interested in him and the woman he'd tried to shoot a line to in the bar about his desert days had turned out to be the widow of a tank colonel who'd got a double DSO and a few other decorations for gallantry and had ended his days happily keeping chickens with the war forgotten, and Houston had finished up a little drunk and full of bitter bawdy comments on her figure. He looked now as though he'd brought out the head-dress merely to bolster up a sagging confidence in himself, as though it were a reminder of the days when slim-legged girls hadn't winced at his jokes and gone off to search for something with a more up-to-date line in beachwear.

'Good God!' I said as he put his head round the door.

He looked sheepish. 'There was nothing to touch 'em,' he explained with a defensive grin. 'Not for keeping the dust out of your mouth.'

'What did young Nimmo say?' Morena asked.

Houston frowned. 'Oh, him!' He gestured angrily. 'He fell off the bed laughing.'

Morena grinned. 'I'm not surprised,' he said. 'Doesn't look the same now, somehow.'

Morena was right. It didn't. During the war Houston's face had been coated with dust and drawn into lines of strain and sleeplessness that had quite obscured the absurdity of the headgear, but now it seemed to drown him and he just looked like part of the chorus from a revival of *The Desert Song*.

He seemed to know it wasn't right, but he was defiant about it. 'All the same,' he said, 'I'm wearing it.'

We were still discussing it when Nimmo came in. He was smiling and I guessed he'd come to tell us about Houston's head-dress. The day had gone better for him than the rest of us because he was younger and he'd been able to pick up one of the girls in the bikinis and later one of the tourists in the bar, taking her into the garden after it got dark. He looked a little put out at first when he saw us all together, then he saw the faded ribbons on Morena's blouse and couldn't resist the dig.

'Zulu War?' he asked gaily.

Morena had been a brave man but never boastful, and I knew he'd never put up the ribbons just to impress us. They'd simply been there when he'd taken the jacket out of the drawer he kept it in, probably with a great sense of pride, and he gave Nimmo a quiet stare that took the smile off his face.

'Oh!' Nimmo edged backwards towards the corridor. 'Sorry! I'll go and hang out the washing on the Siegfried Line or something and leave you old soldiers to fade away together.'

His words grated because, somehow, I knew how he felt. There was a secretive compact between Houston and Leach that irritated me, something I couldn't explain that had set them talking in low voices in corners on the ship or at night near the tent, something that set them aside and made them seem childish and conspiratorial, and Houston's constant references to the war had had a strangely annoying effect.

When they'd gone I noticed that Morena had taken out his penknife and was cutting the stitches that held the ribbons in place on the jacket. Knowing Morena, I guessed that he'd never intended them to remain there, but there was something angry in the way he slashed at the thread, as though he, too, had seen Houston through a magnifying glass and found him not quite the man he'd believed him to be.

He looked puzzled as he pulled the ribbons away from the material, and a little worried too, as though he were wondering what he'd let himself in for. For a moment he held them in place against the breast of the jacket staring at them, then he looked at me.

'Zulu War,' he said, his voice a little shocked, his eyes a little hurt, because it had suddenly come to him, too, that El Alamein to Nimmo was as far away as the Somme and Waterloo.

He sat for a moment in silence, then he stuffed the ribbons into the kitbag and tossed the blouse down on the bed.

'I never realised it was as long ago as all that,' he ended slowly.

three

The Sahara always triumphs over the Mediterranean and when we left the scorching winds were sweeping over the land inshore. The khamsin was blowing with parching dryness and great clouds of dust were coming up towards us, and although we were still in cultivated country with plenty of greenery about, wisps of sand were blowing in little feathery tails across the tarmacadam. The thermometer was already well over a hundred and I could feel the sweat running down between my shoulder blades as I drove.

'Christ,' Leach said longingly, 'what wouldn't I give for a nice cold beer!'

There were already dark patches on his shirt under his arms and down the middle of his back, and he seemed to be feeling the heat – Leach, who used to slave with a shovel all day just to show off his strength!

His nostalgic words started me thinking, because I could still remember the heat down by the Qalam Depression. We'd lived then on a drop of water a day per man and I found myself wondering if we still could.

We turned south out of the town, down towards the desert, passing a dead pi-dog stiffening in the road, and an old rusting bus which had overturned in a drainage ditch. Its wheels had been removed so that its axles looked like amputated stumps, and the panelling had been ripped from the framework, leaving the skeleton like a heap of ancient camel bones. As we passed the squalid native shacks of sack and kerosene tins, I noticed the traffic had changed from cars to shoals of trucks and petrol lorries coming up from the south, and broken-down buses heading for the market with shrieking horns and cargoes of gesticulating Arabs.

'Christ,' Houston said, 'they're all on wheels these days instead of on camels.'

We began to run through an amazingly rich growth of vegetation which I didn't remember because it was all new and post-war, with bright green fields of groundnuts separated by windbreaks of cypresses, so that it looked a little like Provence. There were tamarisks and wispy eucalyptuses, and dirty villages brightened by oleanders, figs, almonds, vines, lemons, oranges and pomegranates. But no date palms. Not yet.

As we cleared the town, I was very conscious of a lifting of the spirits, a feeling of a holiday beginning so that we were like a lot of kids from an orphanage on their first trip to the seaside. I'd noticed it first as we'd left Dover, but now it was so marked as to be almost an emotion, the same feeling we'd all had years before when we'd first felt the hot air of the desert.

Houston's pale eyes grew bright and he began to make a running commentary on things as we passed, and then, from somewhere at the back of his sluggish memory, as though it were an instinct almost, Leach began in his heavy hoarse voice to sing the old song we'd always sung as we'd left the base at Siwa – 'We're off to see the Wizard, the wonderful Wizard of Oz!' It brought back memories of a slender and youthful Judy Garland looking like a wistful elf, with clouds of dark hair and big eyes, and that curious emotional constriction of the throat we'd all felt as we'd left wartime England, a saddened nostalgic feeling that we might never come home again.

By the third day we had begun to settle down a little, shuffling ourselves uncertainly into our new roles, and I began at last to see the first signs of the old comradeship we'd enjoyed so much.

The old songs began to pop up as we followed the coast road to Benghazi, from where we were to drive south-east in the direction of Siwa. We'd decided on this deliberately in spite of the extra miles. Going to Tripoli had saved the long sea journey from Marseille and the run along the coast would give us the chance to bed down together and work out what we needed in the way of extra stores before we entered the desert proper. After three days we would know just how much we were using in the way of fuel and rations and how the vehicles were behaving, and we could iron out the snags at Benghazi before we left civilisation.

Benghazi was still one of the ugliest towns between Tunis and Egypt, with a lot of unbuilt open spaces from which the sand blew into the eyes with every gust of wind from the sea, and it seemed to have more than its share of lean cats and scavenging dogs and more than its complement of flies. It didn't seem to have grown any bigger or any more attractive than when I'd last seen it. Arab music still wailed from open windows even over the sound of motor horns and there were greasy finger marks across the lurid new cinema posters, and donkeys tied to trees between the racy American cars. We decided to eat in a little restaurant we remembered, and the Italian owner, spotting we were English, immediately offered us eggs, bacon and chips. It was just as if someone had rolled back a curtain.

'We had eggs, bacon and chips *last* time,' Morena said with a grin.

'It was raining then, though,' Houston added. 'And there was hail. I didn't know it could hail in Africa. Even the mud seemed to be flying in the wind.'

'I'd got desert sores all over my 'ands.' Leach took up the story. 'We'd just come all the way up from the frontier. I got into an argument with an Aussie. I laid 'im out. He'd got a better greatcoat than mine, so I took it and left 'im mine.'

Houston's face was suddenly sharp-angled and grim. 'They expected brass bands and a military parade when we arrived,' he growled as an unexpectedly bitter memory arose. 'The mayor turned out in a tricolour sash. They didn't think much of us when they saw us and they didn't clap much.'

As he spoke, I caught sight of Nimmo's face, half-amused, half-contemptuous. At first he'd listened to Houston's stories eagerly, like any youngster hearing of something exciting beyond his own experience, but to Houston the war had been the only event in his life and he always tended to go on just too long about it and now Nimmo endured him with a blank face as though he only half believed him.

Houston had sat back, his eyes distant. 'Wouldn't mind nipping on to Tobruk before we turn south,' he went on slowly. 'Just to see what it looks like. Just to see how it's changed.'

'Chap told me,' Leach said, 'that it was just a village built out of old ammo boxes. 'E was 'ere in 1955. He said the Arabs was making a fortune out of scrap – petrol tins, guns, vehicles, tanks even. They broke 'em up by digging out the land mines and detonating 'em underneath with petrol-soaked rags. He said the casualties was a bit 'igh.'

He looked round at us to see if we'd enjoyed his story, then he scratched at the end of his nose, which had begun to peel with the sunshine, and gave a low guffaw. 'He said they was so bloody keen on scrap it was dangerous to walk about at night in the town because they'd even removed the man'ole covers.'

'Wouldn't mind going back, all the same,' Houston said again. 'Just for a laugh.'

From Benghazi we drove through splendid avenues of eucalyptus planted years before by Italian colonists, following the undeviating monotonous ribbon of the coast road towards Agabia. The surface was good and free from pot-holes, and, with the bus in front of us jammed to capacity with fat veiled women returning from market, and vegetables and hens and even sheep, what lay ahead of us all seemed very straightforward.

Only the road seemed to hold any element of danger as wisps and eddies of sand streamed across the tarmac to form dunes, so that there was always the possibility of running into a wind-blown drift and careering off the hard surface. We kept passing gangs of men at work clearing it, and near Braq the encroachment had buried several mud houses to first-floor level and the palm trees were almost submerged by the advancing sand so that the fronds stuck out like carrot tops in an allotment.

We stopped the night at Agabia before setting off south and east the next day. It was our last night in civilisation for a while, but the hotel wasn't the type to offer much comfort. It was still lit by oil lamps and the white walls were covered with finger marks and patches of grease. The tables in the restaurant were covered with oil-cloth and on the wall of the entrance hall there was a picture of the Sphinx with *Welcome to Egypt* written on it in English. There was a jukebox and a few bedraggled flowers in a rusty container that looked like an HE bomb case, and there were a few tourists, too, travelling along the coast to Egypt, all Americans from the airfields they'd established along the coast.

They were singing 'Happy Birthday to You' to one of their number, and the woman on the next table to me was relating some anecdote to her friend – 'She's just celebrated her silver wedding, dear. Do you know what that means? It means she's been married twenny-fi' years. Just think of that. Twenny-fi' years with the same guy' – and somehow it stuck in my throat. Not because they were Americans or because they were enjoying themselves, but because they made the place different, like the *Welcome to Egypt* signs and the heavy bright-blue lorries carrying petrol and stacked bales of halfa grass that pounded past on the road outside every few minutes, their tyres screaming on the hot tarmac. It might just as well have been a pull-in bar outside Oshkosh, Wisconsin.

The landlord spoke English with a guttural accent and it turned out he'd been in the Afrika Korps and had returned to marry an Italian girl and set up the hotel.

'I bet we met you,' Houston said enthusiastically. 'I bet I shot at you more than once.'

Nimmo shoved at the fatty-looking mutton on his plate and frowned. 'Pity you didn't kill him,' he muttered.

The whole family turned out to see us off the next morning, as the pink fingers of the sun rose out of the mist, and the landlord gave us two bottles of wine just for old times' sake.

'Never again,' he said earnestly.

'Never again,' we agreed, jammed full of sentiment.

We shook hands all round, and then his wife brought out a tray of warm beers, and we drank them there alongside the vehicles like stirrup cups before we set off south, the Land Rover leading this time, the lorry just behind.

We began now to see a few faded signs in German that were relics of the Afrika Korps and here and there a battered Volkswagen of wartime vintage, then we passed a long Roman arch, its tall columns gold and long-shadowed in the early sun, and a Fascist victory column with its eagle marked with bullet-holes where the Aussies had tried to shoot off its head. There were palms that were still disfigured by shell-splinters and fields of white crosses where men had died, the geraniums at their feet like new blood on the dusty earth, then we entered the desert at last, and I found my heart was in my mouth, not with fear or doubt, but with the same indefinable emotion that comes to you when you go back to an old school or look on the face of an old love, because you remember it with fondness and don't want it to be spoiled.

We were all itching to get away from civilisation because it was in the desert that the adventure really started and because we felt that there the irksome irritations we'd felt and the disappointments that things were so different would fall away.

We were all glad when we stopped in the evening to stretch stiffened legs. The sky was beginning to show every shade from pink to lavender, with the curtain of the night rising from the east. The vanished sun had been a red ball of fire hanging on the lip of the desert and with its disappearance the plain seemed to be shifting, a changing waste of orange and lilac, and the two vehicles were the only two moving objects in the whole world.

We pulled on to a patch of pinky-red gravel off the track by a deserted village with derelict wind pumps and new dunes and prepared to camp for the night. There were a few Arabs among the broken buildings, not in them but camped in tents in the gardens, and we bought eggs and cheese from them while Houston brewed the tea on the stove.

Nimmo was cooking a bully-beef stew in the back of the lorry and we could catch the odour of it already over the smell of the hot engines. We were all hungry and it seemed delicious.

It was then that Morena surprised us by digging into his kit-bag and producing his mouth-organ, the same old instrument, and the way he got across the heartbreak of 'Lili Marlene' sent the whining notes floating thin and reedy and lost on the clean air, and started the memories flooding round us, almost tearful, so that it was all there again, just as it had been twenty years before.

'This is the time I always liked best,' Houston observed. 'The cleanness, the smell of grub cooking, the silence.'

As he spoke, the high raucous notes of a modern jazz group started as Nimmo appeared from behind the lorry with his transistor, and the mood vanished at once.

'For God's sake,' Houston said angrily. 'Wrap it up!'

Nimmo looked up, startled, and grinned. 'Why?' he said. 'We've got to have a bit of civilisation, haven't we?'

We slept on the sand alongside the lorry that night for the first time, wrapped in blankets among the scattered desert plants fighting for survival. Only Nimmo used a hammock in the lorry.

'You want to get some desert time in,' Houston advised him. 'Get your head down on the sand. Scoop a hole for your hip. Sleep like a log.'

'That's all right, old boy,' Nimmo said. 'I'll leave the hardships to you old sweats. I'll have the air mattress.'

It was surprising how much harder the desert seemed than I remembered it. The hole I'd made for my hip didn't appear to fit in quite the way it used to, and a rolled-up coat no longer seemed a very adequate substitute for a pillow. About midnight I heard Houston swear softly, and as I saw him stand up against the pale sky and shuffle into the lorry, dragging his blanket behind him, I couldn't help wondering ruefully how long it would be before I threw up the sponge, too.

The next morning, long after we'd left the track and were driving entirely by compass, we came up to a group of Arabs working at feverish speed on the stony desert. We were surprised to see human beings at all, but they seemed completely unconcerned, digging little holes with picks and filling them with small cylinders connected by wires that led to a large truck a hundred yards away.

'What the 'ell are they doing?' Leach asked. 'Laying mines?'

'Seismologists,' Nimmo said in a flat patient voice from the Land Rover alongside us. 'They're prospecting for oil.'

'Oil? In the desert?' Leach stared.

'There are wells all over the Tunisian Sahara,' Nimmo pointed out. 'The French opened 'em up. Surveyed the whole place by air. It isn't still 1940, man. They're growing flowers here now.'

The seismologists, two Frenchmen and one American, all of them so young they seemed to be just out of school, allowed us to watch the explosion of the canisters and showed us the zigzag lines they were drawing on a chart of the area. They produced a couple of bottles at lunch, which we ate sitting under an awning near the truck, and their varied foods made our bully beef and biscuits seem very spartan.

'Where are you heading?' they asked.

'Qalam Depression.'

'Hope you enjoy it. It's hotter there than it is here, and it's going to be a scorcher later on.'

As the sun grew higher, a mirage began to form and as we travelled we could see black cliffs rising ahead, beyond what looked like a sheet of water that never grew any nearer. Then the going altered and the land grew more uneven, with large plate-like stones jutting from the ground and flat pebbles rattling away from under the wheels. There were a few low-topped hills too, now, that rose out of a mirage of mountains and floating terraces.

'Two more days on this course,' I said, as we stopped for a brew-up, 'and we should be well below Breba. Then we turn due south. There ought to be some remains of the wire there. After that, Qalam and the well and then the Depression.'

'Two days!' Leach looked up from his mug of tea. His face was plastered with a grey mask where the dust had stuck to the sweat there, and he looked exhausted.

'Two days,' he repeated. 'I never thought it was *that* far!'

'You'll be where no white foot ever trod,' Houston said. 'Remember that, mate. Apart from us and that Paymaster who got himself clobbered, there've never been any white people down there before.'

He wiped his face with a grimy handkerchief. 'Does it seem to you,' he asked, his expression changing, 'as if it's hotter than it used to be? I've got a sore coming on my back.'

'Summers are changing even in England,' Nimmo said sarcastically. 'They say the whole of the Northern Hemisphere's warming up.'

As he rose and moved away, Houston stared after him resentfully. 'I don't wish that bastard any harm,' he said slowly, 'but I'd just love to see him paralysed all down one side.'

During the afternoon we spotted a herd of Loder's gazelle in the distance.

'Fresh meat,' Houston said as he stopped the Land Rover.

We had two rifles and a couple of revolvers, which we'd bought in France just as a precaution, and Houston reached slowly into the back of the Land Rover for one of the rifles.

'Watch me knock him off,' he said.

We saw the dust spurt up in front of the herd as the bullet struck the earth, and the animals bounded off at once, all except one, which seemed startled and stood with its head up.

'Too short,' Houston said, working the bolt of the rifle. 'I'll get him with the next one.'

This time the spurt of sand was beyond the gazelle, and it turned slowly and I knew that at any minute it would be off after the others.

'For Christ's sake,' Leach said urgently. 'Gimme that rifle! I'll get 'im!'

They were still struggling for the weapon when we heard the other rifle fire from the lorry, and the gazelle, which had just started to move, leapt into the air and rolled over, head down, and lay still, and we saw Nimmo running towards it.

'Did *he* shoot it?' Houston asked, startled.

'*You* certainly didn't,' Leach said.

I was glad Nimmo had shot the gazelle. It seemed to restore him to favour in the eyes of the others. He seemed to know what to do with it, too, and he thrust his knife expertly under the skull to make sure it was dead and slit it up the stomach and disembowelled it. Then he hoisted it to his shoulders and trudged back to the lorry with it, while we were all still walking towards him.

'Who taught you to shoot like that?' Houston asked.

'My old man. In Kenya.'

'What was he doing in Kenya?'

Nimmo grinned, that same brash grin his father had had.

'Bit of trouble,' he said. 'It seemed wisest at the time.'

'What sort of trouble?'

'Money?'

'Did he lose some?'

'Somebody else did.'

Nobody made any comment because it came as no surprise.

'Were the police after him?' Houston asked cautiously.

Nimmo grinned. 'Wasn't the first time,' he said.

'Lots of people get mixed up with the police,' Leach pointed out heavily.

The way he said it made us all look quickly at him, but he didn't enlighten us further and we climbed back into the vehicles. Almost immediately we ran into a patch of soft sand and the lorry stuck, its rear wheels up to the hubs in smooth yellow dust.

JOHN HARRIS

Long before we'd got it out, Leach was gasping for breath and Houston was complaining about the raw spot on his back. Young Nimmo worked like ten men, yet when he'd finished he was the only one who seemed untouched by the hard work, sitting in the sun with a mug of scalding sweet tea, indifferent to the heat, slipping into easy immobility, relaxed and unworried with the confidence of a young man sure of himself.

'If we had to dig out once getting back to Alamein,' Houston said slowly, 'we had to do it a dozen times.'

'We shouldn't ever 'ave gone back,' Leach said heavily, gesturing with the slow movement of an overweight man to whom everything was an effort. 'It was a good job Monty came. All them tanks and guns and aeroplanes.'

'Nothing to do with Monty,' Nimmo said quietly, not moving, not even lifting his eyes. 'They'd all been ordered beforehand.'

Their heads turned towards him and I saw Houston's eyes glow, sharp and unfriendly at once.

'Were you there?' he asked with immediate truculence, as though he'd been waiting for the comment to pounce on it.

Nimmo smiled, still not moving. 'No,' he said.

'Were you ever a soldier?'

'No.'

'Then you don't bloody well understand.'

Nimmo grinned. There'd been plenty of better soldiers than Houston, and Nimmo knew it. Somehow, the fact that he talked so much about the things we'd done made them seem dreary and cheap and even to me his stories had begun to have the nagging effect of a stone in the shoe.

'We did our bit,' he was saying now, pressing the point a little too hard, as though he, too, secretly realised that Nimmo had the measure of him. 'We didn't dodge anything. We got the lot.'

Nimmo said nothing, but began to sing softly, 'We're the soldiers of the Queen, my lads, we've been, my lads, and seen, my lads...' and Houston couldn't resist turning on him again.

'Three years we were in the desert,' he said, staring at Nimmo and speaking sharply, deliberately, as though to rub it in. 'We were chewing on a tough tit in those days.'

Nimmo stared back at him, not saying anything, then he suddenly stood up and slashed the rest of his tea down, and it was swallowed up at once by the greedy sand. Nobody spoke for a moment, then Leach looked up.

'What's up with you?' he asked.

Houston shifted restlessly and I was surprised at the vehemence and dislike in his tones. 'He's like all the bloody rest of his generation,' he said. 'Knocking everybody who did his bit. It's something to laugh at now and write plays about on the telly. It was just a bloody game to his lot. His generation's dead jammy.'

'No.' Nimmo laughed, undisturbed by Houston's sudden smouldering hostility. 'It's not that. It's just that *your* generation always liked to do it the hard way.' Like his father, he enjoyed tormenting people, and this time his words had a curious jabbing effect on me, too, like a probe touching a raw nerve. 'Bikes, instead of scooters. Crystal sets instead of transistors. That sort of thing.'

Morena looked up, his face expressionless. 'It helps,' he said slowly, 'if you remember those things were developed during the war to stop men dying.'

Nimmo turned to him and his smile faded. 'OK,' he said, nodding, as though Morena with his long silences impressed him far more than Houston with his quick arguments. 'Take off your girdles and relax, girls. I was only pulling your legs.'

The following day was a scorcher, and the mirage rose long before the sun had reached its zenith.

The land around us was brown and lifeless, without any trace of vegetation, and the bully we ate at midday was tepid and almost poured out of the tins, greasy and uninviting, while the sun beat down on us, searing and breathtaking, as we crouched in the little strip of shade alongside the lorry.

'The oasis this afternoon,' I said. 'The Depression tomorrow. I suggest we go straight on down and get started. We can always send the Land Rover back to the well at Biq Qalam for water. It's not far.'

They nodded, and I noticed they were glad to accept leadership in decisions of this sort.

'Convoy will get under way at 2 p.m.,' I said, trying to sound gay and breezy. 'Troops will wear full kit and carry side arms. Hats will be worn back-to-front and shirts will be worn outside braces.'

They grinned and Houston slammed up a caricature of a salute. The foolishness seemed to inject a little life into him and we rose briskly and began to stuff away the equipment into the van.

We were working from the map now, skirting the little patches of red crosses where I'd written '*Mines*', and not long after we set off we came across the remains of a couple of vehicles. They were so old and blackened with rust it was hard to tell what they'd been. Their wheels had gone, together with anything else that had been detachable, so that only the chassis remained, doorless, seatless, wheelless, like the statute of Ozymandias in Shelley's poem.

We stopped alongside one of them and prowled round, our feet scuffing the sand.

'Austin. Six-cylinder Austin,' Morena said, stalking round the metal skeleton.

He crossed to the other vehicle about twenty yards away, half covered in drifted sand.

'Humber,' he said. 'Staff car, probably.'

'Something clobbered 'em,' Houston said, poking his finger into a hole in the curve of the body. 'Bullet-hole here. Two, in fact.'

During the afternoon, with the mirage growing worse and the cliffs curtseying away from us all the time, we came across a few rusty coils of blackened barbed wire.

'Right on course,' I said. 'This is the fence. The Ities put it up. All the way down from Sollum to Siwa.'

'When will we be at Qalam?' Nimmo asked sharply, interrupting. I could hear the impatience in his voice and I let the clutch in again quickly.

'Two hours,' I said. 'That's all.'

The curtain of the mirage started to dance again as we set off once more, the flat-topped glassy hills moving and swaying. We reached Qalam by late afternoon, but even Qalam was different after twenty years. There were white houses there now and small irrigated fields to which the water was fed by a petrol-driven pump attached to the well. There was a car there, too, belonging to a Unesco official, and a police post to which we reported because they liked these days to know where desert travellers were. We'd already been reported by radio from the last police post we'd passed and they were expecting us.

The sergeant in charge, as he took down our route, told us that Qalam had been opened up since the war and that even one or two farms that had belonged to Italian colonists up to 1940 and had been allowed to fall into ruin had been started up again. There was a school and, with radio, they didn't feel cut off from the rest of the world any more.

But there was still the old village with its endless wail of barbaric music, and there were still the thin hands of children stretched out towards us and the cries of 'Baksheesh', and the old man in the sunshine blind from trachoma. It wasn't so different, in spite of what he said.

After all the dust and the sunshine it seemed strange to see shade, and coarse grass between the palms, and smell the stink of rotting vegetation near the small pool full of brown muddy water where a couple of moth-eaten camels stood with their heads down.

An old man in black rags sitting on a donkey watched us drive past.

'Wotcher, cock,' Houston shouted. 'Long Range Desert Group. Doyle's Boys reporting back for duty.'

The old man didn't move and his expression didn't change.

'Looks browned off' Leach commented.

'What do you expect?' Houston grinned. 'He knows what happened last time. All his dates got pinched, someone peed in the well and he caught his wife offering jig-jig to the troops.'

The oasis had fallen away behind us now and everybody's spirits seemed to have lifted. There was some good-natured shouting backwards and forwards between the Land Rover and the lorry, but it soon died away and there was a curious tenseness that didn't come just from excitement, and then we began to see scattered fragments of white along the track.

'Bones,' I said. 'This is the old camel trail. How much further, Wop?'

Morena's face was set and excited now, his eyes staring ahead of him. 'Tomorrow afternoon, I reckon,' he said. 'We'll be south of the well at Biq Qalam tonight and reach the Depression tomorrow.'

We reached the Depression on schedule, with the horizon growing hazy as the sun dropped. In the distance we could see yellow mounds, faint and far away, like the fleshless backbone of a gigantic skeleton.

'Dunes,' Morena said. 'The Great Sand Sea.'

Nobody said anything and I saw Leach and Houston and Nimmo exchange glances with each other. There was something about them that had me worried, something that had been growing steadily all the way down from Qalam, a sort of controlled, suppressed excitement that somehow didn't include me, and it worried me because I couldn't put my finger on a reason for it.

We entered a stony defile, where the land dropped away in front of us, with angular tilted slabs of white rock like tombstones on either side. The evening shadows were rising to blot out the purples and the greens as we went lower and lower, bumping and clattering over the rocky path. Half-way down we stopped and gazed at the mysterious hazy flatness below us, surrounded by its limestone walls and eroded sections of cliff in prehistoric pillars and columns that were ready to collapse to the valley floor at a shout.

We were all staring when Nimmo pointed. 'What's that?' he said. 'That black thing.'

'Rocks,' Leach grunted. 'That's all.'

'I've never seen rocks move.'

I raised the binoculars and began to focus them.

'There's a fire or something down there,' Nimmo said. 'I can see smoke.'

Something seemed to have dropped away from me and I stood there with a hole in my belly as big as a house, empty feeling and suddenly tired.

'It's a lorry,' I said flatly. 'There's another one further on – and a jeep.'

We all stared, and I could see the disappointment written all over Houston's face. Leach's brows had come down and his stare was almost a glare, then I noticed that Morena was watching them, his eyes narrow, and I realised that I wasn't the only one who was shut out and that the closed little secretive compact lay between the other three alone.

Nimmo had taken the glasses now and was peering through them, frowning heavily, his mouth drawn down in a hard line.

'They're Arabs,' he said. 'No, hang on! There's a white man there, too! And – and – '

He lowered his glasses and stared round at us, then his taut face relaxed and split into a broad derisive grin, as though what he'd seen had overcome his anger in its appeal to his sense of humour.

'Where no white man's ever trod before, eh?' he said slowly, triumphantly staring at Houston. 'You marvellous bloody desert rats! You wonderful wonderful *wonderful* warriors! One of 'em's a woman – a white woman!'

four

We spent the night there, half-way down into the Depression on a flat patch of ground off the road against the rocks, the vehicles under the cliffs, the five of us crouching round the petrol stove and none of us saying much.

There was a look of glee on Nimmo's face that infuriated Leach and Houston, but somehow I didn't think it was only Nimmo's jeers that angered them. Morena sat on his own, his face thoughtful and unemotional as usual, eating his bully beef in silence, and I watched them all while there was light enough, wondering what was in their minds. It had been impossible to see down into the Depression, so we couldn't tell what the lorries were doing there, but the knowledge that white people had got there before us when we'd expected nothing and nobody jarred against our enthusiasm. It was this more than anything else that seemed to infuriate Leach and Houston.

It was difficult sleeping, because the ground was stony, and a short, sharp quarrel broke out between Houston and Leach and Nimmo on who was to have the hammocks.

'Not Nimmo,' Leach insisted. 'Not 'im. He's used 'em all the time.'

He plunged into the back of the lorry and I saw a pair of boots come flying out. Young Nimmo was up in a second and after him, and we heard the thump of a fist against flesh, and we were all there immediately, pushing between them. Nimmo was holding his jaw and he had his hand on the rifle.

It was the first flare-up of temper we'd had, but it had been coming a long time and was by no means unexpected.

Morena snatched the rifle away and pushed Nimmo aside.

'Last time somebody threatened me,' Leach said slowly, his face heavy and forbidding, ' 'e ended up in 'ospital for a couple of months.'

'And I suppose you ended up in clink,' Morena snapped.

Leach nodded. His nose had peeled now and looked uncomfortably raw and pink in the shadows. 'A month,' he said. 'It was worth it.'

All the humour had gone from Nimmo's face and there was a glow of evil in his eyes I'd seen once or twice in his father's face years before. 'Nobody hits me,' he said in a low voice. 'No matter how bloody big he is.'

They shuffled apart at last, but the ill feeling was strong enough to cut with a knife.

We descended into the Depression as soon as the sun began to rise next morning, moving cautiously – not because the going was difficult but because we were somehow unanxious to find out what was waiting for us down there. Leach was in front, driving the Land Rover, and I could see his head turning from side to side as he stared about him, as though he felt the Depression were full of ghosts.

Houston, who was driving the lorry, seemed to be suffering from the same uneasiness.

'Doesn't look the same,' he said slowly.

'It's twenty years later,' I reminded him.

We stopped as we reached the floor of the Depression, and stared along the flat plain to the shallow cliffs rising on either side. The heat was intense now and made you pant as it fought for the moisture in your body.

'It's different.' As we drew up alongside the Land Rover, Leach spoke slowly, as though he thought there were a trick in it somewhere. 'There's more sand at the bottom 'ere.'

'Could have come from the Sand Sea,' I pointed out. 'A steady north wind could have brought tons of it down.'

We were all silent for a moment, aware of the oppressive silence that was menacing in its intensity, then Houston spoke, his voice hushed as though he were suddenly scared.

'It was somewhere here we found the Paymaster,' he said. 'Over there.'

He jerked his hand towards a cluster of rocks, and then we saw for the first time the blackened box of metal half buried in the sand, without wheels, doors, glass or seats.

In the silence it seemed as though it were one of the ghosts that was troubling Leach, and abruptly I had the feeling that we were being watched, as though those eroded buttresses of rock hid figures which never shifted their gaze from us.

Morena had climbed down from the lorry and was staring round him in that manner of his that I remembered so well from the war – standing still, a little apart from everyone else, his eyes moving slowly about him, full of caution and alertness. The others were climbing down, too, now, staring uneasily round them at the high flanking walls of limestone, and I noticed that Leach and Houston had drawn close to one another, as though they drew some comfort from each other's presence.

'This is it.' Morena had walked over to the rusting wreckage now and was peering at it. 'You can see the bullet-holes.'

It was like passing through a time-barrier and seeing things happen that had first happened centuries before, and it gave me a strange feeling of having stepped back into the Middle Ages, because suddenly, with all that had happened since, the war – our war – seemed to belong to the Middle Ages.

We stood by the wreck in silence for a moment, all of us touched, each in his own way, by memories, and I found myself wondering if they'd ever managed to turn up the

77

Paymaster's iron chest. There'd been a hell of a row when we'd got back to base. There'd been an enquiry, with no less a person than a colonel running it, and a lot of accusations had been made. We'd all been questioned and cross-questioned and for a fortnight or so had lived damned uncomfortable lives. In the end the CO had decided to court-martial me, to clear the air a bit.

'I know damned well you haven't got the bloody money,' he'd said. 'But we've got to wrap these Provost bastards up. Now they'll either have to put up or shut up.'

The court-martial had absolved the lot of us, but it didn't really clear the air. Nimmo, Leach, Houston and the others who'd gone to the Depression had been harried by the Provost Department for a long time afterwards, and the first thing that had happened when we broke through after Alamein and swept up to Tunisia was that an expedition had been sent down to the Depression to look for the money. Needless to say, they didn't find it, and in the end they'd just accepted that Sheikh Ghad had got it, and even that had annoyed them, because when Rommel had driven us back he'd swapped sides with all his men and just before his camel trod on a mine that sent him to Kingdom Come he'd actually handed over to the Germans a column of soft-skinned vehicles that had fled his way to get round the Panzers.

I snapped out of the memory, pushing it behind me quickly.

'Where did you bury them all?' I asked.

'Further down,' Houston said. 'Near the rocks. It was too hard here then to dig. We went close to the cliff where there was some loose soil.'

'Let's go,' I said.

The track emerged from the sand as we moved along the floor of the Depression towards the east. We could see the smoke of fires and a lorry and a jeep and a high square vehicle that seemed as though it might contain some sort of laboratory. They were just up ahead of us now blurred a little by the heat that was making the rock faces dance.

As we drew closer, we saw people standing by them, waiting for us.

'It's a woman, all right,' Houston said eagerly.

'Sure it is,' Nimmo grinned. 'I've never seen a man that shape before.'

They began to walk towards us as we approached, a man with grey hair, tall and stooping, and a girl, small and slim and straight, followed by about twenty or thirty Arabs of all ages and in all kinds of dress from ragged robes to modern khaki shorts and shirts.

The Land Rover halted and I stopped the lorry alongside, a few yards from the other vehicles. The man was the first to come up to us, with the girl just behind him, and, behind her, the Arabs in a half-circle, standing motionless – curiously motionless – still as stones, their hands by their sides, their black eyes opaque and unrelenting and full of an unexpected hate. As I stared back at their unyielding gaze, the uneasiness that had been growing on me ever since we'd reached the floor of the Depression increased.

The man had moved forward again now, gesturing with his hand at our vehicles.

'Who the devil are you?' he asked, not angrily but with a frosty, mid-Western American voice that was full of surprise and curiosity.

'My name's Doyle,' I said. 'Alan Doyle. This is Leach, Houston, Morena and Nimmo.'

'I'm Sloan Crabourne. Professor Crabourne. Marston University, Ohio. This is my assistant and my cousin, Philomena Crabourne Garvey. What are you doing here and what do you represent?'

The girl was watching us, saying nothing, her face calm and interested. She wasn't beautiful, though she had the sort of face that grows on you – awkwardly angled but with a pale perfect skin, short fair hair and lively grey eyes that made you feel full of excitement without knowing why. She had an inquisitive look about her at the moment, too, as though she'd been stiff with boredom and welcomed the diversion, and I had to wrench my gaze away from her to answer Crabourne.

'We might ask you the same question,' I said.

Crabourne stared at us for a moment, his eyes resting curiously on Houston's absurd head-dress.

'I guess,' he said slowly, 'to put it simply, we're archaeologists. Though perhaps that's *too simple*. I'm the archaeologist. My assistants are artists. We're copying wall painting.' He gestured behind him with his hand. 'The Ghad tribe discovered the painting of a bullock on the rock face of a cave here. For some reason best known to themselves they were doing some excavating work in the area and found it quite by chance. It probably dates from way back before Christ.'

I saw Houston and Leach glance at each other and I felt a surge of hope as Crabourne's words bore out what Nimmo had told us.

'Since then,' Crabourne went on, 'we've found literally hundreds, probably of Negro origin, though some of the later ones are undoubtedly of Mycaenean or Egyptian influence. There are more at Qahait south of here. I've got an assistant and another group there. We're trying to put them on record. Now I guess you'd better tell us what *you're* doing here.'

'Much the same, I suppose,' I said.

He stared at us for a moment, then he exploded. 'But this is plain goddamned silly,' he snapped. 'Why *two* groups? We got permission to come here.'

'So did we.'

'We got the backing of Unesco and the Libyan Academy of Archaeological Sciences. Who's backing you?'

'Us,' Leach said bluntly. 'Me, him, him, him and him.'

Crabourne stared. 'What do you mean?'

'We put up the money ourselves.'

Crabourne looked angry. 'You guys are poaching on our territory,' he said sharply.

It seemed to be time to lay our cards on the table. 'On the contrary, I said, 'perhaps you're poaching on ours. We were here long ago and found the first of your paintings long before you did. In 1942, to be exact. We were operating just to the north of here. A patrol came down here to rescue a group of men. They'd been caught by Messerschmitts. They're buried here. *We* buried them.'

Crabourne looked interested and the anger left his face. 'Say, those'll be the graves we found. Four of 'em. Up against the cliff. Ahmed says it was a Britisher who'd come to bring money to them.'

I glanced at the girl. 'Who's Ahmed?' I asked.

'He's in charge of the diggers.' It was the first time she'd spoken and her voice was warm and steady and I saw Nimmo and Houston staring approvingly at her. 'He's our interpreter, too, and helps with the photography. He said he was a boy of ten at the time.'

'We'd better have a word with Ahmed,' I suggested. 'The money was never found and I was responsible for it.'

'Is that what you're here for?' Crabourne asked.

I shook my head again and told him the reason for our journey, but his lip curled and he made a derisive gesture.

'There are no ornaments here,' he said. 'There's no trace of human habitation, in fact, outside the pictures. No monuments, no tombs, no mounds that might hide a lost city. The Qalami simply liked painting, that's all, and this Depression and the cliffs at Qahait simply provided a suitable place for it.'

'It seems to tie up with the paintings, all the same,' I insisted.

He gestured again with a trace of irritation. 'For God's sake!' he said. 'For ornaments you'd need a church, and for a church you'd need a city. There's nothing like that here. You're wasting your time.'

He clearly resented us, but I felt we had as much right there as he had. 'Why can't we help each other,' I suggested, 'and pool results? We have a map of where they were found.'

Crabourne gave a twisted smile. 'Treasure Island, eh?' he said. 'Long John Silver.'

His sarcasm irritated me and I answered sharply. 'It was made in 1942. Here. By the men who came down here.'

Watched by the circle of silent Arabs, all of them listening, their eyes moving quickly among each other, Crabourne considered the information for a moment, then he nodded, though not very willingly.

'Well, a map's a map,' he said. 'I suppose, in fact, I'd be mighty interested if you *did* find something, though I don't figure you will. Ask Ahmed.'

Ahmed was a sullen young-looking man with a lean handsome face and a thin nose like the blade of a scimitar. He didn't bow to me as he might have done twenty years before, and I noticed he showed even less interest in Nimmo's treasure than Crabourne.

'There is nothing,' he said softly in English. 'I know. I am a Qalam. We are all Qalami here. From Qalam and Qahait and Qatu. I was here when your people came down to bring us the money during the fighting. I was a boy at the time. I had a rifle. The money never came.'

'I saw it coming,' I said.

Ahmed's eyes flashed angrily. 'It didn't arrive,' he snapped. 'We heard the aeroplanes. We found the dead men. One of them was a Qalam - my own cousin. They'd been buried. But there was no money.'

It didn't seem worth arguing about. Not now. Not after twenty years. The Paymaster and his companions were merely mouldering bones under the thin soil of the Depression now, and the jeep was just a blackened pile of rusting metal. Whoever had taken the money had doubtless spent it long since. But Ahmed seemed still to regard it as important, as though it nagged like a knife under the ribs of his tribe. With his young aggressive face, he reminded me a little of Nimmo.

'My people spoke of it with bitterness for many years,' he went on. 'The soldiers sent lorries and cars and many men. They questioned all my people. But they never sent any more money.'

'They might have done,' I pointed out, 'if you hadn't changed sides.'

His eyes flashed again, but he ignored the comment. 'There were soldiers here for years,' he said. 'All the time. Men from the bases in the north. They pretended they were doing field exercises. But we knew what they were looking for, because there was a shepherd who saw four men with a vehicle on the day the money should have come. One of them a big man like the one with you, and one with hair like fire.'

'Those were my men, Ahmed,' I said. 'I sent them here to find the money. But there wasn't any money. It had gone. Instead, they saw gold ornaments in a cave.'

He spat contemptuously. 'There are no gold ornaments,' he said, and I saw Crabourne nod approvingly. 'My people would have found them long ago if there had been.'

Something in the way he spoke and in the way he held himself, one foot forward, his head up, curiously proud and absurd in his white shorts and baseball cap and sun-glasses, made me start wondering.

'*Your* people?' I asked, feeling sure he'd stressed the point so that I wouldn't fail to take it.

He nodded slowly, his lips thin and tight under the cruel curve of his nose.

'*My* people,' he repeated. 'I am the son of Sheikh Ghad.'

five

We set up our camp within a few yards of Crabourne's, parking the lorry and the Land Rover alongside each other. As we were going to be there for some time, we set about making it more or less permanent and dug out the tent and the fly-sheets from under the stores. With two extra air mattresses we could now all sleep in comfort without a fight every night for the hammocks.

Crabourne's camp was a spartan set of crude stone huts erected by the Arabs and roofed with plaited palm-fronds brought down especially from Qalam. There were also a few olive-drab army tents with the camouflage still on them and the spring gone from the guy-ropes so that the dusty canvas hung forlornly in the heat, and a wired enclosure that was used as a stores dump and a parking area, for the jeep and the five-ton truck and the big van like a pantechnicon that they used for a technical studio and photographic dark room. The place was neat but it had a look of squalid impermanence about it. Somebody had tried to plant some flowers, but they had dried out in the heat and stood up stiff and stark like the withered legs of dead birds, and the palm-frond roofs of the huts, like the tents, were heavy with dust, their colour dulled to a matt brown.

Just beyond the group of vehicles was the Arab encampment, a few low tents covered with red tanned goatskins, with brightly coloured rugs in front. There was a group of goats and camels, supercilious, bad-tempered and ridiculous, that the tribesmen kept with them for transport and for milk, and a few women, blue-tattooed on forehead and chin, in barbaric silver jewellery, who eyed us with bold curious eyes as we passed them. They were offshoots of the Tuareg and doomed to disappear before long – a shiftless, immoral lot who had no word for virginity. Even the prestige that had sprung from their warlike history was fast disappearing against the dazzling competition of the oil men and the mineral seekers who were traversing the desert with fat-bellied planes and helicopters and their magnificent trans-desert highways. There was little left for them now except menial work such as labouring for Crabourne, casual thieving or a little quarrelling with neighbours, incidents that were whipped up by such tribe-minded leaders as Ghad Ahmed seemed to be.

We'd been invited over to Crabourne's camp for an evening drink, but only Morena and Nimmo and I went. The other two pleaded that the heat was affecting them more than they'd expected.

They were still in the strange mood that had come on them as we'd descended the Depression, their light-heartedness draining away as soon as we'd passed Qalam. Inevitably Houston had tried his charms on Phil Garvey, but he hadn't got very far and had returned to the tent full of snide remarks on her figure and her morals, and lewd suggestions about what might happen when we'd been there a little longer. There'd been a brief exchange of words with Leach, when Leach had failed to understand one of his tasteless jokes about her, and now they were silent and remote and curiously angry – as though they resented Crabourne as much as he resented them. There'd been a few muttered remarks during the morning as we'd pitched camp, and a grumbling undertone all through the midday meal from Leach, and, though they'd subsided now to a panting fury at the heat, they still hadn't got over their inexplicable bitterness.

Crabourne's mess hut was a bare sparse building stacked at one end with cartons and packing cases, with a wire screen at the window and a hissing primus on a table, and a rifle on an improvised rack above a tin trunk and a dented wash-bowl. I heard a spurt of music from the workmen's camp as we arrived, barbaric and flat on the evening air, as toneless and thin as the wind itself, then someone started singing in a high-pitched voice that was more a screech than a song, and I saw the lamps yellow and glowing among the low mounds of the tents, and caught the drifting smell of the smoke from where the women cooked over fires made with camel-dung.

Crabourne was waiting for us, together with his cousin and a small Jewish-looking man we'd not seen before, with a narrow face and a tall spire of curling hair that stood up above his forehead like the tuft of a cockatoo.

'This is David Selinski,' Crabourne said as we settled our-selves in the folding chairs that gave them a shred of comfort. 'David's looking after Qahait. He's been having trouble over there with the workmen, so he's joined us for the evening to report. They're too sophisticated these days, I guess. They know all about union rules and proper hours.'

His cousin handed us coffee poured out by a silent Arab and Crabourne splashed spirit into thick mugs.

'Hardly brandy bowls,' he said cheerfully, waving away the flies. 'But I guess they suffice.'

He pushed aside a pile of paper clips and measuring tapes and manila envelopes, to put his mug on the table, then he sat back and sailed into me without preamble.

'You guys are barking up the wrong tree, you know,' he said. 'There's nothing here.'

He gestured in a peremptory manner, as though what he'd said should be sufficient to convince us, and reached for the mug again as though the matter were settled. I saw Morena glance at me and I shrugged. 'We'll look, all the same,' I said.

Crabourne frowned, as though stubbornness in anyone irritated him. 'Look,' he said, 'this place was found only by chance. Though, God knows, it's been searched often enough since the war by Ghad Ahmed himself.'

'There were paintings at Faras,' I pointed out. 'I've seen pictures of them. There were plenty of other things, too.'

He was unimpressed. 'Doesn't mean a thing,' he said. 'The desert's full of paintings that have no connection with anything else. They found masses of them at Djanet in the Tassili Hills, and more at Jabbaren and Sefar and Adjefou. The French copied thousands.'

'The Poles found pictures of Christ at Faras,' I pointed out. '*And* remains of churches.'

He shrugged again. 'Some of these goddam churches that are found are so unimportant the tribes use them for goat-pens.' He swung round on Selinski. 'David,' he said. 'Do you figure anyone ever lived here?'

'How could they?' Selinski spoke with the soft sycophantic voice of an intellectual yes-man. 'The paintings are spread over a dozen miles. That doesn't seem to indicate a settled community.'

'*Or* a treasure,' Crabourne put in with a faint note of contempt in his voice as he looked at me. 'The Qalami are nomads, in spite of their villages. And nomads don't carry treasure with them.'

We stayed for a while, fighting off the insects that came towards the light in terrifying swarms, with Nimmo hogging the girl in a corner while Crabourne lectured the rest of us rather like a teacher with a set of students. He had a lecturer's manner and most of the conversation was taken up by his opinions. His cousin kept glancing over Nimmo's head at him, with a hint of amusement in her eyes, as though she knew his faults and had learned to live with them, but Selinski obviously took them seriously.

It was dark by the time we left, and as Selinski had to drive back to Qahait, we all turned out to see him go. The jeep moved away down the Depression, a black slug trailing a cloud of dust behind the long white beam of the headlights, then we said good night, Nimmo lingering over Crabourne's cousin a little longer than he need have done.

The night had come as abruptly as if a whole lot of lights had been dimmed in a theatre, and there was even something of the same theatrical effect. One minute everything was bright and in clear visual contact, and the next it was in darkness. But the stupefying hostile heat had vanished also and, driven by an urgent longing to find something of what we'd lost over the years, I let Morena and Nimmo go ahead and walked off alone into the Depression, past the low mound of soil they'd dug out of the caves to get at the paintings.

There was a great humming silence, with a sliver of moon coming over the edge of the cliffs dead ahead, flooding the land with faint pale light that showed up the rocks with softly radiant contour lines and left the hollows as black patches like holes in the earth. I could see a fire flickering palely in the shadows, and there was a smell of food in the air coming from Ghad Ahmed's camp. Above me was the full sweep of the night sky, a dark bowl riddled with stars that didn't twinkle as they did in England but seemed to burn, enormous and brilliant, just above my head.

The sense of being watched came over me again, as though the whole Depression had eyes, as though all those thousands of paintings that Crabourne was copying were staring at me, and I found myself listening suddenly, half expecting to hear the rumble of guns and see the rose-red flashes of light towards the north and feel the vibration through the soles of my feet of far-off heavy blasts. Then I relaxed, knowing it was my surroundings that were causing me unconsciously to reach back into memory. The Garden of Allah, the Arabs called the desert. The place where you could find a paradise on earth.

I sighed, knowing I was searching for something from the past that didn't exist any more. I was full of peculiar embitterments and ecstasies that were hard to bear, and was just about to set off back to the camp, my heart tight, my chest constricted, when I heard the chink of a stone nearby, and I whirled round.

It was Crabourne's cousin, a small slender figure emerging from the shadows.

'Enjoying the moon?' she asked as she appeared.

I laughed. 'At my age,' I said, 'the romance has drained away a bit.'

She chuckled and gazed at me for a second. 'How long are you going to he here?' she asked.

I shrugged. 'God knows. How about you?'

'I don't know. Nobody knows. Not even Sloan. There's so much to do.' She laughed. 'There were five of us originally, but now we're down to three, and David Selinski's over at Qahait all the time. The other two just vanished.'

'Vanished?'

'She was German. Bit of an expert, I guess, and Sloan's right hand. I came along originally to chaperone her, or her me, I don't know which. She was fat and ancient. At least thirty-five...'

I held my tongue like a coward and didn't tell her I was forty, as old as some of the dug-outs I'd sneered at in just the same way during the war.

'I guess the heat got them,' she said. 'It sure bowled them over.

'Sunstroke?'

She laughed. 'No. Sex. They couldn't work for pawing each other. Like a couple of hippos making love. After a fortnight she claimed she was ill and had to go to the coast, and he insisted on taking her in one of the jeeps.' She chuckled again. 'They never came back.'

She paused, as though she had something on her mind, and suddenly I realised she'd been not only bored but a little scared, too, with only Crabourne and the Arabs down there in the silent Depression. Then she seemed to draw herself up, as though she were pushing her apprehensions out of sight to the back of her mind.

'It's funny to think that people once lived here, isn't it?' Her voice came slowly and sounded awed. 'Lived here and left nothing but the paintings to show they'd ever existed or where they went. There must have been a lot of them, too. The paintings give quite a detailed picture of the life.'

She stopped, as though afraid she were talking too much shop, and looked up at me. 'I'm sorry Sloan's so – so boorish about everything,' she went on. 'Personally, I find it a pleasure to see someone around. Particularly as Sloan always seems as though he's just been taken off a shelf and dusted after not being used for a long time. It's his job, I suppose.'

'What about Selinski?' I asked. 'You've still got him.'

She smiled. 'He's what you'd call "devoted to his work". We don't really get on.' She paused and went on in a faintly resentful tone: 'It's such a pity everybody objects so much to each other. Sloan to your party. Your friends to us.'

I shrugged. 'I think *they* find the desert more crowded than they remember it,' I explained. 'It's a little disconcerting. Besides, perhaps they don't like having people disbelieve them.'

'Like Sloan?'

'And Ahmed.'

At the mention of the name the worries that I'd guessed had been plaguing her burst out as she let her guard down, and there was a note of relief in her voice as she replied.

'Whatever Sloan says,' she pointed out firmly, '*I*'m glad you're here. I prefer it that way.'

'Why?'

'I don't know.' She moved her shoulders. 'Sloan's a professor. He has his head in a book all the time. The only things he sees are what are written in the sand. Perhaps it's because I'm a woman, but I seem to see more.'

'What, for instance?'

She jerked her shoulders again. 'I wouldn't know,' she said helplessly. 'Something. Something not quite right. Suspicion. Dislike. Watchfulness. Something like that. Ghad Ahmed's people are hardly Ivy League types, are they?'

I laughed, and she went on quickly.

'The very sight of you coming across the Depression did me good.' She gazed around her. 'What is it about this place?' she asked, her voice unexpectedly sharp and nervous. 'What is it that gets everyone on edge so?'

'Are they on edge?'

'Sure they are. Ghad Ahmed doesn't like us. In fact, I think he detests us. Yet his people are working for us. They're *always* working. In spite of their union rules, they work when we don't want them to. They do no harm, but I wonder why.'

I laughed. 'Perhaps *they*'ve heard of our treasure, too.'

She looked up at me, puzzled. 'Do you really believe there is a treasure?'

'I saw the bowl,' I said. 'I really did. Nimmo's father had it. He said it was from one of these caves where he saw the first of your paintings – long before the Qalami found them and reported them. He was impressed enough by the pictures to make drawings and take bearings. He felt the pictures were important enough for someone to come back one day and find more like them and copy them. Leach was with him and so was Houston.'

She was silent for a while, thinking, then she looked up at me. 'It's a bit like Zerzura, isn't it?' she said. 'The Place of

Little Birds. The legendary city in the desert with the sleeping king and queen.'

'*You*'ve heard that one, too?'

'I don't believe that, either.'

'Look,' I said, desperately keen to convince her. 'Those Messerschmitts that killed the Paymaster back there. Nimmo said their bombs had disturbed the rocks. And why not? A bomb might well have unearthed the first of your pictures by moving soil or stones that wouldn't be disturbed by normal things like wind or rain. So why not a cave with treasure?'

She seemed impressed, in spite of the smile on her face. 'Perhaps that's what Ghad Ahmed's after,' she agreed. 'It would certainly explain all his eagerness.'

She stared around her, her face pale in the moonlight.

'What is it about this place?' she said again, half to herself. 'I noticed it even when we first arrived. There's something I don't like about it. There are too many people interested in it and what we're doing. First us. Then Ghad Ahmed. And now you.'

s i x

It was the heat that woke me next morning. I was bathed in sweat and the glittering white light outside was without shade of any kind. I could hear the chatter of voices against the cliff and through the open flap of the tent could see that Crabourne's party were already at work.

'They start early,' Leach commented heavily, squatting on the ground with an enamel mug in his hands, his eyes on the basket-boys near the spoil-mound and the slender figure of Phil Garvey moving about near one of the caves.

We'd not got into any kind of routine about rising or starting work, but Houston, more by accident than by design, had found himself crouching unwillingly over the stove, and we breakfasted off beans and bacon. The bacon was soggy and the beans were over-cooked into a brown mash and Houston was only vaguely apologetic as he served it up.

'Sorry, mates,' he said. 'I seem to have lost the knack.'

'You never *'ad* the knack,' Leach growled. 'It was always like this when you cooked the grub.'

And then I remembered that it was, and I began to recall all the other little things that Houston had always failed to do, the way he'd always been carried on everybody else's shoulders, the way he'd always been quick to draw attention from his faults.

He was shrugging now at Leach's complaint, indifferent as he had always been to criticism.

'Well, it *is* a bit tiresome, all this cooking, isn't it?' he said fretfully. 'Why can't we mess with that lot over there? They've got a Wog to do it. It might even be company in the evenings. Something better to look at than your ugly mug.' His eyes strayed across to Crabourne's compound, bright and shining and faraway. 'That girl's got a pair of pippins,' he said. 'Wonder who she gets to scrub her back in the bath, because she can have me any time.'

Nimmo, who'd been watching Phil Garvey through the tent flap, turned and gave him a sharp look, and Houston shrugged.

'Well, she has, hasn't she?' he said.

It was soon breathtakingly hot and seemed to be growing hotter all the time, but someone had to go to the well at Biq Qalam and I decided to start off by being friendly with Crabourne's group and offering to fetch water for them. Morena offered to go with me, chiefly, I think, because Houston and Leach were already getting on his nerves, too.

Biq Qalam was off the direct route between Qalam and the Depression and we'd not bothered to go out of our way to it the day before, feeling that there'd be plenty of time to collect water later, and Crabourne jumped at the chance and even offered us one of his drivers, because both he and Phil Garvey were overworked and he needed Ghad Ahmed with him to keep the men at their soil shifting.

Out of the Depression there was an unexpected breath of wind from the north that was surprisingly cool and refreshing, and we reached the well in good time and, in return for a few tins of bully beef the Qalami there helped the Arab driver to fill the cans and stack them on the lorry.

It grew hotter as the day progressed and the wind faded almost to nothing. The plain seemed to be heaving in waves as the air shimmered, and I was already looking forward to the blessed relief of evening. We sat in the shade of the trees, among the tufty grass where flakes of encrusted salt gleamed, and Morena played his mouth organ softly as we smoked and waited.

'You ever go to any of those Old Comrades' dinners?' he asked suddenly, the words coming unexpectedly from nowhere, as though he'd been thinking about them for a long time.

'Once,' I said. 'Only once.'

He nodded. 'Same here. It seemed to be run entirely by blokes who never got nearer the desert than Cairo. Came as a bit of a disappointment. Wasn't the same.'

He gestured. 'This is different, too. Something missing nowadays.'

His words had mirrored my own thoughts exactly. 'Yes,' I agreed. 'It's different.'

'Funny how disappointed you feel about it, isn't it?'

He nodded at the desert. 'It used to get me, this lot,' he said. 'You know how it did. I remember sitting at the top of the Depression waiting for the others to come back with that Paymaster. We couldn't see what was going on in the Depression and we were alone, but I wasn't scared. I sat up there with Gester and Smollett, with old Morris reading his poetry and pretending he liked it, while Nimmo went down with Bummer Ward and Leach and Houston. I wasn't a bit disturbed about it. Now...' he shrugged and frowned '...well, now it's not the same. There's something wrong somehow.'

'You've noticed, too?'

'Yes.' He threw away his cigarette. 'It worries me. I keep wondering what's going on in that black hole Ghad Ahmed calls his mind. And then there's Leach. He's just a fat slob now. And Houston's a bit of a wash-out, too, when you think about, it, isn't he?'

He sighed. 'But it's not that. It's not just because it's twenty years later and we're older. There's something else. Something I don't like.' He paused and looked hard at me. 'I think there's something bloody queer going on around here,' he ended.

Work had finished by the time we got back to the Depression. The Arabs were listlessly packing up for the day and Ghad Ahmed was by the spoil-heap placing sheets of drawings into folders.

We climbed down slowly from the lorry, our knees stiff aware how dry and desiccated we felt under the blazing sunshine, and conscious all the time of a row of eyes watching us from near the low heap of the spoil-mound, where the workmen were just downing tools and squatting on dusty haunches with their baskets and mattocks. Ghad Ahmed began to move among them, smarter-looking than the rest, definitely a chief's son in his neat trousers and shirt, a baseball cap on his head and dark sun-glasses on his curved nose. He was peering towards the tent alongside our vehicles, scrutinising it carefully.

Against the bleached empty light they all had a faded dun look like blurred images on an old photograph, and they seemed, somehow, to be waiting for something to happen. I glanced at Morena and saw him staring aggressively back at them, his square body brown under the sun, his hands thrust deep into the pockets of his shorts, his feet wide apart, the dusty stockings rolled down round his ankles over his scuffed boots. His eyes were narrow and puzzled and his face was expressionless, and I knew that he'd noticed it, too, and that it was worrying him under the surface as much as it was me.

As we watched, Ghad Ahmed closed the file he was working on and walked across to supervise the unloading of the water. He was still hostile and even almost rude.

'What's the matter, Ahmed?' I asked. 'Don't you like us?'

'This is a young state,' he said sullenly. 'We are no longer an Italian colony, and we are inspired by strong feelings of nationhood.'

I put him down as an Arab Nationalist and decided to warn the others that when we came to find what we were looking for it might he a good idea to keep it quiet. A man with Ghad Ahmed's feelings might well consider it belonged to *him*.

'We are striving to build up the country,' he was saying arrogantly. 'Assisted by specialists from Egypt and Italy and Germany.'

'No British?'

He shook his head. 'No British.'

I was aware of humiliation and I began to wonder just why all those hundreds of men had died at El Alamein and Tobruk and Knightsbridge.

'One day,' he went on stiffly, 'we shall not need even these people either. Recent finds of oil promise well for the future. We are opening schools everywhere. You must have noticed at Qalam. For girls as well as boys. Trees are being constantly planted to improve the climate, and dams built to provide water. All the farms of the former Italian colonists are being cultivated again.'

He directed the stacking of the last of the jerricans and walked away, his whole body stiff with unrelenting pride. I stared after him for a while with Morena, then Morena shook his head. 'Funny, isn't it?' he said. 'When we were here before I always used to feel it was the Arabs who were the intruders.'

When we reached the tent Nimmo was sitting in the shade of the lorry, his transistor to his ear, and the most he could do when we greeted him was nod. Leach and Houston were stretched in their underpants on the air mattresses in the tent, gasping for breath.

Morena stared round at them as he entered behind me, his eyes cold. 'You lot still here?' he asked, sounding exactly like a sergeant again, doing his rounds at Reveille.

We ate our meal in silence and, afterwards, with Morena sitting a little to one side reading an old magazine he'd borrowed, I wandered off to where Crabourne's group was working.

The limestone of the cliffs had been worn away by the winter winds that swirled round the floor of the Depression, to make deep erosions and caves, and outside one of them Crabourne's pantechnicon truck was standing, running on an advanced throttle, wires stretching from the battery into the cave.

Lights had been rigged inside and I found Phil Garvey balancing like an acrobat on a rickety stepladder, taking tracings on a cellophane sheet with a felt pen. She wore brief shorts and a frayed straw hat and her face was serious and absorbed. There was a clip block of smaller sketches alongside her, and an array of colours and pens.

She looked down and smiled quickly as she saw me.

'Ghad Ahmed always insists on proper hours and union rules for *his* people,' she said. 'Except when it suits him to work extra. But not us. Sloan gets all he can out of us.'

She glanced at me curiously. 'I thought it might be your young screwball Nimmo,' she said. 'He's been here once. He seems to like watching me work.'

'I'm not surprised,' I said, my eyes on her figure.

She climbed down and drank from the chatti that hung against the rock. The painting she was working on showed shapes which seemed to represent gods looking down on groups of women crushing corn in stone mortars, and men on oxen with children riding pillion behind them, and great herds of cattle covering the whole wall of the cave from top to bottom. Part of it was even on the roof, fifteen feet high, and another part was so low that to copy it she must have been on her knees – as though through the centuries the floor of the cave had risen.

'It's always cramped like this,' she said, enjoying the curiosity in my face. 'We have to wash the walls first because of the layers of dust over the paintings. That's why we need the water.'

'I bet it was quite a job,' I said, staring upwards into the shadows.

'It gets so hot in here sometimes,' she agreed. 'That's the chief trouble. We had to bring huge stocks of paper and drawing materials, and paint and tables. A lot of the ladders were made at Qalam.'

I gestured at the paintings. 'They're quite something, aren't they?'

She nodded enthusiastically. 'There's one wonderful fresco in one of the other caves that we haven't even started on yet,' she said. 'A hundred feet square and no relation to any of the other paintings. It's probably the earliest example of Negro art known, and a record of the prehistoric population of the Sahara.'

She led me along the walls, directing the light against the cave's surface, and I saw women working in fields and men seated by huts, and horses and chariots.

'Herodotus refers to chasing Troglodyte Ethiopians in chariots,' she said. 'And he died in 425 BC, so at the latest these paintings date from then. Further down there are some of horses going at full gallop, similar to Cretan pictures, and the Cretans landed here in 1200 BC to use the country as a base to attack Egypt, so the paintings might even date from then.'

'There are a hell of a lot of them,' I said. 'Will you come again next season?'

She shook her head. 'It's not really a woman's job, is it? You have to be such an acrobat and I've already lived too long on macaroni and spam.'

'What will you do?'

'Go home,' she said with a laugh. 'Look round for a man and get married. I'm the domesticated type, really. Sloan says I'd be much happier here if I could just hang up a few chintz curtains and go round with a feather duster.'

Her mood seemed to change, as though the warmth had gone out of her abruptly. She had become uneasy and uncertain again and I remembered her worried look the night before in the moonlight.

'Have you found anything yet?' she asked.

I thought of Leach and Houston stretched out on their beds, and of Nimmo quiet and uncommunicative outside the tent, and the strange atmosphere of remoteness about them all that excluded Morena and myself, and I shook my head.

'Do you think you will?'

'I'm beginning to doubt it,' I said.

'Your young friend, Jimmy Nimmo, seems hopeful enough,' she pointed out.

I stared at her, remembering Nimmo's apparent indifference. 'What makes you say that?' I asked.

'I saw him. This morning early. It was light enough, but only just. We start early, as you know, and I'd just gotten up.'

'Where was he?'

'About a hundred yards away from here. There's a rock fall and a patch of broken rock up there and a cave with an entrance shaped like a pear. He was walking up and down, kicking at the ground and staring at it.'

'Why?'

'Perhaps it covers something he's interested in. Old bones. Hidden plans. Buried treasure. Take your pick.'

'Thanks,' I said. 'That's worth knowing.'

'That's OK,' She gave me an odd look. 'I hope I haven't brought any disruptive influences to bear on your expedition.'

I shrugged. 'I shouldn't think so,' I reassured her. 'None that weren't there before.'

She watched me light a cigarette, then began to climb back up the ladder on slim brown legs.

I stayed for a while watching her work as she reproduced the blacks and whites and the faded reds and blues, then I walked slowly out into the sunshine.

As I came out into the heat I glanced instinctively down the Depression towards the rocks she'd mentioned. Without surprise, I saw a figure moving slowly in the glare, and as I watched I saw it stop nervously and stand, staring at the cliff face, its feet scuffing the dusty earth. It was Tiny Leach, and right opposite him was a cave whose entrance was shaped like a pear.

The Arabs had gone from the top of the spoil-mound now and it seemed to be empty of life, then, briefly, as I stared down the Depression, I caught a movement against the sky and realised there was still a figure up there, sitting down, half hidden, as though he didn't wish to he seen.

I saw a glint of sun-glasses and realised it was Ghad Ahmed, and all that Morena had said and tried to say as we'd waited for the lorry to be loaded by the well at Biq Qalam came back to me. Suddenly the desert seemed more hostile, and the bare rocks and bloodless earth of the Depression seemed to hide a whole host of enemies.

Part Two

The Empty Desert

Somehow, from the moment we'd reached the Depression I'd been sure that trouble was coming. I hadn't known what shape it would take, but I was as sure of it as I was of day following night.

The sense of expectancy grew during that evening. Ghad Ahmed's camp seemed oddly quiet, as though they were listening, and the breeze was shifting the grit so that I could hear a tent canvas flap-flapping in a flat monotonous beating. Ghad Ahmed's men were squatting by their fires, but I had the impression that they were still watching us, with opaque black eyes that were entirely hostile. The Depression seemed to be full of phantoms in the fading light, a terrible vacant space where no life stirred, where there was not even a bird to break the silence, or a wild animal to bring movement to the stillness. Soon the stars would be moving silently above with the moon on its cold remote course, and all at once I was stiff with fear at the emptiness, a sudden unexplained panic I'd experienced more than once in the desert, a feeling of minuteness in the infinite vastness, a sense of vulnerability and weakness.

I could hear Morena humming softly to himself as he tinkered, stripped to the waist, with the engine of the lorry, but somehow the normality of it failed to break through the thin skin of apprehension. Leach and Houston seemed as much on edge as I was, and ready for a fight. They'd been bickering in the tent with Nimmo for some time, arguing as usual across the straight bright flame of the lamp.

It had started off with a few tasteless comments on Phil Garvey by Houston, and it had suddenly dawned on me that, far from being the lady-killer he liked people to believe he was, Houston was a sad little man whom no woman ever took seriously, and his frustration took the form of tall stories about his conquests and lewd remarks about every woman he saw.

But it hadn't been me who'd turned on him, but Nimmo, who'd offered to knock his head off if he didn't shut up and, when Houston had taken refuge in sarcastic suggestions that Nimmo was anxious to get her into a corner himself, they'd set about each other in a noisy series of threats that could have been heard a hundred yards away. It was over now, but things were still a bit strained and to escape the tension I walked down the Depression for a while then went across to Crabourne's camp. My excuse was that I was interested in the paintings, but in my heart of hearts I knew it was Phil Garvey who drew me there.

There'd been only one other woman who'd ever drawn me like this – the girl I'd married towards the end of the war and lost in the bitter days of the disappointing peace, and, although it was years since now, I could still only think of her as she'd been then, as if my mind were the camera that had caught the colour of her eyes, the way the wind had blown her summer dress; as though, after she'd gone, I'd become her immortality. Since then there'd never been anyone else, and because I'd long since given up hope of finding another woman who could attract me as much again, I found it disturbing that Phil Garvey could, particularly as she was as young as my wife had been years before, as young as I still saw her in the secret rendezvous of my mind.

I was annoyed to find Nimmo had got there before me and was hanging around her, but she seemed to shrug him off neatly as I arrived and before he knew where he was he was inside the hut staring unwillingly at Crabourne's pictures.

We drank coffee together sitting outside the hut in canvas chairs, while Crabourne muttered to Nimmo inside over the files of drawings. Phil was in an odd mood, however, and the liveliness that had first drawn me to her had given way to a strange sort of nervousness that was heightened by my own feelings of uneasiness.

'There *is* something about this place, isn't there?' she said, and I nodded, pleased and warmed to find she had the same awareness of things that I had.

'Yes,' I agreed. 'There is.'

She gave a little shudder of apprehension. 'Something happened here in this Depression,' she said. 'Something between when your patrol arrived and now. I don't know what it was, but this place has got a secret that isn't just a set of paintings on a cave wall. It's something I've been trying to tell Sloan all along. But I guess he's too much of a scientist and, because there aren't definite signs in the sand, he doesn't believe me.'

We were still there, talking to Crabourne and Nimmo, who had joined us with mugs of coffee, when I heard cries from beyond Ghad Ahmed's tents, and I felt no sensation of surprise because I'd been waiting for hours for it to come.

One of the workmen ran up, shouting and pointing, and stopped in front of Ghad Ahmed who was standing with Crabourne. He was staring in the direction of the thin gesturing brown hand and his expression seemed to change, as though a shadow had passed across his face.

'He says it's a motor vehicle,' he pointed out to Crabourne. 'Coming into the camp.'

We moved away from the hut and walked through the tents towards the dusty track that ran along the floor of the Depression to Qahait. Morena had left the lorry and was staring into the distance, his hands deep in the pockets of his khaki shorts, the white scars on his shoulders where he'd been wounded in Italy plain in the fading light. Just behind him were Leach and Houston, both staring towards the cloud of dust in the distance.

'Jerry,' Houston said with a grin. 'Rommel.'

'Dry up,' Morena said without turning his head, just as if he were a sergeant again and Houston were a flippant private who was interrupting his thoughts.

After a while it was possible to distinguish a jeep in the yellow cloud and Crabourne's eyebrows came down.

'That's Selinski,' he said. 'What in hell's he doing here? He ought to be keeping an eye on things at Qahait.'

The jeep drew nearer and slid to a stop in the soft sand, the dust drifting past it as it halted, then Selinski came towards us in a stumbling run. His high parrot crest of hair was rumpled and matted with sweat, and he looked strained and scared under the mask of dirt that lay on his face and eyelashes.

'What the hell are you doing here?' Crabourne demanded.

'They've gone.' Selinski stopped in front of him and jerked his hand backwards into the empty Depression.

'Who've gone?'

'The workmen!'

'What the hell are you talking about?'

'There's nothing left!'

Selinski's face looked thin and drawn and his features were taut under the pall of dust.

'For God's sake, man,' Crabourne said quickly, 'pull yourself together. What are you trying to tell me?'

Selinski gestured again, uneasily, jerking his hand nervously once more. 'There's nothing left,' he said his voice high-pitched and uneasy. 'They've all gone. I was on my own just outside the camp, working on a drawing, and when I turned round I realised they'd all disappeared.'

'Disappeared? They can't have disappeared.'

'They have, I tell you. I was entirely alone. The whole place was empty and silent. It's enough to put you in a panic. Have *you* ever been alone in this goddam Depression?' Selinski had obviously been badly scared. 'There'd been half a dozen of them with me, with the rest of them further back towards the camp. I called out for help to move a ladder and when nobody came I realised I was on my own. I went to look for them because I thought they were skulking somewhere – you know how they do – but there was no one about. Then I thought they must have lit out back to camp, so I got into the jeep and went to look. But there was nothing. Their goddam tents had disappeared, too. *And* the camels. And all the drawings were blowing about the desert like so many leaves.'

Crabourne's face was set now and uneasy. He glanced quickly at Phil and then at Ghad Ahmed.

'Ahmed,' he said. 'What's all this about? You must go over there and get them back to work.'

Ahmed shrugged. 'They have gone back to their villages,' he said.

'Then you must get them back.'

'They'll not come. They have had enough. They have been there five weeks already.'

'But, God damn it, Ahmed, we made an agreement! In Qalam. There's work here for months.'

'There will be no more work done at Qahait,' Ahmed said calmly. 'When a Qalam decides there are ghosts in the Depression there is nothing I can do about it.'

Crabourne stared at him silently. The Arabs had moved up from their camp and had formed their usual semicircle behind us, ragged, watchful, reflecting somehow the whole mood of the camp.

Selinski was unloading a big file from the jeep now. 'I collected all the drawings,' he said. 'They're all here, though a few of them'll have to be done again. The lousy s.o.b.s had walked over them.'

Crabourne drew a deep breath and let it out noisily. 'You'd better put them in the hut with the others,' he suggested, his face defeated and tired. 'We'll have to abandon Qahait for the time being and concentrate on this place. We'll get over there tomorrow and see what we can do.'

Selinski nodded and seemed to shudder, and as he moved off with Crabourne, Phil Garvey came up alongside me.

'It's starting,' she said coolly. 'Whatever it is that we both know about, whatever it is we've been expecting.'

She was smiling, but even through the warmth I could see the nervousness in her eyes.

I looked across the camp, dun-brown in its flat monotones of colour that hardly differed from the background of the Depression. The Arabs were standing in groups, talking in undertones, their eyes moving shiftily, as though they had somehow expected Selinski's appearance. The wind muttered a little and I saw a wisp of sand suddenly get up like a top, spin for a while, moving along the track, then collapse again.

As the dust settled, the Arab voices seemed to die and the Depression became twice as silent.

'Yes,' I said, 'it's starting.'

Morena and I sat outside the tent until late, talking about Selinski's arrival, smoking and trying to make a couple of cans of warm beer last forever. Morena was in a thoughtful mood, not nervous, because Morena was never nervous, but alert and cautious.

'Crabourne's got trouble,' he said quietly.

'Yes,' I agreed. 'He has.'

'I wouldn't trust that damn Ghad Ahmed as far as I could throw him.'

I looked round at him, wondering if he'd seen something I'd missed.

'Why not?' I asked.

He shrugged. 'Dunno. Just something about him. I got like that in the army. Sergeants were closer to the blokes than you lot' – he smiled, faintly apologetic – 'and you got so you could size 'em up. I wasn't often wrong. I just don't trust Ghad Ahmed.'

I spent some time that night writing up my diary. I'd been taking great care with it, because I'd decided if I were to get a book – or simply a story – out of the trip, then it would be as well to have as many facts down as I could, and the others were asleep long before I'd finished. I was tired when I turned out the lamp, but I lay sleeplessly in my blanket for some time, my mind groping towards half a dozen unformed little questions that seemed to need an answer and yet wouldn't frame themselves properly. My eyelids began to droop at last and I was just on the point of dropping off when I became aware of noises somewhere outside that resolved themselves into confused shouting. I sat up abruptly and against the pale canvas of the tent I saw Morena and Nimmo sit up, too.

'What the hell's that?'

I was just getting out of my blanket when we saw that the light outside had turned to yellow, a ruddy yellow that told us immediately what had happened. I'd seen that colour too often through the canvas of a bivouac tent not to know what it meant. Something was on fire and there were only a few things in the stony bowl of the Depression that would burn – the Arabs' tents, our own tents, the crude huts that had been erected for Crabourne, and the vehicles. And judging by the noise it was more than a tent.

We were out of the door in a flash, trampling on the sleeping figures of Houston and Leach.

It was one of the lorries that had gone up and the first selfish thought that crossed my mind was 'Thank God it belongs to Crabourne'.

It was the big five-tonner and it was blazing like a torch, with a column of black smoke rising straight into the air. Fortunately, there was no wind, but people seemed to be running from every point of the camp in all sorts of undress, and I saw Selinski jump into one of Carbourne's jeeps and drive it away to safety.

I'd thought I was first out of the tent, but I saw the Land Rover move away with Nimmo at the wheel as I dragged open the driver's door of our lorry, then, with my eyes full of smoke and my skin shrinking from the fierce lash of the heat, I got the engine going and roared after him, the wheels spinning in the soft sand. Morena got Crabourne's laboratory van away, and I saw Phil driving the other jeep.

We stopped the vehicles in a ragged line and headed back towards the blazing five-tonner. There was nothing we could do, however, except stand around in a circle and stare, because we had no water to spare and the fire extinguishers would have been useless.

Ghad Ahmed was with a group of workmen, smarter and cleaner than the others, his face expressionless, his hands hanging down by his sides. A few of the women were chattering, but I noticed – though I don't think anyone else did – that the men showed no signs of surprise or excitement. Even carrying coal on to a ship in Alex or Suez was always enough to get a crowd of Arabs worked up into a frenzy, but these men were standing like Ghad Ahmed himself, with their hands at their sides, their faces expressionless.

The fire died down at last, leaving the lorry a smouldering wreck on lopsided wheels with melted tyres. The air was full of fluttering black fragments of charred paper which had been snatched away by the up-draught of the flames and were now coming slowly back to the ground, and overhead the stars shone, mysterious and cold and indifferent. The walls of the Depression seemed to swallow all sound, and everyone was quiet now, subdued and depressed, because there was nothing we could do until morning.

We parked the vehicles again, carefully, nervously rechecking that they were in no danger. Crabourne seemed to be almost in tears.

'How did it happen?' he was demanding in a wail, standing in his pyjamas. 'That goddam lorry hadn't been used all day.'

'Don't take it too hard, Sloan,' Phil Garvey was saying. 'After all, it didn't have the work on it.'

He stared at her, unconvinced. 'It's sabotage,' he snapped, coming to life with a jerk as his anger swept over him. 'It's plain goddam deliberate sabotage. I'm going to contact the police at Qalam. After all, that's why we brought the transmitter along, isn't it?'

He walked away through the darkness towards the huts, his figure tense and urgent, and we stood in a group, waiting for him to return none of us speaking, all of us busy with uneasy thoughts.

Within a few seconds, it seemed, he came running back, his eyes wild, his mouth working, and stopped in front of us, gasping, his hands flapping in desperate gestures of rage as he struggled to speak.

'The transmitter's been smashed,' he panted at last. 'Someone's smashed the front in!'

Beyond the Depression the flinty aridness of the plain was an intense blackness like thick felt, a world that was flat and empty and forbiddingly full of secret shapes, and I felt another momentary pause of unreasoning, illogical fear as the phantoms moved closer, then Morena's brisk, matter-of-fact voice brought me back to my senses.

'What the hell did they do that for?' he asked.

As he spoke, I saw his expression change and he spun round on his heel and dived for our lorry, swinging back the canvas cover and switching on the torch he carried, as we all crowded round the tailboard after him.

'Christ!' I heard him say.

I didn't have to climb into the lorry to see what was wrong. The front of *our* transmitter was smashed in, too. There was even an iron bar still lying across it.

The equipment was tumbled everywhere and papers and maps were scattered among the tin trunks and cans of food. For a moment it didn't dawn on me what it was all about and I couldn't quite see the reason for it, then it all clicked into place and I knew at once what they'd been searching for and the reason for the blaze. Nothing had been thrown out of the lorry in the search, or, if it had, it had been thrown back in again so that we shouldn't notice it as we salvaged it.

'What were the bastards after?' Houston asked, but I was already swinging round and looking for Nimmo.

'The tent,' I said. 'Get back to the tent – quick!'

The same thought seemed to have occurred to him, too, and he'd set off running before I'd even finished.

Houston and Morena watched him go. I hadn't seen Leach on the scene near the blaze and I hoped like hell that he'd stayed in bed.

By the time we reached the tent, Nimmo was standing in the doorway, his face dark.

'Some bastard's been in here,' he said. 'The place's upside-down.'

We lit the lamp and saw the uproar inside. Blankets had been flung everywhere and every kit bag and suitcase and pack had been tipped out on top of the ruin.

Leach appeared at that moment, stepping out of the shadows as though materialising from nowhere.

'What's 'appened?' he demanded, his big body bulky against the glow of the dying flames.

'Where were you?' Nimmo demanded angrily.

'With you. Up by the lorry.'

'More's the bloody pity!'

'Why? What the 'ell are you talking about?'

Nimmo glared round at us, his face taut, that strange vicious glow in his eyes that I'd seen before. He seemed to have trouble in getting his words out.

'The bastards have got the map,' he said.

t w o

Crabourne had no sympathy for us next day. In fact, he clearly considered us indirectly responsible for the loss of his lorry and the ruin of his transmitter.

They were having a conference when I joined them. The morning was bright and luminous, sharp with an inhuman gleaming, as though every scrap of grit and every stone in the Depression had been polished and reflected the sun's rays. They'd got the basket-boys working and you could hear the shovels scraping and the shuffling feet and the low muttering further down the Depression where I could see the white-clad figure of Ghad Ahmed directing operations.

The burnt-out lorry stood on its own, a blackened shell surrounded by scraps of charred paper, and a circle of scuffed sand where we'd all waited and watched.

Crabourne looked tired and worried, but Phil still managed to look efficient and smart. Selinski looked thinner than ever and his cockatoo's crest of hair seemed to wilt in the heat.

'It's obviously connected with this goddam map of yours,' Crabourne said, his face taut and angry. 'Somebody set fire to my lorry to get us all into the vehicle park, so they could steal it.'

There was no answer to him and he went on accusingly:

'We're in a fine mess now, aren't we?' he said. 'With no transmitter and one lorry short.'

116

Phil interrupted his self-sympathy. 'We don't need a transmitter, Sloan,' she said. 'Nothing's happened that need stop us working.'

He gestured impatiently. 'We can't be without contact with the rest of the world,' he pointed out irritably. 'We've got to pack up.'

'That's what they want us to do,' she said quietly. 'Go away from here.'

He swung round at once. 'Who does? What do you know?'

She shrugged wearily. 'I don't know anything,' she said. 'But *somebody* does. Somebody's obviously trying to drive us away.'

He stared at her, Only half comprehending her fears. 'What the devil for?' he demanded.

'Because,' I said, 'they obviously consider what *we're* looking for of far more value than what *you're* looking for.'

He stared. 'What in hell are you suggesting?'

'I'm suggesting that this treasure you say doesn't exist very definitely does exist.'

'It can't exist,' he exploded. 'There's no reason for it – no explanation!'

'Good God,' I said, trying to hang on to my patience, '*something* exists and whoever burned your lorry knows about it and wants it. And it's big enough to make them willing to do this to you.'

Crabourne stared at me unbelievingly, almost as though he couldn't comprehend that anyone could set a greater value on anything than they could on his paintings.

'They've probably been looking for it on and off for years,' I went on. 'When you came it was obvious they'd have another go. You were paying 'em to do it. It must have been a godsend to them when we turned up with a map.'

His stubbornness irritated me and I insisted on a search being made of the Arab compound, but in spite of his anger

Crabourne only gave way unwillingly, afraid still for his paintings.

'It'll cause trouble,' he said. 'Ghad Ahmed's not going to like it.'

'Sloan,' Phil said sharply, the anger clear in her voice. 'Ghad Ahmed's not running this damned camp! We are!'

We all trooped outside, Crabourne still nervous at the thought that the dispute might halt his work, and set off towards the Arab compound past the burnt-out lorry. It was only then that we noticed that the chatter of the basket-boys had stopped and that there was no one at work near the spoil-mound.

'They've stopped,' Crabourne said at once, turning to me, his voice full of resentment. 'I said they would.'

There was no sign of any work going on, and we walked through a camp that was ominously silent. As we reached the Arab tents and picked up the first acid whiff of camels and the reek of dung-smoke we saw a procession similar to our own heading towards us.

'Trouble,' Crabourne said, eyeing me with smouldering dislike.

He stopped dead, licking his lips, and waited for the other group to approach. Ghad Ahmed was in the lead, his cruel young face set and tense. Behind him came the workmen and there was an atmosphere of hostility about them. The thought that crossed my mind was of two truce parties meeting to come to terms.

The two groups stopped about ten yards apart and for a moment nobody said anything. Then Crabourne spoke.

'Ahmed,' he said, 'during the blaze last night there was a thief in the camp. We think he deliberately set fire to the lorry to help him.'

Ghad Ahmed said nothing, his face masked and enigmatic, and Crabourne went on nervously, obviously hating the job.

'The transmitters were smashed and a map was stolen belonging to Captain Doyle's party.'

I saw Ghad Ahmed's expression flicker at last and he glanced at the man on his right, a small man in black rags with flinty eyes like a snake.

'We have no map,' he said, and there was something about the way he said it that somehow made me think he was telling the truth.

'The map's gone, all the same,' Phil said angrily. 'And none of *us* have it!'

Ghad Ahmed's eyes shifted again. 'Very well,' he said calmly. 'I will permit you to make a search. On one condition. If you are to question us, then we reserve the right to question *you*.'

Crabourne stared. 'God damn it, Ahmed, you're not suggesting one of *our* party has stolen the map, are you?'

Ahmed shook his head. 'I am not referring to the map,' he said.

'Then what in hell are you referring to?'

Ahmed signed to the men behind him and the group opened and it was then for the first time that we saw there was a body lying on the ground between them. I saw a bundle of rags, covered with a fragment of dirty blanket, and two limp brown feet sticking out from the bottom. The men on either side of it stared silently at us, their eyes like stones.

Ghad Ahmed jerked a hand, his gaze all the time on Crabourne's face.

'*I* am talking about murder,' he said.

three

We tried to go about our work as though nothing had happened.

We buried the dead man that afternoon. There was no knife wound on him and nothing to indicate who'd killed him. He'd simply failed to return to his tent after the blaze and his woman had finally reported his absence to Ghad Ahmed. The search party had found the body near the scattered rocks along the fringe of the camp near our tents, lying in a hollow, its neck broken.

His death took all the wind out of our sails. Nothing more was said about searching the Arab compound and Ghad Ahmed dropped his request that our own half of the camp should be searched. It was an uneasy truce, however, because it was obvious now that each side distrusted the other.

There was nothing else to be done, though. There were no police and there was no coroner to hold an inquest. Crabourne held a nervous enquiry into both incidents, but nothing came of it and there was nothing he could do after that except record them as fully as possible in the expedition log and let the matter drop. With tuberculosis and bilharziasis and the other odds and ends that the nomad Arabs suffered from, death was normal enough in the desert.

The sense of events building up around us grew stronger. The workmen went about their duties, but the excited chattering that had gone on when we'd first arrived had become subdued and the atmosphere was different, resentment and disappointment going hand-in-hand with the feeling that Ghad Ahmed was still waiting for something.

We watched them bury the shapeless bundle in a grave alongside the cliff wall, and the puffs of dust as the sapless earth was shovelled over it. We could hear a little muttering and the wailing of women, then the Arabs returned to their work without saying anything.

It was from that point that I noticed there was *always* a man squatting on top of the spoil-mound with his eyes on our tent, a figure that never moved and never turned its gaze from our direction.

I didn't say anything to anyone until Morena was standing alone, then I pointed it out to him.

He nodded. 'I'd spotted him, too,' he said.

'What do you think he's up to?'

He looked uneasy. 'There's something I didn't tell you,' he said.

'Go on. Let's have the lot.'

'That bloke. The one who was murdered. I had a look at him. Someone had hit him hard at the back of the neck. Bang. Just like that.' He paused uncertainly. 'It wasn't an Arab,' he ended.

'How do you know?'

'Did you ever see an Arab fight with his bare hands? Always a knife or a baulk of timber. This wasn't a baulk of timber.'

'Go on.'

He gestured. 'You know as well as I do who could kill a man with a single blow across the neck.'

'Someone who'd been trained in unarmed combat.' His eyes narrowed. 'I dare bet,' he said, 'that none of the Arabs have. *Or* Crabourne *or* Selinski *or* the girl.'

The inference was obvious.

'Good God!' I said.

I indicated the silent figure on top of the spoil-mound. 'Do you think that's why he's watching us?'

'Could be.'

'Or do you think it's because they're waiting for us to make some sort of move?'

He glanced up at the silent silhouette. 'The bastards are watching for something,' he said.

It grew hotter as the sun rose higher and the floor of the Depression began to heave in waves as the air shimmered, and the cliffs at the far end kept fading then shooting forward in a mirage.

I had thought Crabourne's group might not work in the heat, particularly in view of what had happened, but there was no sign of a halt. Our party ate its lunch early, but we kept very much to ourselves because Crabourne obviously resented us as he had from the very beginning, and clearly considered we'd brought with us all the trouble he was suffering from now.

The atmosphere in the tent was heavy, muffled with suspicion and alertness, and it seemed to stick out a mile that there were things that were not being brought out into the light. The discussion on what we should do now that we had lost the map was not acrimonious but it was certainly not friendly, with Leach surly in his corner of the tent, Nimmo noisy and indignant, and Houston artificially flippant in an acid, unreal way. Morena could barely conceal his contempt for them all.

'Well,' he said. 'What are we going to do?'

'What the hell *can* we do?' Nimmo growled. 'We haven't got the bearings.'

Houston grinned, his eyes sharp and watchful. 'I suggest we get the old jeep out,' he said. 'Check the guns, and attack from the flank.'

'Oh, for Christ's sake!'

Houston's smile vanished at once. 'Well, somebody pinched the map, didn't they?' he said angrily. 'It'll be us next.'

In the end we decided in desperation to explore the Depression in the Land Rover, pooling memories and hoping that someone would remember some feature of the land. It was a hopeless move from the start, but there seemed to be no alternative, and, having come all this way, none of us wanted to go back without making a try.

We climbed into the Land Rover, Morena driving, me alongside him and the other three in the back, Leach perched up on the side, his big behind hanging over the edge, his eyes screwed up in the glare of the sunshine. Morena drove slowly along the track through the Depression, among the stretches of stony hardtop where the loose rock glittered with flecks of mica and dried-out crystals of salt, while camel-humps of blown dry sand spread a riddle of heat waves in the dead hot silence.

Morena and I, as the two who had *not* been on the patrol into the Depression, attended to the driving and the watching of the track, while the others did the talking, but they all seemed confused or unwilling, and we got nowhere.

'That looks like it,' Houston said, gesturing at the cliffs.

'Can't be,' Leach growled sullenly. 'We never came as far as this.'

'It had a sort of column like that, all the same,' Houston said brightly, speaking with a strange brittle glibness that was manifestly false as he pointed at a buttress of limestone which threw jetty shadows across the cliff face.

But it wasn't the place we were seeking, as I'd known it wouldn't be, and we followed the Depression for miles towards Qahait, until the Land Rover was covered with dust and it was ground into our faces like masks. In the end we stopped the vehicle and the three in the back got out to stretch their legs. Nobody said anything and suspicion was clearly in the air. Everyone was withdrawn and solitary, Leach off on his own, staring up the Depression, apparently indifferent to what we were doing, and Houston and Nimmo, well apart, their brows down, constantly giving each other watchful glances.

Morena and I sat in the Land Rover waiting for them to return, both of us puzzled and angry.

'I don't get it,' Morena said softly. 'I don't think those three bastards *want* to find it. Not now, anyway. Not while *we*'re with 'em.'

None of them had anything to say as they climbed back into the Land Rover, but I noticed there were a few odd glances among them, as though the distrust that had touched me and Morena had touched them, too.

Nobody spoke as Morena started the engine and my mind was full of misgivings, then Houston's voice came, sharp and acid and ugly, and as full of artificial good humour as it was possible to be.

'Oh, well,' he said. 'We can always go back and make way with Crabourne's cousin. Twenty smackers that our honourable and gallant captain lays her first. Any takers?'

I had begun to detest him by this time and was just on the point of turning round to him when Nimmo spoke.

Whatever it was that they had shared had been thrust aside abruptly at Houston's words, and Nimmo reached up his hand and jerked the frayed head-dress over Houston's eyes, so that he looked like some cartoon Arab out of a television programme.

'Listen, you bloody dehydrated Lawrence of Arabia,' he said quietly. 'You just make one more remark like that and I'll personally take you apart.'

'Well, Christ' – Houston was still too full of bounce to hear the menace in his voice – 'you don't think Nature gave her a backside like that just to sit on, do you?'

'Shut up!'

Houston stared at Nimmo for a long moment and Morena waited with the engine idling, his eyes mild, obviously enjoying himself.

'Yes,' Houston's eyes dropped. 'All right.'

Nobody said any more and in a stony awkward silence we drove slowly back towards the camp. As we turned the Land Rover round, I saw a small moving figure on the spoil-mound. I nudged Morena and indicated it without saying anything, and his eyes narrowed.

'The bastards are determined not to miss us,' he said.

Nobody moved very far during the afternoon, and there still seemed to he a sort of wary watchfulness about the camp.

A slight breeze had got up and somehow it managed to reach even the bowl of the Depression, so that you could hear the rustle of the sand against the tent, the gritty whispering of millions of tiny paws scratching away at the canvas, but by evening it had died away again and the place seemed touched with evil. There were a few disconnected noises, curiously muffled by distance and the walls of the Depression – the murmur of voices from the Arab compound, and the splash of water, and the stomachic grumble of a camel. It had been a spectacular sunset and now the moon was up, remote in the black dome that shimmered with mysterious light from half a million unknown worlds. The silence – the utter soundlessness – seemed to come from the deep spaces to the stars.

To avoid further incidents, we'd decided that we should split the nights up into three three-hour watches, with two men remaining undisturbed each night. I took the first watch until midnight, with Leach following to 3 a.m., and Houston from three until six. After 6 a.m. we didn't expect trouble.

I sat on a box outside the tent, smoking, feeling the air grow cooler. For some time I heard Nimmo's transistor faintly beating out pop music, then Leach's sour growl stopped it abruptly and I saw the light in the tent go out. I walked around for a while, between the tent and the vehicles, and could see the yellow lights in Crabourne's camp and the faint glimmer of oil lamps among the Arab tents, and I wondered if the look-out was still squatting up there on the spoil-mound.

There were a lot of things in my mind. Suddenly I had no trust in the others and the whole operation seemed to fall apart because of that. The whole be-all and end-all of the journey for me had been to rediscover something of what we'd missed after leaving the desert, and without that absolute trust we'd always had in each other, the very thing I was hoping to find had disappeared before I'd even started looking for it. The grandeur had not come just from the desert alone.

The moon was shedding a cold light over the Depression and the great empty plain beyond seemed to stretch its barren emptiness to the end of the world. I felt minute and afraid, then I pulled myself together abruptly. Every man with any imagination who'd fought in the desert had felt this same desolation and you had to be careful not to infect yourself with the fear it bred all too easily.

At midnight I called Leach. He was wide-awake, a fact which surprised me, because normally he went out like a light and slept like a log. He grunted and went outside and I rolled myself in my blanket, but I found I couldn't sleep for thinking. There were too many 'whys' there in the darkness with me.

From time to time I heard Leach moving around outside, then after a while I noticed he'd moved way and hadn't returned. I lay listening for what seemed hours, but I didn't hear him. I wasn't even sure what I was listening for, but I wasn't surprised when I heard someone in the tent sit up slowly. I didn't move and as I heard shufflings I guessed he was climbing out of his blanket and putting on his boots.

After a while, through the slits of half-opened eyes I saw the tent flap move and a black figure against the pale sky. By its size it seemed to be Nimmo.

I lay for a while, wondering what to do and half-expecting Houston to follow him. I was rather surprised when he didn't, and, in the end, I decided that whatever the other two were up to it didn't include him, and that he really was as much asleep as he appeared to be. Finally, I climbed out of my blanket and pulled on my boots, and placed my hand quietly over Morena's mouth. I felt a small start as he came to consciousness.

'Quiet,' I whispered. 'Outside. Bring your boots.'

The moon was dripping its icy light across the Depression so that we could see the shape of Crabourne's huts and the line of sagging tents in front of the stark serrations of the cliffs.

'What the hell's going on?' Morena whispered.

'I don't know, but I've got a shrewd idea it doesn't concern you and me, Wop. Nimmo's out there somewhere with Leach.'

He didn't waste time with questions and we walked quietly away from the camp, past the silent mess hut in Crabourne's compound and the dark shape of the Arab tents, and it crossed my mind that if Ghad Ahmed was as interested in us as he seemed to be the look-out might at that moment be waking him, too.

A camel grunted and we caught the strong ammonia stink of the animals above the clinging burnt-dung and charcoal smell of the camp, then we were walking slowly up the Depression with the limestone buttresses sharp in the starlight.

As we came to the patch of rocks, I led Morena in among them and warned him to be quiet.

'What the hell are we up to?' he asked, and I could see his good-humoured face was blank with bewilderment.

We moved through the rocks for a while, then as we stopped I heard the chink of stones from somewhere on our left. At first I thought it was Nimmo or Leach, but as we sank down behind a flat piece of shale, I saw Nimmo in front. He was quite recognisable even in the poor light and seemed to be crouching.

'Just in front,' I said softly.

Morena raised himself gently, then he turned and stared at me, bewilderment on his face.

'It's Nimmo,' he whispered. 'He's watching someone.'

'Leach, I expect.'

'He's supposed to be on guard.'

'It seems he isn't. And if Nimmo is watching Leach that means Leach is in front of *him*. So what was the cause of those stones clinking over on our left a second or two ago?'

Morena's face came round to me, pale in the faint light.

'Ghad Ahmed,' he said.

I nodded and his eyebrows rose. 'What are we going to do about him?'

'Nothing at the moment. Let's concentrate on one thing at a time.'

We raised ourselves gently. Nimmo was just ahead of us still, crouching as we were, and beyond him I could see the limestone wall of the Depression and, faintly, the shape of two buttresses of rock. Ahead, out of sight somewhere, was the cave with the pear-shaped entrance.

Briefly, in a whisper, I told Morena of seeing Leach there and how Phil Garvey had seen Nimmo.

'I think there's something in that cave,' I said. 'Or near it.'

'What we've come for?'

'It looks like it.'

Morena's expression changed and his brows came down. 'They said they hadn't been able to recognise it,' he breathed. 'I bet the bastards are intending to fish it out themselves and nip off without us.'

I could tell from the sound of his voice that it wasn't just the thought of losing what lay hidden in the cave that was worrying him so much as the disappointment of finding that the trust he'd put in his old comrades had been misplaced.

We watched Nimmo move slowly round the rock where he was crouching. From his manner it was clear he had no more desire to be seen than we had, and it came as something of a relief to realise that the opposition was at least split among themselves. A lot was suddenly explained to me, a lot of incidents and a lot of the atmosphere of suspicion and secrecy and distrust that had been worrying me.

I nodded to Morena and we moved on until we could see Nimmo again, and then the pale blur of Leach's bulky frame against the shadows. He appeared to be standing, staring towards the cliff face, then we saw him turn, apparently listening, and drop out of sight.

'He's seen Nimmo,' I said.

We listened for a while, then, sharp across the silence, we heard the clatter of stones and a cry.

'Come on,' I said.

They were at it hammer and tongs when we arrived, clutching each other and rolling over and over in the dust. There was already blood on Nimmo's face, black-bright in the light of the moon, but Leach was panting heavily with a middle-aged man's lack of steam, and in spite of his extra strength he wouldn't have been able to keep it up much longer.

As we came up to them, Nimmo broke free and stood up, grabbing for a lump of rock, and I took a swing at him without thinking. He went down like a log, and I saw the dust puff out as he hit the ground. Morena stuck out a foot as Leach jumped up and dived for him, and Leach went down also, with a yelp of pain as his knee struck one of the projecting spurs of shale.

It seemed to stop them dead. Nimmo sat up, holding his jaw where I'd hit him, and Leach dragged himself upright, moaning with pain from his injured knee, and it was only then that I looked round and saw Houston standing among the rocks behind us and knew that he'd wakened and found the tent empty and got up to join the party.

'It might be a bloody good idea,' I said, 'if somebody told us what this is all about.'

There'd been a time when I'd been faintly scared of Leach. He'd always been an uncertain number during the war and, as he was so big, I'd been a little in awe of him because of his sudden moods and sullen tempers. But now he was just a big fat middle-aged man and I was tougher with the toughness of experience.

'The bastard was following me,' he growled.

Nimmo paused before answering. 'He was supposed to be on guard,' he said. 'What the hell is he doing here if he's supposed to be on guard?'

'What did you think he was doing?' I asked.

'I think he knows where that bloody stuff we're after's hidden and he was looking for it.'

Leach began to shout. 'I saw somebody scouting round the tent,' he yelled. 'I followed him!'

'Well, it might interest you to know you missed him,' I said. 'Because he was watching you both. And probably us as well.'

There was silence for a moment as the fact sank in.

'What were you looking for, Tiny?' I asked.

Leach's heavy face lowered and what I'd been expecting for some time came out. 'You're not the bloody officer any more,' he growled.

'The bastard was looking for the treasure,' Nimmo said again.

'And you were making sure he didn't find it on his own,' I replied. I turned to Houston. 'And *you* were afraid of being left out in the cold, eh? Is that treasure we're after round here somewhere?'

'I don't know,' Nimmo said quickly. 'I wasn't here. I wasn't even born.'

'And I was waiting by the wire,' I pointed out. 'And Wop was at the top of the Depression.' I turned to Houston and Leach. 'That seems to leave you two,' I said. '*Was* this the place?'

Houston's eyes flickered to Leach's as though they'd talked the thing over secretly and his reply came slowly and with a marked reluctance. 'Looks a bit like it,' he agreed. 'But then, on the other hand, it looks different.'

'Memory *has* a habit of playing tricks,' I agreed. 'That's something I've found out, too. You were never a pretty bunch, but it seems you were even less pretty than I thought.'

Nobody spoke and I could see Morena watching the three of them carefully. I let what I'd said sink in before I went on and when I spoke again I couldn't keep the disgust from my voice.

'I'm beginning to think,' I said, 'that that bowl I was shown in London didn't come from here at all.'

Morena's face turned quickly towards me and I could see the surprise in his expression.

'I expect,' I went on 'that it was picked up cheap in the East End. But not *too* cheap because it had to look good enough to put it across me and Morena, me for my map references and Wop to see that nothing broke down on the way. But it wasn't a set of gold ornaments you were after, was it?'

Morena looked blank again.

'That was a good story,' I went on bitterly. 'And I might have gone on believing it if it hadn't been for Ghad Ahmed. Because I'll bet a year's wages it isn't gold ornaments *he's* interested in.'

'What the hell is he interested in, then?' Morena's words burst out of him in an explosion of anger.

'What he's been looking for, for years,' I said. 'What he came here for with Crabourne. What he's been digging for all the time he's been clearing soil for them. What he's been watching us for, ever since we arrived – from the top of that mound, so that he could see where we went.'

Morena's eyes flickered round the others. 'Go on,' he said. 'What?'

'What he considers belongs to him,' I said. 'The same thing as this lovely lot consider belongs to them – that chest the Paymaster was carrying. Crabourne was right all the time. There isn't any treasure. There never was.'

I saw Leach's eyes move towards Houston's and I knew I was right. Morena stared.

'Well, by God!' he said.

'They found it here,' I went on. 'They found it when they found the jeep and the bodies and they thought then it would be nice to keep it. But they knew they couldn't get away with it, with the rest of us waiting up there for them. So they hid it. For all I know they were probably the bastards who shot the Paymaster.'

'He was dead,' Houston said quickly, his face suddenly scared. 'They were all dead!'

'OK, they were dead. And that left only four people who knew about it, didn't it? You, Leach, Nimmo and Ward. And Ward made your shares bigger because he was unfortunate enough to get himself killed at Alamein. Perhaps he was lucky. He never knew his friends were bastards.'

'Christ!' Morena breathed.

'It does come as a bit of a shock, doesn't it?' I said. 'Especially when you remember they were just waiting for us to turn our backs to pick it up and nip off without us. I suppose it had even entered each one of their rotten little minds to dig it up on their own and leave the lot of us in the lurch.'

'Look' – Nimmo drew a deep breath – 'there's no harm done. The dough hasn't been touched. It hasn't even been found yet. We just know it's here.'

Houston nodded. 'It's here,' he said quickly. 'Somewhere in front of the cave.'

'Unfortunately, though, you've lost the map,' I pointed out, 'and the bearings were too complicated to remember.'

'*He* should have made a note of the bloody things!' Houston nodded at Nimmo, whose eyes glowed viciously.

'Perhaps I should have let *you* have 'em,' he growled. 'So you could have done the job on your own, like Leach.'

'It *is* a pretty big area to dig up without knowing exactly, isn't it?' I said, almost enjoying their fury.

'We can do it,' Nimmo said.

'From memory?'

'We can work together. Nothing's different. There's nobody else knows about it but us.'

He was trying to bargain, I could see. 'Just us,' I said. 'Each one of us wondering when he's going to get a knife in the back. Just us – and *Ghad Ahmed*.'

Nimmo's face fell.

'Christ, man,' I said disgustedly, 'you might have told Morena and me. It might become rough. Ghad Ahmed's hard enough to push things to the extreme if he has to. He believes that dough's his. He's been looking for it ever since his father died. I'll bet that's the only reason he's here with Crabourne. His Qalam shepherd saw the Paymaster being buried and it didn't take Ghad Ahmed long to guess the chest they'd been expecting had also been buried.'

They didn't say anything and I went on bitterly, speaking chiefly to Morena: 'I bet the late lamented and beloved Jimmy Nimmo, senior, would have been back long since if he could,' I said. 'It wasn't the distance that stopped him. It was because this place was a forbidden military area or because he couldn't raise the fare or was in trouble with the police. That and the uproar. When he hid that chest he didn't expect the questions and the court martial and the Provost people searching for so long. He didn't realise, of course, that there was enough money in that chest to start another war. We were trying to buy a lot of help with it, and it was worth burying and coming back for, even after twenty years. But, unfortunately, there were too many people watching for them coming. That's why he never dared to make a move. Because, if anyone had the nerve, *he* had!'

We walked slowly back to the camp, with Leach limping in the middle, as though we were all suddenly afraid he'd run out on us, all of us knowing things could never be the same again. They didn't even look now like the men I'd known during the war. Then, nobody could ever do without anybody else and out of that knowledge had sprung the comradeship that had overridden all undercurrents of bad feeling; but now, where once the issue had been a straightforward and uncomplicated one of duty and nothing else, we were hag-ridden by ambition and greed.

Nobody spoke on the way back, but you could literally feel the distrust moving from one to the other of us. There was a lot of noise from the Arab compound and the camels seemed to be restless. The breeze had started again from nowhere, stirring the sand into small gritty whirlpools, and I decided it must be that which was unsettling them. I saw a camel move across the dying glow of a fire and decided it must be a stray, then I saw a man run after it and there was silence again.

Just as we reached the camp, sullen and angry with each other, we heard the roar of an engine from the Vehicle Park and we all stopped dead and tried to stare through the darkness. For a moment we seemed to be frozen, then, as a chorus of yells started up in the distance, Morena shouldered us aside and set off running.

'The bastards are pinching the trucks!' he yelled.

four

In the semi-darkness it was hard to see just what was going on, but as we pounded towards the vehicle park I saw what appeared to be a whirlpool of figures milling around in a cloud of moon-laden dust.

Sharp-edged by one of the camp-fires, I saw a tent go down and realised it was ours, but, as we swung towards it, a jeep moved off; its engine screaming in the hands of an inexperienced driver, knocking down a stake as it went. It began to increase speed, jolting and rolling as it lurched over the flattened boundary fence, trailing a strand of wire and a broken stake behind it, and we swung round and ran to head off the shadowy bulk.

We were far too late and turned again towards the Vehicle Park. As we reached it a figure rose in front of me. I lashed out instinctively and it vanished from sight, sending a pile of empty petrol cans clattering. I jumped over the sprawling figure, hearing the yell as I trod on it, then I was grabbing at the shirt of one of Crabourne's Arab drivers who was just climbing into the lorry. I felt the material rip as I heaved him back and I caught a quick glimpse of the startled look on his face. He landed flat on his back, yelling, then he picked himself up and started to run.

Nimmo was scuffling with someone near the Land Rover and I could hear shouts all round me. The night seemed to be full of running figures, and the bulky shapes of camels barging against tents, then suddenly it was silent again and empty, and we were counting noses to see if anyone had been hurt.

Our vehicles didn't appear to have been touched and I was just congratulating myself on our luck when I saw Phil approaching, followed by Crabourne and Selinski. She came towards us in little frightened runs ahead of them, as though she found more assurance among our party than her own, and it dawned on me they were seeking help. Her hair was over her face and she seemed to have been crying, and it was then for the first time that I realised that the silence around us came from the fact that the Arab camp was empty.

The camels had gone and the fires were dying and the tents were down. The running figures we'd seen had scattered like leaves before a wind and there wasn't a single moving shape in the darkness now apart from our own.

We were all left with a lost feeling, a blind sense of uncertainty and frustration that emptied us of anger so that only a futile hopelessness remained.

We checked the rest of the vehicles and gathered near Crabourne's mess hut, where Phil handed out mugs of coffee. Nobody had much to say, but we were all aware of waves of dislike and suspicion that moved about between us.

In only one thing did we seem to be united, and that was the need to protect ourselves. This, at least, was a common cause.

Without speaking, almost without thinking, the group split up. Crabourne went to his hut, his head bent and looking somehow older in the pale light of the lamp. Phil stared after him, and then at me, her face worried, then she too moved away to her own hut.

For a moment the rest of us stood in silence, then Morena seemed to jerk us to life.

'There'll be a lot to do in the morning,' he said sharply. 'It'll be a good idea to get some sleep.'

We worked for a while on the collapsed tent, but in the end we left it and just salvaged our blankets and lay down on the rocky ground. Nimmo had agreed to stand watch for the rest of the night and we selected places near the vehicles, but we were all of us hungry and tired, and the night seemed cooler than normal.

I lay a little apart from the others, out of the moonlight in the shadow of the huts, my eyes prickling with the need for sleep, yet unable to stop my mind churning over all the things I felt we had to do. There seemed to be so many precautions we suddenly ought to take.

After a while I heard the scuff of a shoe in the sand near me and the chink of a stone. I lifted my head and sat up abruptly, thinking immediately that Ghad Ahmed was back, but as I did so Phil came towards me out of the shadows in a nervous rush and threw herself down alongside me on the cooling sand.

'Let me stay here,' she begged. 'Please let me stay here!'

She moulded herself to me as I took her in my arms, small and cold and trembling like a frightened child.

'It seemed like the inside of a tomb in the hut,' she said with a shudder. 'I just couldn't take any more of it. I had to be where there was someone alive.'

She seemed terrified and I could feel her shaking against me. 'I woke up,' she said. 'I was scared. Please let me stay here.'

'Take it easy,' I whispered. 'You're all right now. Nobody's sending you away.'

'It was the thought of the camp just emptying like that. Everybody just disappearing in the darkness. I woke up and couldn't hear anything and I suddenly felt I was alone in the whole of the desert. Please don't send me away!'

I put my hand on hers and was surprised at the strength of her fingers as she grasped it. She put her cheek down on it in a spontaneous gesture of affection and tenderness, then she lifted it to her breast and left it there. For a moment I stroked her hair, murmuring to her, then as I took her chin, she turned her face quickly towards me. I kissed her gently, but she put her arm round my neck and pulled me towards her, urgently, with all her strength, her young body firm against me, her mouth on mine, her hand under my torn shirt against my skin, suddenly murmuring wild endearments as she returned my embraces. In the desperate flow of emotion it seemed as though we were carried away on a flood, drowning and blinded, while she made little abandoned sounds by my ear and ran her fingers feverishly against my flesh.

Then the madness passed and we drew apart, both of us a little dazed and startled, and there was a starry look in her eyes. Her face seemed blind and bewildered and I was filled with pity and tenderness and a sad lost longing to be as young as she was.

'I'm sorry,' she said quickly in a shaky voice. 'That wasn't why I came. Truly it wasn't. I'm sorry, I'm sorry.'

'Christ,' I said, more roughly than I intended, 'don't start apologising.'

My hand found hers again and our fingers grasped harshly, entwining fiercely, and she kissed me as though she were starved of love, dishevelled and heedless, her hair tumbled, her skin silken, her eyes ecstatic.

After a while her kisses grew softer and tender and I knew the reaction and shock had passed because when she spoke her whisper was steadier, though still full of bewilderment.

'This is a damn funny time to go in for tomcatting,' she said. She was silent for a while, motionless in my arms as I stroked her hair.

'Shall we have to leave?' she asked. 'Shall we have to go home – now that they're all gone?'

'It depends a bit on Crabourne,' I said. 'It depends a bit on how much nerve he's got. It depends on how much nerve we've all got.'

'If we do leave, can I ride with you? Just to be near.' I kissed her again in assent and her tones became possessive and needy.

'I just have to,' she said. 'I just have to. Don't make me go with anyone else. Not now.'

'Not with anybody else,' I said, and she squeezed my hand. She was still trying to squeeze it, still trying to make certain that I didn't take it away, when she fell asleep.

five

The cooking hearths were cold and on a stick a scrap of rag hung forlornly in the brilliant sunshine which seemed to highlight the scene with a garish glare. There was nothing else, just a few fragments of broken water pitcher and a discarded Arab slipper. Where the Arab compound had been there was now only a lot of stirred sand, a few heaps of camel-dung and one or two scattered piles of charcoal.

And what was worse there was now silence, utter silence, the deep daytime silence of the empty desert that filled us all with a sense of misgiving. Before, even during the period of distrust and suspicion, there had always been the grunt of camels, the low chatter of the women by the tents and the subdued murmur of the workmen and their shuffling feet, and Ghad Ahmed's imperious commands. Now there was nothing under the high sun, only the hollow sound of our own voices that were thinner in the stillness as they bounced back at us from the deserted caves in a deep velvety brilliant silence that muffled every sound, swallowing it, it seemed, in its greater immensity, so that we found ourselves, as we erected the flattened tents, whispering, even in the daylight, in awe of it.

There was nothing we could do now except pool our resources, throwing in our lot together and messing as one unit, taking it in turns to do the cooking. It was quite clear that Selinski's trouble at Qahait had been connected with our own disaster and the one thing that stood out above all else was that Ghad Ahmed was trying to force us to withdraw from the Depression.

Phil welcomed the suggestion of integration, bustling around at once to make sure it became fact, but always sticking as close as she could to me. From time to time her eyes met mine. At first she wasn't able to meet my gaze, but then she began to stare back defiantly, with a little secret half-smile, as though proud of what had gone between us. Nimmo seemed to suspect what had happened and his face was thoughtful, and Houston, his grubby little brain always full of unpleasantness, also seemed to know and there was a bitter twist to his mouth as he went about his work, his eyes always greedily on Phil, as though the dark recesses of his mind derived some satisfaction from the fact that what he had predicted had come true.

Crabourne, of course, was almost in tears and mute with fury, but it was obvious we couldn't carry on as separate units, and he had to accept what we had all decided. His face was like thunder with disapproval, as though he felt he was losing control of his expedition, and in the end it was decided that Selinski should take Crabourne's remaining jeep and report the incident to the police post at Qalam, at the same time trying to raise more workmen there. It wasn't too far and it didn't seem an impossible task, and we drew lots to decide who should go with him. Houston lost and I saw his face fall at once.

'Don't worry,' I said shortly. 'We'll make bloody sure you aren't left out if anything's found.'

We loaded the jeep with water and tins of bully and biscuits and armed them with a rifle just for safety, and watched them set off across the Depression away from the blinding light of the sun. At Qalam, with luck, they'd find help enough for us to finish the jobs we'd come to do.

When they'd vanished from sight we turned back towards the camp, which had drawn closer together now, as though for protection, the tents alongside each other and a vehicle beside each one. Nobody spoke much to Leach and he limped around with a surly look on his heavy features.

Lunch consisted of melted bully beef and biscuits, because we'd spent the morning reorganising ourselves and hadn't made any roster for cooking, and it was a scratch affair eaten in the mess hut that Ghad Ahmed's men had built for Crabourne.

Crabourne was in a bitter mood and clearly held us responsible for all that had happened.

'All right,' he said, the resentment bursting out of him at last. 'So they were after this damned money that was lost! And that's why they were helping us – so they could do a little private searching while they were at it. But it didn't matter, did it? It didn't matter why they were here. I'm not interested in the money. We were getting on with what we came for. Slower than we expected, but we were making progress. Now we've nothing left. We'll have to get our air force to help us from Wheelus Field or somewhere like that.'

'How do we contact them,' I asked, 'without radio?'

He looked at me bitterly. 'We could have gone on for ever until you people came,' he said.

'For God's sake, Sloan,' Phil said angrily, 'they weren't to know we'd be here when they arrived. It's not *their* fault.'

We tried to carry on during the day, with Crabourne and Phil wrestling half-heartedly with the drawings with occasional assistance with ladders, while the rest of us scratched around in front of the pear-shaped cave. It was a hopeless task from the start without the map and we just had to dig where Leach's memory of the place and Nimmo's memory of the bearings told us to dig. I, for one, never expected much because Leach's memory was clearly faulty or deliberately blank and the bearings weren't clear enough in Nimmo's mind to be much help.

143

Eventually, I suppose, we'd have stumbled on the chest, but it would have been a long hard grind, and all the time I hadn't the slightest doubt that somewhere Ghad Ahmed had his eyes on us from the lip of the Depression, with his group of Qalami camped round the camels and the stolen jeep. By the end of the afternoon our muscles ached, and our hands were blistered, and our backs were hot with the sear of the sun. It was years since I'd done work of that kind and I was filthy with sweat-caked dust.

Morena had gone back into the camp ahead of us to prepare stew from bully beef, noodles and dried tomato and rice, and when we returned he was tinkering with the engine of the lorry.

'Trouble?' I asked.

He gave me a slow smile. 'Not really,' he said. 'I'm just taking the bung out of the lifeboats.'

I didn't understand what he meant at first and he held up the rotor arm from the distributor. 'They can't pinch 'em if they won't go,' he said. 'Surely you remember? Regulations against surprise. We used to bury 'em in the sand near the offside front wheel.'

Night came with its usual unexpectedness. One minute the whole length of the Depression was in view, with its caves and buttresses sharp against the shadows, then it was blurred and everything had a distant violet vanished look, and in a few minutes it was dark.

The camp was silent – so silent you could almost hear the desert breathing. There was none of the scratched barbaric music from the Arabs now, none of the clink and tinkle of implements and the splash of water or the grunt of camels, or a wailing voice raised in song.

I was standing outside the mess hut staring into the darkness with a cigarette in my mouth when Phil appeared alongside me and slipped her hand into mine.

'Thinking?' she asked.

'Yes.'

'What about?'

'All sorts of things. One of them that up there somewhere Ghad Ahmed's got a man, perhaps a couple of men, staring down here, doing what I'm doing, thinking, watching the lights and listening to the sounds, waiting.'

'What for?'

'I wish I knew. Perhaps till we've decided we've got to move.'

'Do you think they'll try to make us move?'

'I'm damn sure they will. They've got Nimmo's map, remember? And apart from wiping out the lot of us, the only way they can get that money, which legally doesn't belong to them now anyway but to the British Government, is to get rid of us from here.' I paused and went on slowly:

'Did anyone ever come this way?' I asked. 'I mean, did anyone ever come through the Depression except you and Ghad Ahmed's people – anyone we might expect to be able to help us?'

'No.' She shook her head. 'When we first arrived we got a rice merchant or two on the way to Qahait and one or two Arabs with dates or offers to fetch water. But I think Ghad Ahmed must have discouraged them. They never came a second time.' She paused and seemed to shiver. 'What do you think their next move will be?'

'It depends,' I said. 'It all depends on Houston and Selinski.'

We'd half expected the jeep to return by the next afternoon, but by the evening there was no sign of it and I began to grow worried. Morena saw me staring along the Depression and stood with me for a moment watching for the little cloud of dust, which would herald its approach.

He squinted into the lowering sun that changed the light to orange and then to rose pink, his square body relaxed, the sheen of sweat on his face.

'If they don't make it,' he said slowly, 'we're really up the creek, aren't we? Without a paddle.'

I stared round at the cliffs, aware of the silence, and the desolation of gravel and scattered rocks. The heavy air was cooling a little as we watched the sun go down, blood red, beyond the edge of the Depression, and the purple shadows flooded out immediately from the cliffs. The silence became more oppressive as we stood there watching the night come, a tremendous silence that was heavy with foreboding. Ghad Ahmed was there, I knew, waiting for us to make a move and knowing we couldn't make it without being seen.

A sudden spurt of desperate optimism moved me to hope that Houston and Selinski would succeed. The route was rarely used and off the beaten track, but they had everything they needed – food, water, petrol, a good vehicle and a good weapon. Surely, I kept telling myself, even Houston, in spite of his twisted humour and inherent laziness, would remember enough of his desert skill to get the jeep through. The opposition couldn't be all that strong and they'd be rank amateurs in spite of their knowledge of the desert. All sorts of questions were revolving in my mind. How much did Leach and Nimmo really know? How much were they to be trusted? What was Ghad Ahmed up to? Where was he now? It was for all the world like 1942 all over again.

It had been like this when we'd waited in the hollows looking towards the west, trying to out-guess the Germans, all senses alert for the Panzers, all eyes watching the sky for the Messerschmitts and the Junkers 87s; probably with the burnt-out wrecks of vehicles around and somebody you'd known crouched against the wheel of his lorry in a soggy muck of blood and sweat; and your nerves on edge because you'd got too much to think about and not enough eyes to watch the whole of the limitless desert around you all at the same time.

By the next morning I was uneasy enough to be really worried, and decided I'd better go and look for Selinski and Houston. We still had our Land Rover.

I made up my mind to take Nimmo with me, chiefly because he was young and he'd already proved he could shoot. With his youth and sharp eyesight, and my own remembered knowledge, surely what had happened to Selinski and Houston – if something *had* happened to them – wouldn't happen to us. This way, Morena would be left to keep an eye on Leach, and more and more I trusted Morena as less and less I trusted Leach.

'Watch where he goes,' I said. 'There's only him you've got to watch, so if he slips off, slip off after him.'

'You think he knows where it is?' he asked.

'I don't know. But that Arab with the broken neck – I don't think Houston's the man to do that, and Nimmo probably doesn't know how.'

Morena nodded. 'OK,' he said. 'I'll watch him.'

'It'll leave you two vehicles,' I pointed out. 'You sleep in one and get Crabourne to sleep in the other. Without the rotor arms that ought to stop anybody pinching 'em.'

It appeared that in addition to the rifle we'd seen in the mess hut, Crabourne had a shot-gun and a couple of revolvers which he'd brought along as a safety measure, but he didn't like the idea of loading them.

'I didn't come here for a fight,' he said. 'I came here for a peaceful scientific purpose.'

I ignored him and gave one of the revolvers to Phil and made her promise to keep it with her all the time.

'You never know,' I said as I fastened the belt round her waist.

She hadn't wanted me to go and, long after everyone was asleep, she'd been pleading with me from the circle of my

147

arms not to leave her. But there was no alternative, and in the end, her eyes full of tears, she'd nodded and accepted it.

She managed a shaky laugh now as I hitched the belt into position, my hands resting on her hips for a moment as I looked down at her.

'I'd like you around when I come back,' I said.

She tried to hold her head up. 'Captain Doyle,' she said. 'At first I began to wonder if you were human.' Her eyes rested on mine, frank with a shared secret. 'I guess you are, though, after all.'

'I'll let you know even more about that,' I told her, 'when I come back.'

Her smile faded rapidly. 'See that you do come back,' she said earnestly. 'Please!'

We loaded the Land Rover with water and supplies, in the same way that we'd loaded Houston's jeep. I did the driving, with the second revolver strapped round my waist, while Nimmo sat beside me holding the rifle.

'No bloody nonsense this time,' I told him. 'If you see anyone, be ready to shoot first. If anything's happened to Houston and Selinski it's because they *didn't*.'

We climbed out of the Depression, following the track that ran like tramlines up the rocky road, the sound of the labouring engine rattling back in echoes off the cliff. I half expected some of Ghad Ahmed's men to be waiting at the top of the hill for us, but there was nothing but the limitless yellow desert, unoccupied and unrestricted in its ominous waste spaces that were marked only by small patches of rock near the lip of the Depression and clumps of camel-thorn up ahead.

'We're all right,' Nimmo said. 'Nobody about.'

'Don't kid yourself,' I told him, faintly uneasy at the very emptiness of the plain. 'This desert isn't as flat as it looks, and it only needs a ten-foot dip to hide a jeep.'

It was a pleasure to get out of the Depression, nevertheless. Up here the air was cooler because we weren't surrounded by those heat-reflecting walls and it was possible to throw off the feeling of claustrophobia that they brought.

The whitish-yellow hue of the flinty earth threw back the glare with a blinding brilliance as we churned through the strips of wind-blown sand that had drifted across the track, then, after a while, the flatness changed to awkward hummocks, with spiky grass and scrub tufting the sandy ridges, and I grew more wary as the track rose and fell.

'Gives you the creeps,' Nimmo commented in an awed voice. 'There's such a bloody lot of it, and it's so bloody still!'

'Don't worry about the desert,' I said, still worried and puzzled by the absence of opposition. 'That won't hurt us. We've got food and water and petrol. Watch the ridges. You might see a man's head.'

Strangely, in spite of my unease, I felt suddenly sure of myself. Twenty years before I'd grown wise in the normal skills of killing. I'd learned to navigate by the stars and study terrain, to judge distances and use my eyes, and I found I could reach back to that experience and I hadn't forgotten.

Nimmo, however, was nervous and kept glancing round him quickly, as though his eye had caught something that had alerted him and made him start, and he was fingering the rifle uneasily.

'Keep that bloody gun out of my face,' I said.

'I've got the safety catch on.'

'It might be a good idea to have the safety catch *off*,' I pointed out. 'If anything comes it might come quickly.'

He glanced at me and I thought he might snap back at me, but he didn't.

'OK,' he said, willingly enough as though for the first time he was aware of his own inexperience and was weighing it up against his youth.

'Divide the horizon into quarters,' I went on, trying to sound more friendly. 'Cover each one methodically. You can't look in two directions at once so don't try. Make sure you cover what you're looking at when you do look at it, though. That's all. You're the one with the good eyes, not me. If they happen to pop up when you're looking the other way it's just our rotten luck. You take the two rear quarters. I'll take the two forrard ones.'

He gave me another odd look, then he nodded. 'It's your show now, soldier,' he said, and for the first time there was no hint of a jeer in his voice. If anything, there was a faint sign of respect, as though he'd decided at last that for once I knew more about it than he did.

Curiously, I was glad to have him with me. I think he'd found it trying occasionally with the rest of us twenty years older than he was, and there'd been many times when I'd not felt very sure of him. Now I was. Behind all his youth there was a great deal of his father in him, and there'd never been anything wrong with Nimmo, senior, when it came to a tight corner.

He settled down after that and didn't fidget so much, as though he drew a certain amount of reassurance from me. Actually, I was as nervous as a cat on hot bricks, but Morena had taught me twenty years before that once you started to show your nervousness everybody else got nervous, too.

We bypassed Biq Qalam and I grew more uneasy at the absence of any signs of life. We stopped for something to eat at midday when the only shadow the Land Rover threw was directly below us, remaining in our seats so that our view of the horizon wouldn't be impeded, and ate the bully beef out of the tin. After a swig at the water and a cigarette we relieved ourselves, one on each side of the vehicle so that we didn't have to take our eyes off the horizon. A lot of people had probably thought during the war that I was over-cautious because whenever I'd stopped I'd always made a habit of assuming that the Germans were just over the next rise also having a brew-up. But I'd never been jumped, so perhaps there was something to it, and I applied the same rules now.

'Keep your eyes peeled,' I said. 'If Ghad Ahmed's around he'll be watching the route to Qalam. You always watch the oases because sooner or later the other side has to come for water.'

He nodded and grinned at me, the first time I'd had an honest-to-God grin from him for a long time, and I began to feel much better.

We'd parked in the shelter of a low sandhill and as we set off again, breasting the rises and small scarps, we began to flounder through soft sand-strips and stretches of shaly rock that spread across the track. Once or twice we disturbed flights of small brown thrush-like birds that swept up ahead of us in great arcs out of the scrub, to be lost against the dun colour of the desert. Once it was a small fleet gazelle, bounding lightly out of a bush and heading for the skyline, and Nimmo's rifle came up at once.

I slammed it down immediately. 'Leave it,' I said sharply, trying to look in every direction at once in case it had been someone else than us who had disturbed the antelope, my uneasiness fed by the emptiness of the land around us.

'Fresh meat, for God's sake!' he pointed out eagerly.

'Listen,' I told him. 'Listen to the silence! You can hear a rifle a hell of a long way when it's as quiet as this. You can hear a car door slam miles away. And Ghad Ahmed's probably listening, even if he isn't watching. If he hears your rifle *we'll* probably be the fresh meat.'

He nodded. 'OK, Captain,' he said.

The sun was sinking and the brassy gold of the day was turning to yellow, so that the whole colour of the desert changed from a white glare to the bronze-yellow of late after-noon. You could see the folds of the land now as the lowering sun began to throw shadows, and the track began to look sharper as the ridges picked up the sun and the hollows were thrown into clear relief.

'Be there soon,' Nimmo commented.

'Hold it!'

I stopped the Land Rover so abruptly he was thrown forward, and he turned and looked quickly at me.

'There,' I said, nodding my head.

He stared in the direction I indicated his eyes narrowed.

'Christ,' he said. 'Your eyes aren't so bad as all that.'

I accelerated to where I had spotted the flattened shape lying like a punctured haybag in a hollow alongside the track, and we stopped in a drifting puff of dust.

It was Selinski. He was lying flat on his face, and I could see a brown-red mess of bloodied dust beneath him.

Nimmo jumped down after me as I climbed slowly from the Land Rover and I swung round on him sharply.

'Get back,' I told him. 'And keep your bloody eyes skinned and the engine running.'

Selinski didn't seem to be anyone I knew. The hours he'd been lying there in the hot sunshine had changed him out of all recognition. Nimmo's face was dry and vacant-looking. He hadn't shaved and his gingery hair was covered with a coating of dust, and for a moment I thought I was looking at his father.

'Gun?' he asked.

'Something better than a rifle,' I said. 'You can see the poor bastard's ribs.'

His face suddenly looked drained and sick, then he swallowed quickly and licked his lips.

'Stay here,' I told him. 'If you see anything, fire a shot.'

'Where are you going?'

I indicated a lengthening shadow about thirty yards off. It was the only one within reach.

'If I know Houston,' I said, 'he probably ran for that.'

Sure enough, Houston was there, lying on his back with his arms and legs wide apart. The sun had played havoc with him and I felt quite sick, because his throat was cut. It looked as though they'd probably wounded him and then murdered him. There were flies about and I wondered briefly where the hell they always came from.

Surprisingly enough, nothing else had touched him, though I could see the prints of half a dozen small animals that had probably come up to him in the night and sniffed at him. There was dust on his staring eyeballs and no sign of the rifle.

As I walked slowly back towards Nimmo, I saw at once that he'd changed. His face seemed thinner and more tired and the roundness of youth had given place to the alert tense look of a soldier I'd seen so many times before.

'He's up there,' I said. 'I'll bury him.'

I unclipped the shovel and walked back towards the hollow while Nimmo sat in the Land Rover with his rifle across his knees.

It was difficult burying Houston because he'd stiffened, and I had to dig a wide shallow grave. I was panting when I'd finished and I was glad to shovel the last of the earth across the accusing expression he wore.

I straightened up at last and looked round for a few stones to put on top of him, but there was nothing worth collecting, so I found the biggest I could and placed it where his head lay. Then I stood for a moment, looking down at the disturbed sand. It seemed to call for something out of a prayer book but instead I just picked up the shovel and started to walk back.

As I went down the slope, my boots scuffing the sand, I kicked a scrap of cloth and I saw it was Houston's Arab head-dress. He'd always been proud of it, so I picked it up and stood looking at it for a moment, then I walked back and put it under the stone.

Nimmo was still sitting in the back of the Land Rover when I returned.

'OK,' I said, indicating Selinski. '*You* can bury this one.'

He gave me a sharp look, as though I were unnecessarily callous, then, while I wiped the perspiration off my face with my shirt, he handed over the rifle for the shovel and climbed down while I sat in the back of the Land Rover in his place.

We knew we couldn't get back to the camp in the Depression before dark, but it seemed to me that if we tried to get to Qalam we'd probably run smack into Ghad Ahmed just as Houston and Selinski had done. I was nervous and worried, and the silence was beginning to play tricks with my imagination.

From the signs it looked as though Houston and Selinski had been surprised and, knowing him, I guessed that the wretched Houston had failed to keep a good lookout. Then, when the shooting had started, he'd run. I was surprised he'd got as far as the hollow.

Suddenly it seemed wiser to get back to the Depression. Somehow that was where instinct told me we should be, and we kept going back on our tracks until dark, on beyond Biq Qalam, then I stopped the Land Rover a few miles short of the Depression and left the lights on for a while in case any-body was watching.

'Let 'em see where we are,' I said.

After ten minutes I started the jeep up and very quietly, keeping the engine as silent as possible, I moved on for another half-mile or so without the lights, then I turned off the track and stopped.

'This'll do,' I said. 'We'll go down at first light tomorrow.'

We ate bully beef again and drank tepid water, listening to the hot engine ticking and creaking, then we drew lots for watches. I won and decided to take the first one.

'Get some sleep,' I said to Nimmo. 'You might need it later.'

'You think the bastards'll come?' he asked uneasily.

'I don't know,' I said. 'I don't like it. They've got two jeeps now to our one. *And* weapons. Houston's as well as their own. We know that. And I can't understand why they haven't been near us. There's something going on I don't like.'

'How can you tell?'

'I don't know. Sixth sense, if you like. I can smell trouble. It's a long time since I last smelled it, but I don't think I've lost the knack.'

He smiled nervously. 'The old desert lore,' he said. 'Sand in my shoes.' But he wasn't jeering and might even have been grateful.

I took the rifle and walked slowly to the top of the neighbouring ridge and flung myself down in the soft sand, listening, straining for the slightest sound that might come out of the coarsely grassed undulations ahead, looking for an improbable geometric shape that was at variance with the soft curves of the desert. There was a chill in the air, and a drifting scent from the dew-wet earth that was faintly aromatic in my nostrils.

I was tired but far too unsettled to sleep, and I lay in the sand, not smoking in case anyone was watching for the glow, and as I stared northwards the feeling of having been there before was so strong I half expected to see the pale fingers of searchlights probing the heavens, and the rose-red glow of shell-flashes.

After a three-hour stretch I woke Nimmo. He came to consciousness at once and sat up.

'OK,' he said.

'Keep your eyes skinned for the shape of anything that doesn't seem to fit – squares and oblongs that might mean a jeep, or a knob that might mean a man's head. Get down low, then you can see them against the sky.'

'Right.'

I heard him shuffle off through the sand, and rolled myself in my blanket alongside the Land Rover. I seemed to wake almost immediately and found him standing over me.

'You'll probably think I'm a bloody fool,' he said apologetically, and I noticed at once the sudden absence of cockiness and the new admission of inexperience. 'I thought I heard shooting.'

I threw off the blanket, rolled it up and tossed it in the Land Rover.

'It sounded like a machine gun,' he said. 'I've never heard one except on television, but that's what it sounded like.'

'You're not such a bloody fool as you think,' I said. 'That's probably what it was. It was a tommy gun that killed Selinski.'

'You sure?'

'I've seen men killed by tommy-gun bursts at close range before now. I expect the bastards have had them ever since the war.'

We drove the rest of the way as though the hounds of hell were after us. The track was hard and flat except for a patch of ridges now and again that threatened to shake us to pieces, but I hardly seemed to notice them. Suddenly I was very worried. It just hadn't been natural for Ghad Ahmed to leave us as much alone as he had and I'd started to wonder if he'd just let us get out of the Depression to slip down into it behind us.

The Land Rover rattled and bumped over the rough track with all the equipment in the back bouncing like a lot of mad things. Once we lost the shovel and had to reverse to pick it up, and I found my jaw was hanging open like a panting runner's, and I was crouching over the wheel as you do when you're coming back from the sea and the traffic's getting thicker and the sun's gone.

'Think there's something up?' Nimmo shouted above the clattering behind us and the roar of the engine.

I nodded. 'They've killed two men and there's nothing to stop 'em doing the lot of us. The desert's big enough to hide it.'

We saw the flames as soon as we reached the top of the Depression and we knew at once that they'd set fire to the huts.

We rattled down the track at full speed, taking a wild chance in the dark, bouncing and swaying over the rocks and slewing wildly every time the front wheels bounced out of the wheel-carved track. Several times I thought we were going over and at the bottom we almost capsized the Land Rover as it hit the soft sand. It swung sideways and came to a stop with the engine cutting out on us, and we were almost thrown out of our seats. Working the gear lever frantically, I got it back on to the track and went bounding across the Depression with the lights switched off again.

As the flames drew nearer, we heard shots and saw black figures moving about in silhouette and once the shape of a moving jeep. It was Ghad Ahmed, all right.

I saw a man running and there was something vaguely familiar about the dark shape of the weapon he had under his arm, and I drove the Land Rover close up to him, working the revolver out of its holster as I did so. Then, as he suddenly became aware of the sound of the vehicle and it dawned on him it wasn't one of his own, he stopped dead and swung round.

I stopped the Land Rover so abruptly Nimmo almost fell out. I flipped the light switch so that the man in front was framed in the glare and shot him smack in the chest as he lifted the tommy gun. We were so close it seemed to lift him off the ground and slam him down flat on his back in a puff of dust.

'Get that gun,' I said, and Nimmo jumped from the Land Rover and was reaching for it almost before the man had stopped twitching.

'That was bloody quick,' he said breathlessly as he returned. There was a burst of firing in our direction and I switched the lights off at once and changed position quickly.

'The bastards have seen us,' I said.

As we drove into the camp I caught a glimpse of jeeps racing off and for a moment, knowing they were on the run and that now was the time to hit hard, I was torn with the itch to go after them. The chase in the darkness and the bullets made it all too familiar and I was reacting instinctively. But even as I swung the vehicle round I realised that Nimmo didn't know how to use the tommy gun and that a rifle was about as much use in the dark as a pea-shooter in a fog, and I stopped again. As I swung the Land Rover round and drove into the camp, the shouting seemed to die away and the drone of the jeeps' engines faded in the darkness into silence.

s i x

The camp was a wreck. Several of the tents had gone up in flames with the palm-frond roofs of the huts and half our supplies and petrol, and there were scattered objects like blankets and fly-sheets and cooking pots lying around in the dust.

A figure with a rifle appeared out of the shadows with a soot-blackened face and white eyes and I saw it was Morena. He managed a twisted grin.

'Thanks,' he said shortly. 'You were just in time. I got one but there weren't enough of us to go round and Crabourne was about as useless as a wet hen with a gun.'

'Where is he now?'

'He was over there somewhere when I last saw him.' He jerked a hand.

'And Phil?'

'I saw her a minute ago. She's all right.'

'What about Leach?'

'He was here. Getting in everybody's way. He's too bloody fat.'

'OK, never mind him now,' I said. 'Let's find the others.'

He scrambled into the back of the Land Rover, and as we drove into the middle of the camp I saw Phil coming towards us, silhouetted by the flames, the heavy revolver hanging from her hand as though it weighed a ton.

'Did you shoot anybody?' Nimmo asked cheerfully still a little excited by all that had happened.

She shook her head numbly, her expression full of shock and horror, and as she stopped in front of us I saw there were dried tears on her face among the marks of soot and dust. I jumped out of the Land Rover and ran towards her and she flung herself into my arms.

'Sloan's been shot,' she sobbed. 'I think he's badly hurt.'

I heard Morena swear softly and I turned to Nimmo as we started after her.

'Bring the Land Rover,' I said. 'We might need the lights.'

We found Crabourne lying on his side near one of the huts, hugging the earth in that grasping intimate way the dead always have. There was blood across his face and in his hair.

'Is he bad?' Phil asked as we turned him over.

'He's dead,' I said.

'Oh God!' Her face crumpled and she dropped the revolver and put her hands to her mouth, her eyes shut.

Morena looked sharply at me, as though he'd noticed for the first time that we'd come back alone. 'What about Houston?' he asked. 'Didn't you find 'em?'

'We found 'em,' I said. 'Houston's dead too. They were both dead.'

Morena's arm moved slowly as he began to polish the butt of the rifle with the heel of his hand, in an instinctive movement as though he were removing the dust. Then he looked up, his face expressionless.

'The bastards mean business, don't they?' he said softly.

There was little we could do but salvage what was left of our belongings. We still had the lorry and the Land Rover and Crabourne's heavy van, but our circumstances had changed considerably. The huts were burned out with most of their contents and the tents were down and torn. Food was suddenly short and for the first time we knew we could not replenish our water when it was gone.

We covered Crabourne's body with a scrap of tarpaulin for burial at daybreak and wandered disconsolately about the wreckage, trying to save what was saveable and it was only when we'd been working for some time, listlessly kicking aside the charred planks and remains of tents, that we noticed that Leach had not reappeared.

For a moment we were all silent, then I jerked my head.

'Come on, Nimmo,' I said. 'Let's go. We haven't finished yet. Wop, stay here. We shan't be far away.'

We left Morena staring after us, the rifle trailing from his hand to the ground and Phil by his side, and walked quickly through the camp. I still had the revolver strapped round my waist and Nimmo had picked up the rifle again.

The smoke from the burning huts was still rising across the sky, making the moon dust-dim, so that it shed a weird glow that was more brown than silver, but there was enough light to see the cliffs and the blurred shape of rocks.

We found Leach outside the pear-shaped cave, and he'd been digging again, thirty yards from where we'd been tearing up the ground two days before. There was a solitary hole and turned earth and he'd obviously known where to look because the hand compass from the lorry lay on the ground beside him and there was no indication that he'd been searching.

'OK, Tiny,' I said. 'You can come out now.'

He'd been driving down with the spade into the stony ground and he hadn't heard us approach, and his head shot up and he came bolt upright, his jaw dropped, his eyes big and round.

'You bloody rotten liar,' Nimmo said, in a low vicious voice, the rifle pointed at Leach's chest. 'You knew where it was all the time!'

Leach stood in the hole as we approached, then his hand reached out slowly for the spade.

'Leave it, Tiny,' I told him. 'One more dead man won't make much difference now.'

He climbed slowly out of the hole, limping and throwing his weight away from the knee he'd injured in the fight with Nimmo, and stood with his hands at his sides, a big, awkward, unhealthy-looking man with tousled hair and a surly face, his nose peeled and raw where the sun had taken off the skin, his eyes fixed on the muzzle of Nimmo's rifle.

I stuffed the revolver back in its holster and began to dig in the hole. It didn't take me long to unearth what Leach was looking for and in the light of the torch I recognised it immediately as the chest I'd seen in the back of the Paymaster's jeep twenty years before.

'How the hell did he know where it was?' Nimmo asked.

'Because he'd got the map,' I said.

His jaw dropped. '*He* stole it?'

'Not from you. Ghad Ahmed's man did that. He just saw him leaving and killed him for it. I expect if you search him you'll find it.'

As Nimmo approached, Leach backed away, his mouth working, and Nimmo swung at him viciously with the rifle barrel. Leach went down, the blood coming from his nose, and as he lay on the sand, half-stunned, Nimmo fished the papers from his shirt pocket.

Although I expected it, I was full of shocked disappointment. The comradeship I'd thought could last a lifetime had existed only because of the conditions that had made it. When those conditions had gone we'd gone back to the old original dog-eat-dog, and this bloated, ugly man with the bright peeled nose and puffy knee wasn't the Leach I remembered, any more than I was the naive, unsuspicious boy he remembered.

Nimmo was watching me, his eyes on the chest.

'What are you going to do with it?' he asked.

'Take it back,' I said. 'Where it belongs.'

'Nobody'll thank you for it,' he said quietly. 'It's a drop in the ocean to a government. I expect they wrote it off years ago.'

I shrugged, and he went on persuasively, still obviously not abandoning the idea of keeping it: 'Money's like everything else. Comparative. If you've only got a hundred, a thousand's a lot. The government won't miss it, and it'd do *us* a power of good.'

'We'll take it back, all the same,' I insisted.

His brows came down. 'For Christ's sake, why?' he snapped.

'Because I was once accused of pinching it.'

He stared at me, but he didn't argue any longer and the two of them carried the chest back to the camp, while I walked alongside the limping, snuffling Leach with the revolver in my hand. He seemed quite subdued, his head hanging, a look of surly bitterness on his face, though if he'd tried to make a break for it I don't know what I'd have done. I'd probably have hesitated too long and he'd probably have got away.

Phil came towards us as we reached the camp, close on Morena's heels, as though she were afraid to be left alone. She seemed to have recovered a little now, but Morena's face was twisted with contempt and disgust as he stared at Leach.

'I never thought I'd live to see one of our lot nip off when there was trouble,' he said quietly. 'Probably thanks to you a man's dead back there.'

We stood for a moment, surrounded by the wreckage of the camp, the smell of the smoke in our nostrils.

'We'll get some sleep now,' I suggested. 'And take a look at what's in the chest in the morning. For tonight I'll keep it beside me. You'd better make sure the vehicles are properly immobilised, Wop, and remember our sweet friend Tiny might have a spare rotor arm hidden away somewhere. As for the rest of it, the problem now seems to be to get out of here and to the coast. I'll lay a year's wages Ghad Ahmed knows we've got the money and will try to stop us.'

Morena lifted the rifle and slipped it under his arm. 'And *I*'ll lay *you* a year's wages,' he said flatly, 'that he'll be smart enough to keep between us and the coast. He'll probably have men sitting up there now, some at each end of the Depression waiting for us to go either to Qalam or Qahait. And by the look of 'em they've got plenty of guns.'

'We'll think of something.'

Phil gestured with her hand. She looked shocked still, but seemed to be coming out of it a little. 'There's a camel track,' she said. 'Over there. There's a wadi and the track leads up it towards Qatu. Or it did. There's no village there any more, though, and it's never used now.'

I glanced at Morena and then back at Phil. 'Can you get a vehicle up?' I asked.

She shrugged. 'There are rock falls. We didn't go all the way.'

'Does Ghad Ahmed know about it?'

'I expect so, but he might think *we* don't. He hadn't arrived when we found it. We were looking for more of the paintings, but as there weren't any, we never went there again.'

'Could you lead us to it?'

She nodded, and as I patted her shoulder I felt her give a small shudder under my hand.

'OK,' I said. 'We'll try it. We've *got* to try it.'

The dawn came in a silver glow and as I woke I moved gently away from Phil so as not to disturb her. Nimmo was already awake and standing alone a little distance away, tall and slender in the mist, his head down, thinking.

As I stood up, he nodded to me and offered me a cigarette. The first puff of smoke in the cool air was like heaven and Nimmo gave me a twisted smile that hid his anxious look.

'When are we leaving?' he asked.

'Tonight.'

He gestured with his cigarette towards the lip of the Depression.

'That lot,' he said shortly. 'They'll see us, won't they? They'll see us as we go up.'

I shrugged. 'We'll go up without lights.'

He protested again. 'They'll see us leaving. And even if they don't, they'll know we've gone once they see the lorries have disappeared.'

'They'll not see the lorries have disappeared.'

He stared. 'What do you mean?'

'We'll make 'em think they're still here,' I said. 'Camouflage. They're not going to come near us – not after last night. It wasn't as easy as they expected, so they'll sit and hope to starve us out. And from where they're sitting they can't see as much as they'd like, not even with glasses. Tomorrow we'll still appear to be here.'

He nodded, apparently satisfied, and jerked his head towards Leach who'd gone to sleep in a small hollow, his big body crouched against a rock, as though he'd clutched at his limbs to bring warmth to them. He had no blanket and no one had bothered to offer him one, and he'd made no attempt to get away because now there was nowhere to go.

'What about him?' he asked.

'He's coming with us.'

'Can you trust the bastard?'

'We've got to. We might be glad of him.'

In the daylight the camp looked like a battlefield, with the burnt-out ruins of the huts with their collapsed roofs and the lorry that had gone up on the night the map had disappeared and the radios had been wrecked. There were scattered blankets everywhere with scraps of canvas and broken camp-beds and torn fly-sheets, and camp-chairs lying about in the harsh grey light of morning, among the charred poles from

165

the huts, and the scattered cinders and burnt fragments of thatch. Even the main compass was smashed. It all seemed so familiar I wanted to cry. It only wanted a few more wrecks, with gun barrels askew and bright red blood on the armour plating. At the very thought of it my stomach knotted with nausea.

We ate breakfast silently and nobody bothered to see that Leach got any. Phil woke in a pallor of lingering terror as we finished, sitting up abruptly with a cry and feeling about her as though she were seeking me. As I went to her, Morena followed me and silently handed her a chipped mug of tea and a bacon sandwich and she took them just as silently, Nimmo watching her with an expressionless face, withdrawn and absorbed in his own thoughts.

The hollow of the Depression was blurred by the mist that swirled and rolled on some hidden draught round a spur of rock where Crabourne had pitched his tents to obtain shade as early as possible. The top of it was out of the mist and picking up the sunshine.

I stared at it for a while, wondering, as I'd been wondering half the night, what was the best way of getting out of the Depression. Behind me the long dusty bowl stretched beyond the rock fall near the pear-shaped cave, blue-grey in the mist and hidden still from the sun.

When we'd finished eating I put some of the soggy bacon on a biscuit and took it with a mug of coffee over to Leach who was sitting up now, rubbing his injured knee and staring towards us.

'Thanks,' he said quietly.

'I'm not doing it for love of you,' I pointed out. 'When you've finished it get hold of a tin of bully beef and a water bottle and get up there on that spur of rock and keep your eyes peeled for Ghad Ahmed. They've got two jeeps and there may be a camel or two. And let 'em see you occasionally. I want 'em to know we're watching.'

He picked at the raw spot on his nose and eyed me, but he said nothing, and later I saw him climbing the spur, limping heavily, his face puffy where Nimmo had hit him with the rifle.

By this time we'd got one of the flattened tents standing again among the scattered packing cases and bedding and all the equipment Crabourne had brought for painting – paper, crumpled like broken bodies, and the sheets of cellophane and splintered ladders. We placed the chest inside it and as soon as Leach's back was turned I got Morena to one side because I felt he was the only one I could trust now.

'Wop,' I said quietly. 'Get one of the tin trunks into the tent when no one's looking and get that chest open. Transfer everything inside it to the trunk, then fill it up with sand and rock and tie it up again.'

He grinned. 'In case friend Tiny decides to bolt with it?'

I nodded. 'We'll put it in the Land Rover. Then if he does make a run for it he'll not get much. I've thought this one out and the lorry's best for us. It'll carry more and it's probably newer.'

I left him to it, under the guise of sorting out spares, while Nimmo and I scouted round the camp to see what we could find. The man I'd killed was still lying where I'd brought him down, flat on his back, staring blindly at the brassy sun. Behind a rock there was another one whom Morena had shot, huddled against the stone as though doing his penances towards Mecca, his face on the sand, his knees up under him, kneeling in the way we seemed to find so many bodies during the war, ugly and ungainly and with none of the dignity so often associated with death. His brown hand clutched a rifle of ancient Italian vintage that was doubtless a relic of the war, like the tommy guns, and there was an ugly stain in the sand underneath him.

We rolled them both into blankets and brought the Land Rover towards them, then we buried Crabourne under the cliffs alongside the Paymaster and his men and erected a crude cross over him, and put the Arabs in the soil a little to one side.

I saw Phil's eyes on us, empty and vacant-looking, as we finished, and I noticed that she made no move to shrug off Nimmo's hand as he placed it on her shoulder in a gesture of reassurance.

By this time we'd separated the undamaged equipment and placed it in a pile near the tent. Everything that had belonged to Crabourne we loaded into the van, packing the completed drawings with care under the supervision of Phil. Then, slowly and carefully, we loaded the lorry and the Land Rover, taking care that everything on the Land Rover could be done without if necessary. If Leach decided to bolt I wanted to make sure he'd take only what I wanted him to take. We made sure there was water and food and petrol, however, because I wanted each vehicle to carry its own supplies in case of emergency, and if the Land Rover was taken I wanted to be sure it would be taken quickly, without any interference with the supplies we had on the lorry. Then, finally, we placed the chest – now full of sand and rock – in a prominent position in the back of the Land Rover where it couldn't be missed.

'All set.' Morena gave me a bleak smile as we finished.

'Fair enough,' I said quietly. 'If he takes off now he can take off without worrying us. I don't want him to take off and if I can stop him he won't. But just in case he does he won't be going with anything we shall need.'

When we'd finished we drove the vehicles behind the fall of broken rock near the pear-shaped cave and parked them so that only the hood of the lorry was visible, then we packed everything that remained and lit a couple of big fires, burning all the torn fly-sheets and tents to make as much smoke as possible, because I wanted Ghad Ahmed to see them. During the afternoon Morena made a check on the vehicles, revving the engines a lot so that Ghad Ahmed would hear them, and when he'd finished he rigged a light from one of the spare batteries ready for the evening.

Just before dusk we decided to have a decent meal, but we discovered we had nothing but a small primus stove to cook it on. One was twisted out of shape, crushed at some point during the night by the wheels of the vehicles prowling through the camp, and the others had simply disappeared, stolen, I supposed, by Ghad Ahmed's men.

Morena shrugged and cut one of the empty petrol cans in half with a pair of cutters from the tool-kit, then, scooping sand into one of the halves, he poured petrol over it and threw a lighted match on to it. It went up with a 'whoosh', then died quickly into low flickering flames in the growing shadows, and he silently filled the other half of the can with water and bully beef and tinned vegetables and placed it on top.

'Haven't lost the knack,' he grinned.

While we ate, we spread a blanket on the ground and opened the maps on it. 'We'll skirt the well at Biq Qalam and the oasis,' I said, 'because if Ghad Ahmed expects us to head anywhere it'll be there. There's a road runs up to Breba and if we go due north from the top of the camel track we can try to turn towards it. We'll soon recognise it because there's a bridge there – Roman, I believe – that crosses the ditch they cut near the well. There's a police post there and if we can reach it we'll be safe.'

'It's a hell of a way,' Morena pointed out.

I managed a quick smile. 'It always *was* a hell of a way,' I said. 'But if they miss us at Biq Qalam and the oasis they're bound to watch the direct route and we'd best not be on it. Besides,' I added, 'we've done this trip before – almost exactly – up to Tobruk during the war.'

When we'd eaten we made tea, the old sweet sergeant-major's tea, and drank it standing, cradling the mugs in the palms of our hands, all of us silent and busy with our own thoughts. Just before dark Morena went up to relieve Leach, as though for the night and I saw him climbing boldly along the skyline so that he was in full view. A little later Leach came down the same way, to eat what was left of the stew we'd cooked. He was subdued, but his eyes were alert and cunning as he prowled round the lorry and the Land Rover, missing nothing. I didn't interrupt him because I knew he'd got one eye on the chest and was making sure of the stores that went with it.

As the night shut down, Morena appeared in the camp and stuck one thumb up.

'OK,' I said. 'Let's get going.'

Leach was slow to respond and Nimmo aimed a kick at him. 'Get cracking, you bastard,' he growled. 'You heard what the man said.'

Before we could get to them they were circling round each other in the dust, Nimmo, his eyes glowing, chopping viciously at Leach's puffy face as though he were enjoying hurting him, and Leach slogging wildly back at him, missing him all the time, his brows drawn down in a stolid expression of hate.

We dragged them apart and pushed them away.

'For Christ's sake,' I said to Nimmo, 'grow up. We've got better things to do than fight.'

'He asked for it,' he said with a savage grin. 'I was glad to give it him.'

Leach said nothing, but he didn't hesitate any longer to help, and, working now as fast as possible, we moved the van and the Land Rover up the Depression and removed the canvas cover from the lorry, and then the tubular frame that supported it. Then, as Morena drove the lorry away, we erected the frame and the canvas cover on piles of stone where the lorry had stood, with Nimmo showing off a little in front of Phil, who was watching both him and Leach with a scared expression on her face. When we'd finished, with as much of the cover showing as had been visible before, we connected the light that Morena had rigged up and stirred the fires until there were two good blazes and enough light to illuminate the top of the cover. With luck, it might fool Ghad Ahmed into thinking the vehicles were still there for a while after sun-up the next day.

'Let's have your radio,' I said to Nimmo, and we set it on a rock and turned up the volume control as far as it would go.

During all this time Morena had been revving the Land Rover as though he were still testing the engine. I wanted Ghad Ahmed to get used to the sound of engines and the blurt of the radio. I wanted him to imagine we were still there, preparing to move up the road towards Qalam the next day. I wanted him to be still waiting there while we were climbing up the camel track towards Qatu. Out of the Depression, I'd feel better because I'd have the whole width of the desert to manoeuvre in and once there we'd at least give him a run for his money.

When we set off it was well after dark but before the moon had got up. We left the fires blazing and the battery light burning and the radio blatting out pop music from Algiers, and slipped away slowly up the rocky track along the Depression, without lights and with the engines as quiet as we could keep them. I had Leach driving the Land Rover with Nimmo alongside him with a revolver. The lorry was in front and the van behind so that he couldn't bolt.

'Keep an eye on him,' I'd told Nimmo, and he'd given me a quick savage grin in the firelight that reminded me of his father.

'Don't worry,' he said. 'If he tries anything I'll take the greatest possible pleasure in shooting the bastard.'

Phil was quiet in the lorry alongside me. She was making a great effort to be brave, though I knew she was feeling pretty low in spirits. She'd made no further reference to Crabourne or Selinski and I knew she was trying hard to put them out of her mind.

Just before dark I'd seen her standing in the entrance to one of the caves, staring round at the paintings with a lost look on her face, and I knew that, although she'd been no archaeologist, she'd somehow become attached to those pictures in the way that you can always become attached to a job you're doing.

'It seems such a pity,' she'd said softly, staring round her at the ancient glowing colours. 'God only knows what damage they might suffer now we've disturbed them.'

'They've stood up to thousands of years,' I pointed out.

'They had a layer of dust over them then that protected them, and the paint isn't new now. Objects as old as these are as frail as gossamer.'

She sighed and managed a quick smile. 'It's here somewhere,' she said. 'That treasure that you came to find. In spite of not being the one you got. I've thought about it often. Somewhere there's got to be something. This land's been covered by everybody from the Phoenicians to the Byzantines, and by the caravans of slaves that came up from the Congo. In spite of what Sloan said, there's a door here somewhere, all covered with soil and rock, a gold door maybe; and behind it a chamber, full of skeletons of men and women who were ritually murdered thousands of years ago. And beyond them the treasure, all gleaming gold, weapons and hunting implements for the men, and domestic things and sex fetishes for the women. All of it waiting to be found and all of it with a curse on it for the finder. It's here and now it'll just go on gathering dust in the darkness, in some vast chamber with the skeletons of the guards and all the scrolls to say why it's there.'

She seemed to choke over the words and as she turned away, she brushed against me. For a second she stared up at me, then she flung herself into my arms, her forehead against my chest, struggling to control the dry retching sobs that tore at her.

By midnight, following her directions, we reached the camel trail at the end of the wadi, with the rising moon shedding a wisp of remote cold light over it that was hardly stronger than the stars. We stopped at the bottom, shocked by the narrowness of the track and by the number of camel bones that lay about, startlingly white in the pale glow from the sky.

'Christ,' Nimmo said. 'It's not very wide!'

Morena stared upwards, his expression calm and unmoved. 'We can't go back,' he pointed out. 'Not now.'

'Suppose we stick?'

'We've got two chances. Either we do or we don't. Either way, we're no worse off.'

Simply because we had no alternative we began to crawl upwards, the engine noises beating back softly from the walls of the Depression. At first it wasn't too difficult, though we were soon slowed down by a series of potholes, but after three hours' climbing, it began to grow more tricky. First it was a fall of rock that blocked the path, so that we had to turn out of the vehicles and throw the stones over the edge, and later it was a drift of wind-blown sand that obscured the track for what seemed thirty yards. It was a heartbreaking job, scooping at its dusty surface and moving the vehicles forward inch by laborious inch, searching the track all the time for stones to jam under the wheels as they bogged down.

We worked until our finger ends were sore with lifting stones and our shoulders were stiff with shovelling sand, but we made steady progress, though I was constantly looking nervously up the slope, waiting for the burst of firing that would tell me that Ghad Ahmed had discovered what we were doing and was waiting for us just above. But nothing happened and, as the moon sank lower, we got nearer and nearer to the surface of the desert.

Then, just when we seemed to be winning, we ran into the landslip. It had cut away half the road and it was impossible to get past it.

'We can't go back,' Morena said again. 'We've got to dig into the cliff face.'

Fortunately, there was more earth than stone and we only had to hack it away, but it was still hard work and I was getting worried now, because I could see a lightening in the sky and I wanted to get up to the floor of the desert and away from the edge of the Depression before daylight. By then the wireless battery would have faded and the fires would have died and it wouldn't take Ghad Ahmed long to realise he'd been fooled.

In sheer desperation we decided to take a chance and move ahead, although the wheels of the lorry crumbled the edge of the track.

'It'd be a tit of a wreck if it went,' Morena said grimly, as he edged it forward.

We got the lorry and the Land Rover safely across the gap, but it was obvious immediately that Crabourne's big laboratory van was too weighty and top heavy.

'It's not wide enough,' Morena said, squaring the vehicle up and standing back to see how much room we had. 'We ought to make it wider.'

I indicated the sky. 'We haven't time,' I said, my voice sharp with nervousness. 'We've barely enough as it is. We'll have to abandon the bloody thing!'

In the end we decided at least to make an attempt, and Morena agreed to drive. We all knew it was a risk, but it was a risk we had to take.

Carefully, we barred the route to the Land Rover with the lorry so that Leach couldn't slip away and make a dash for it, then, for safety, we lifted the flat wooden cases of tracings from the van and placed them alongside. I could hear Leach muttering about them to himself and I knew he was still weighing up his chances.

As we laid them down, Morena climbed into the cab of the van, his face set, and with the engine grinding in low gear he edged the heavy vehicle forward, while I shone the torch along the edge of the drop for any signs of danger.

'Easy!' I called. 'Easy! And for God's sake be ready to jump if I shout. We don't want to lose *you*.'

There had been many times when I had blessed Morena's imperturbability. For a man who had Latin blood in him he was always remarkably difficult to rattle, and I never blessed him more for it than now. The heavy wheels crunched forward in the sandy soil and I could see the broken edge still crumbling away under their weight, then, when he was almost across, I saw the outside front wheel beginning to dip.

'Go!' I screamed. 'Full revs!'

He wrenched at the steering and as the engine shrieked we all flung ourselves against the back of the van, spitting out the sand that the wheels threw into our faces, while it canted more and more sharply to one side.

'Keep it going!' I was screaming. 'Keep it going!'

The rear wheel, now also almost in space, was spinning uselessly, while the inside wheel threw up loose sand in a gritty shower that filled our mouths and eyes and nostrils. By the light of the torch I saw the whole edge of the track begin to crack and crumble in front.

'Jump!' I screamed.

I saw Morena's face, a quick blur of white as he looked out of the window, then it disappeared once more as he struggled to hold the vehicle on the track.

'Jump, you fool!' I yelled again.

As the front wheel dropped and the bonnet canted downwards at a fearful angle, I ran forward, still screaming at Morena to jump, and I saw him fall against the wheel, his head jerking forward. The engine howled as he made one last effort, then he scrambled from the cab, knocking me flying. The yellow dirt flew as the wheels tore at the edge of the track, then the nose of the van dropped in an excruciating lurch.

Clouds of dust rose as it dipped again, and the wheels carved deep grooves into the lip of the track, then it slid forward with a terrifying screeching sound, with bits of scrub and a shower of yellow rock and stones cascading in front of it, and surged down the slope in a fearful plunge, plummeting forward in a dust-enshrouded slide with the awesome grandeur of its own tremendous size.

We saw it bounce, incredibly high considering its weight, roll over and bounce again, with the roof breaking adrift in splinters and all the equipment flying out at angles, and listened to the crunching and the rending of woodwork and the moaning of torn metal as it rolled over and over and over, flinging soil and stones and sand up like a great animal in a dust-bath.

At last the noise stopped and we climbed to our feet, still spitting out the sand, all of us silent and awe-stricken, and I saw Phil was crying softly.

'I'm sorry,' I said. 'We hadn't any option. We had to try it.' She shrugged, curiously untouched by the disaster in spite of her tears. 'We've got the pictures,' she said. 'The rest doesn't matter.'

For a while we stood in a group, staring down the slope. Further down, it levelled off and the van lay on its side just below us with its nose buried in the earth, the ground wrenched away by its fall into a big swathe of torn soil and scattered stones. At first it seemed a calamity, then I realised that we'd lost nothing of real importance.

I told Nimmo and Leach to go down the slope with torches to see what they could salvage, and Nimmo set off at once unquestioningly. Leach hung back, staring downwards, one hand picking at the raw spot on the end of his nose. When he didn't follow, Nimmo stopped and looked back, waiting.

'I can't get down there,' Leach said slowly in a whine. 'My leg'll go. I can't 'ardly bend it already.'

'Get down,' I said.

'Look' – his voice rose angrily – 'we've got all we want! Let's go! It'll be daylight soon and them bloody Wogs'll be after us soon!'

'Get down, you bastard,' I told him, 'before I knock you down.'

He stared at me for a second, while the others watched silently, then he turned, limping heavily to impress us all with his suffering, and began to climb down among the rocks after Nimmo.

I watched him for a second, then I gave the revolver to Phil.

'Sit in the lorry,' I said. 'If anybody tries anything, use that. Can you do it?'

She nodded. 'I'll try,' she said.

The constant strain of having to watch all the time, not only for Ghad Ahmed but for Leach also was beginning to weary me. It required so much forethought to remember that he wasn't to be trusted and to take precautions all the time so that he couldn't simply slip away.

With Morena, I followed the others down the slope and we managed to salvage a few unpunctured water cans, a tent and some food. We'd not come off too well with the petrol because two of the jerricans had bounced out of the van, and one had been punctured and the other simply flattened, but Morena scrambled back up the slope and topped up the tanks of the other vehicles to the limit from a sound can, then we siphoned the contents of the van's tank into the half-empty container. Finally, he took off his shirt and emptied on to it the contents of the big tin of tea we carried, and filled up the tin with the rest of the petrol from the tank. Then, quietly, efficiently, not wasting time or energy in telling us what he was doing, he tied up the tea into a bag with the sleeves of the shirt and started up the slope.

The sky was distinctly lighter by this time and I was growing worried now about being caught on the track. We were all exhausted with labouring up and down the slope, but nobody questioned what I told them to do – not even Leach, now. It was just as though we were right back where we'd been twenty years before, with me in charge and Morena to back me up with his stripes.

With the sky paling into a yellow light along the eastern horizon, and the earth sweet with the scents left behind by the darkness, we reached the surface of the desert, and at last felt able to breathe and stretch our aching limbs without those constricting walls of the Depression hemming us in. The surrounding land stretched away to infinity, empty and silent and menacingly beautiful.

We stopped the two vehicles alongside each other among the scattered rocks, and boiled tea on the primus and opened a couple of tins of bully beef, eating it off hard biscuits with our fingers.

I could see the blunt form of Morena against the Land Rover, his socks over his ankles, dusty, shabby and stooping with tiredness, sharing a cigarette with Nimmo. Leach, big and fat and cumbersome, his shirt damp with sweat, sat on the sand, his back against the wheel of the lorry, his elbows on his knees, his hands hanging down, a blue whorl of smoke rising slowly from the cigarette between his fingers.

Phil came towards me as I stood by the tailboard, cradling a mug of tea in grimy hands. She looked tired and dusty as her eyes searched my face. 'Are we going to be all right now?' she asked quietly.

I shrugged. 'We've got room to move,' I said.

'Will Ghad Ahmed know that we've got the money?'

'If he doesn't, he damn soon will. As soon as he knows we've gone. He'll send someone down to make sure.'

'What do you think he'll do?'

'Try to get it back. There's a police post at Qalam and another at Breba, so he won't want us there. Not now. If he's half as smart as I think he is he'll sit where he can force us off the road – so that he can get rid of us in safety.' I shrugged. 'But Ghad Ahmed's not the only one who wants us in the desert. So do I. It's too big to search easily and as far as we know he's only got two jeeps and some camels.'

'Shall we be all right for water?'

With the sun coming up over the spiked-grass ridges and throwing sudden elongated shadows across the sand, I lit a cigarette and tried to sound optimistic.

'We'll manage if we're careful,' I said. 'It'll mean no washing and things like that because we've got to keep all we've got for drinking and for the radiators. Still,' – I managed a smile in an effort to reassure her – 'we'll be all right. We know how to live in the desert. We've done it all before.'

She looked up. 'Twenty years ago,' she reminded me.

My smile faded and I eyed her soberly. 'Yes,' I agreed. 'Twenty years ago.'

seven

We set off northwards as soon as we'd finished eating, taking a big swing towards the west to get away from the road. The desert was a vast place, unromantic and arid, but big enough to hide us as well as Ghad Ahmed and I was relying on that.

We lurched along slowly, with Leach on the back of the lorry searching the dusty track ahead. I didn't trust him at the wheel of either vehicle – not now he'd got elbow room to get away – so I gave him the job of keeping his eyes skinned for the dust-cloud in the still air that would show where Ghad Ahmed and the stolen jeeps were.

Morena rode with Nimmo in the Land Rover behind, while Phil sat alongside me in the lorry. We all of us had some sort of weapon – except Leach, whom I wouldn't have trusted now with a peashooter. Perhaps it was that more than anything else that made me realise how difficult it was going to be.

Phil had been right. It was the same desert, the same sun, the same sky and the same sand, almost the same vehicles and weapons. But we weren't the same men. It was a long time since there'd been any light-hearted laughter, and there was no nostalgia now because we weren't dreaming it any more. We were living it again, in harsh black and white, and this time we hadn't every scrap of equipment that an anxious government could give us, and lorries that had been serviced by experts in good workshops. We had old vehicles, which had probably been rotting in War Department dumps for longer than they ought and only half the equipment we needed. And, what was worse, we had a woman with us to be responsible for, and, last of all, treachery within our own lines.

The land was like a huge beast stretched in the sun, tawny-coloured, a dead land, empty of life and sound, even empty of echoes, so that the sound of the engines seemed to wing away into the distance with nothing to throw it back in that friendly note of close-grown land. The dust that was coming up irritated the membranes of the throat and nostrils and it was already hot and uncomfortable in the cab, but I felt much more at home now with the feeling of spaciousness about me.

Glancing back, I saw the tyres tracing delicate little ribbed marks in the sand, and the darker strip of the camel track fading away behind us. Already it was impossible to see even the rocks that marked the lip of the Depression, which had faded into the general yellow flatness of the desert.

'We have one advantage,' I said. 'It's harder to find than be found, and this time the enemy's not got aircraft to spot us from the air.'

It was slow going over the soft surface and more than once we had to stop to get sand-mats under the wheels of the lorry. It was bad enough to do that alone, but, all the time, too, I had to make sure that the vehicles were properly immobilised and that Leach was nowhere within reach of them. Nimmo worked like a madman, slaving in the hot dry air as though he didn't even notice the sun beating down on his bare shoulders, while most of the time Phil waited near the Land Rover with the revolver, or sat behind the wheel of the lorry as the rest of us worked. I was hoping she wouldn't have to struggle like the rest of us, but if she had to I was trying to conserve her strength as long as I could.

We stopped at midday for food, because we were all empty-bellied and faint after the work we'd done. I searched for a little hollow between two dunes, and sent Leach up to the top of the highest one to keep his eyes skinned.

'Why me?' he demanded in a whine.

'Why do you think?' I said. 'Because I can't trust you anywhere else.'

'It's always me. And I can't walk properly. You know I can't.'

'That's the cross you've got to bear,' I said unsympathetically. 'But you made it. You can wear it.'

He picked at his peeling nose and his hand strayed down to his puffed knee. 'You might at least give me one of them rifles,' he said, his eyes shifty. 'Then if I see somebody coming I can stop 'im.'

'No dice, Tiny. You asked for it. You've got it. Get cracking.'

He went off muttering, his feet sinking ankle-deep in the soft sand as he climbed. But I knew he'd keep a good lookout for us, for the simple reason that *he* wanted to get back to safety, too. He'd probably make his chance later, but until then he had no desire to walk or fight his way home.

We pooled our cigarettes, which were in short supply now because most of them had gone up in the blaze in the Depression, and we ate our meal without saying much, sitting alongside the vehicles, and trying not to move more than necessary because of the heat.

'We'll keep on our present course for another sixty miles by the clock,' I said to Morena as we studied the map. 'Then we'll try to edge over towards the road. By that time we should be well north of Qalam. There's a well at Bir Baku, and though it's not much good for drinking, if I remember right, we can use it for the radiators.'

Morena wiped his spoon on the seat of his pants and scoured his plate with clean soft sand.

'Which,' he said flatly, 'will be a good thing.'

The way he said it made me look quickly at him. 'Something wrong?' I asked.

'Radiator's leaking,' he said shortly. 'On the lorry.'

The lorry was an ex-WD vehicle and had probably lain in vehicle pool after vehicle pool, deteriorating all the time as it made the rounds, and I knew he wasn't exaggerating.

'Can't you repair it?' I asked.

'No such luck. Not on the move. I can fix something but it won't last long. It'll drip. I've got a can under there now.'

Everybody became silent at once and we heard the distinct plop-plop of dripping water above the tick and creak of the cooling engine.

By this time it was so hot that you couldn't put your hand on the metal sides of the vehicles, and our movements were sluggish as we began to put the equipment back. I was just on the point of sending Nimmo up to relieve Leach when I saw him back down slowly from the lip of the ridge and make a sliding descent down the hill, his feet kicking up puffs of dust as he approached.

Everybody stood up and watched him and he stopped in front of us, panting, the sweat drying in the dust on his face. 'There's a jeep out there,' he said. 'Between us and the road.'

'Only one?' I asked.

'Just one.'

I went up the slope with him, feet sinking in the soft sand, and threw myself down just behind the lip of the dune. In the distance I could see the dust of a vehicle that was churning southwards at a laborious pace, hanging in the windless air like yellow smoke. It seemed to be moving back the way we'd come.

'Watch it,' I told Leach. 'I'll send you some grub up.'

I sent Nimmo up with a mug of tea and some biscuits and bully beef while I spread a blanket on the sand and laid the map on top of it again.

'We'll sit tight for a while,' I said. 'We'd be best to sit tight. If we can see their dust they could see ours. We'll just lie low until dusk and then move. Keep your voices down and no slamming of doors. You can hear 'em a mile away.'

We settled down to wait, clinging to the sides of the vehicles where there was now the beginning of a faint shadow. I sent Nimmo up after a while to relieve Leach, and then Morena. When it had grown cooler I asked Phil if she'd take a turn.

'We've a long way to go,' I pointed out, 'and this is one job *you* can do. Will you have a try?'

She nodded, her eyes dark and heavy, and strangely remote. 'Don't shout if you see anything,' I told her. 'Just come down and tell us. There'll be enough time to do it without hurrying. Keep your head down, though, and remember *they're* watching as well as we are. I'll fetch you down just before we leave.'

Her eyes flickered anxiously. 'You won't forget me, will you?'

I put my hand on the soft flesh of her arm. 'Not on your life,' I promised.

The night came suddenly, as it always did. One minute the outlines were sharp and clear, orange-coloured in the setting sun, then the sky was full of brilliant saffron streamers and the orange had changed to pink and then purple, and then suddenly it was difficult to see things sharply and finally not at all.

I left Morena in charge, with instructions to watch Leach, and walked up the soft slope towards Phil. The sky seemed remote with a few early stars pricking the green-blue dome, and the land was a dark sepia-purple wash, empty and soundless and still. The air was thankfully cooler, and the sky paler than the land now, and dew had laid the dust so that there was the old familiar sweet smell in my nostrils. Down in the valley I could hear the faint reedy notes of Morena's mouth organ.

I flung myself down alongside Phil in the darkness and she gave a little cry as she saw me.

'Oh God!' she gasped in relief. 'I didn't hear you. I've been waiting here ever since it grew dark for someone to come and fetch me. I thought you'd forgotten. If you'd started the engines I think I'd have died.'

I lay on the sand beside her, staring cautiously over the lip of the dune.

'What are you looking for?' she said.

I put one arm round her and drew her to me, still staring across the top of the dune. 'Lights,' I said.

She moved closer. 'There's nothing,' she pointed out. 'I've seen nothing.'

She was close against my side so that I could feel the soft living breathing vitality of her body, and the desert seemed to be quivering with its own breathless stillness. There were no engine noises, no voices, nothing that indicated Ghad Ahmed was near.

'Come on,' I said.

I climbed to my feet and pulled her up after me. She was lighter than I thought and came up into my arms, her bosom brushing my shirt. For a second she stared up at me and I could see her face pale in the starlight, her eyes wide, her lips parted a little. Then I smiled and patted her shoulders.

'Later,' I said.

She didn't reply, but she took my hand, holding it tight, and we slid down the slope together, ankle-deep in the dust.

Morena was waiting by the cab of the lorry, cleaning the tommy gun we'd captured during the fight in the Depression, and Nimmo was in the Land Rover, holding the rifle. Leach was sitting on the sand, smoking and staring sullenly at his feet.

'Let's go,' I said.

Morena put aside the gun. 'No lights?' he asked.

'No lights. We'll do this in darkness and chance soft sand. Ghad Ahmed must know we've got out of the Depression by now and he'll have his camel-boys on every scrap of high ground looking out for us.'

The desert was a dead flat mottled expanse, smooth as water, over which the night had descended like a curtain, with nothing to see ahead but mysterious purple blackness that stretched to the horizon and the splendid stars.

We started off slowly, feeling our way a little, trying to get used to driving without lights. This time, Morena drove the lorry, with Phil alongside him and Leach crouched in the back, while I followed in the Land Rover with Nimmo. I'd have preferred Phil with me, but I'd seen Nimmo's expression once or twice and I was being careful to avoid comment.

We drove with about thirty yards between the two vehicles, watching the stony surface slide back beneath us. Nimmo chattered for a while, but eventually I felt him leaning heavily against my shoulder and guessed he'd fallen asleep. I didn't mind because we were unlikely to be jumped, on the move at night. The following day was the one to worry about, because by that time Ghad Ahmed would have found our tracks and be following us.

With this in mind, Morena and I had decided to pick up every scrap of shale and rock that might obliterate the tyre marks, and every now and then the lorry in front turned slightly along the soft slopes of sand to run, bumping, over a patch of stony ground where the tracks would disappear. After about four hours of slow moving, with the lorry bucking and moaning and the speedometer showing we had covered about twenty-three miles, we came to a stretch of dunes. Morena stopped as we'd arranged, and I drew up alongside him.

Nimmo woke up at once, as you wake up in a train when the swaying movement stops.

'What's up?' he asked.

'Nothing,' I told him. 'Thought you'd like to powder your nose.'

Morena, with a sure instinct, had found the only dip for miles around, and while he immobilised the vehicles we brewed up quickly, with petrol on a canful of sand. Phil was still crumpled in the cab of the lorry, her head down, her short fair hair over her face, deep in an exhausted sleep.

'Let her stay,' Morena said, his voice gruff and fatherly.

We lit cigarettes and stood beside the Land Rover, one of us all the time between Leach and the driving seat and the weapons that lay there.

We glanced at the map in the weak glimmer of the side-lights and the glow of the stars that was brushed thin by a strip of hazy cloud, and I studied the faded pencilled comments I'd made twenty years before.

'It's all soft sand from now on,' I said. 'Undulating, with patches of scrub. We might find it more difficult.'

I looked up towards the first of the dunes that stood in front of us, as high as a house, and soft and yielding and no route for a vehicle.

'Are you thinking what I'm thinking?' Morena asked with a grin.

'I expect so,' I said with the ghost of a smile.

'This'll be the beginning of Katanak Dunes,' he said. 'There's a bypass over to the west. I heard they built one. Goes right round the end.'

I nodded. 'And Ghad Ahmed'll have somebody sitting on it just to the north, waiting for us to be turned towards it by this lot.'

He smiled. 'There's not much of 'em this end,' he said.

'Too bloody much.'

He shrugged. 'I don't know. They're not all that high.'

I grinned. 'High enough for them not to expect us to go *over* 'em.'

He nodded, his eyes glinting. 'That's what I was thinking,' he said.

We changed seats again, and in response to the silent appeal in Phil's eyes as I woke her, I let her get into the Land Rover with me, while Nimmo climbed into the lorry with Morena.

The map was accurate enough and we made slow time. The ground fell into long waves like the ribs of a giant animal and we crept up them slowly, churning through the wind-blown sand. The slopes didn't vary in angle in all their length, smooth, unbroken and silver-grey under the stars, and every time we had to stop, our feet sank in and the powdery sand ran over our shoes in a hurrying persuasive way. Then, as we progressed, the dunes grew higher and steeper so that the vehicles went up with their bonnets swinging from side to side like spirited horses, the sand shooting out from the wheels behind, the sound of the engines swelling and falling in a sustained sobbing.

The Land Rover made it without too much difficulty, but the slopes grew progressively worse, with sharply angled lips and contorted summits that had been whipped by the desert winds into strange, twisted shapes and queerly moulded tongues of sand that balanced incredibly in mid air, and the speed dropped until finally the lorry, with its higher point of balance, began to slide sideways and finally sat back on the rear axle, the back wheels sunk to the hubs in sand.

We climbed down slowly and got out the spades and the sand-mats to dig her out, with the Land Rover hitched in front to give an extra heave. Nimmo was a tower of strength and seemed to be everywhere at once, his face shiny with sweat and the beads of moisture gathered in the stubble of his beard. After a great deal of hard work, however, we seemed further back than when we'd started and the lorry began to boil and we had to wait until it cooled down, limp against its side and covered with grit and dust, the insane look of exhaustion in our eyes.

'Look,' Morena panted. 'Let me unhitch the Land Rover and have a run at it. I'll get the bastard up, you see.'

Nobody argued, because we were all too exhausted for words, and Morena climbed into the cab, his face grim.

'If she slows, shove,' he said.

His first run at the slope ended with the bonnet dug deep into the sloping wall of sand and the back wheels filling our eyes and mouths with grit. Morena swore softly and backed the lorry away, so that the sand ran off the bonnet like water, and in the end the slope became furrowed like a ploughed field by his repeated charges, before he finally wrestled the heavy vehicle to the top, flinging it at the overhanging lip with the engine screaming, so that it shouldn't come to rest with both sets of wheels above the sand.

It dropped to the sand on the other side with a shuddering crash and seemed to slide sideways all the way down to the valley in a swelling bow-wave of dust that left it half buried. As Morena climbed from behind the wheel, we walked slowly back, exhausted and ankle-deep in the dust, towards the Land Rover, and as I drove it up in the lorry's tracks in the churned sand, we caught a glimpse of a flashing light away over on the right behind us, just a sudden glow arcing across the sky, rather like a lighthouse beam, and we knew at once that it was Ghad Ahmed somewhere in the rear on our trail.

'Perhaps it wasn't such a bloody good idea, after all,' Morena said with tight lips as we stopped in the valley and passed round the water bottles to moisten the parched dryness of our throats. 'The bastards must have been able to hear us in Cairo.'

e i g h t

As we set off again, the slopes began to grow shallower and we were able to increase our speed a little and, as the dunes levelled off and the driving became easier once more, Phil huddled against me, warm and comforting, hugging me in her sleep, the feel of her flesh agony to me in the cool expanse of the night.

The light we'd seen had disappeared, and it seemed we'd thrown them off, but by the time we reached firm ground again it was pale in the east and a sword-blade of morning silver stretched low along the horizon. Morena climbed down from his cab as we stopped, and we lit cigarettes, catching the dry smell of the tobacco over the scrub and wild thyme as it drifted away. For a moment, neither of us spoke, just standing there smoking, a little apart from the others, cut off from Leach by his treachery, and by our age and knowledge from Nimmo and the girl, each of us absorbed in our own silent thoughts and drawn together by half-forgotten experiences.

We'd experienced a hundred dawns like this, and the memory flooded back strong and powerful as if it had happened only the day before – half a dozen men crouched by their vehicles, catching a brief vision of beauty in the cool sweet morning air. We were each moved in our own way by the timeless grandeur of the desert that was still undisturbed by man's corroding influence, in spite of the petrol lorries and the aeroplanes and the Shell guides, in spite of the technologists with their air-conditioned cabins and their newspapers and their post offices, and the pumped water that made the international refuelling stations into gardens. It was ridged now as it always had been and always would be, in spite of the bypasses they built round the dune country, seamed by a hundred features that had been hidden by the darkness until the ecstatic dawn changed its contours and its colours as the sun began to rise in the cloud-free sky. Even as I watched, I saw the ground grow more rugged, and the line of dunes and plains and the clumps of tall scrub appear.

'We lost 'em,' Morena said at last.

His voice seemed to explode like a mortar bomb in the silence, and I nodded.

'Yes,' I said. 'We lost 'em.'

Leach limped grumbling to his post on the lip of the dune while the rest of us cooked bacon and beans and brewed tea. Phil had agreed to act as cook, and as she slopped the water from the container into the billycan, she caught it with her foot and it tilted enough to slosh a pint or two out into the greedy sand.

'For God's sake,' I said sharply, 'be careful.'

She glanced up, her eyes faintly resentful in her tired face, and, though I knew she'd been doing her best and the spilt water was an accident, I didn't withdraw the reprimand because I knew she had to realise just how precious it was.

Nimmo stared at me for a second, then he crossed to her and took the container from her. 'I'll do it,' he said quietly.

He put the can on to the stove and began to brew the tea, measuring the water in precise drops. There was a faint breeze getting up now, I noticed, a fragment of the wind that had stirred the bowl of the Depression while we'd been down there, whipping up the tops of the sandhills and covering the food with a fine gritty dust that floated on top of the tea and crunched between our teeth as we ate.

191

'Remember that time when we were coming back from Bardia?' Morena asked quietly, his eyes moving slowly round him. 'It was blowing up just like this then.' He looked at Nimmo. 'We thought we'd lost your old man that time,' he said. 'He ran over a mine. He was lucky.'

Nimmo looked up and for once there was no irritation in his face at the reminiscence, because Morena, in his wisdom, had managed to make him feel part of it through the reference to his father.

'What was my old man *really* like?' he asked. 'I never knew him much.'

He seemed to be seeking something to admire, and Morena nodded. 'He was all right,' he said firmly, in a way that made it a compliment.

'Better than me?' Nimmo asked with a grin that was malicious but still friendly. 'With all *my* knowledge?'

Morena nodded again. 'They always are,' he said. 'Still, you'll have the pleasure of knowing that you'll be better than *your* son.'

'The way we're shaping, I might not get the chance to have a son.'

'Don't let's shout, "All is lost" till the bloody ship sinks,' Morena growled. 'We've got two good vehicles and we're all fit and well. And you're luckier than most. You've got enough good looks to pinch anybody's girl.'

Nimmo grinned and glanced at Phil and the tired look on his face seemed to drain away.

'Think they'll try to rush us today?' he asked.

'God help 'em if they do,' I said. 'If we're ready for 'em, there's nothing more dangerous.'

Because it wasn't hot yet, I sent Phil up to relieve Leach. It looked as though we might be in for a blow and, if we were, the sand whipping off the top of the dunes would make keeping a look-out a damned uncomfortable pastime, and I thought she ought to get her share in first before it grew too unpleasant.

As she rose slowly to her feet, tiredness showing in every movement, Nimmo scrambled up, too.

'I'll do it for her,' he said quickly, but I waved the offer aside.

'Christ, she's tired, man!' he said.

'I'm tired,' I pointed out. 'Morena's tired. You're tired. It's the one job she can do that'll relieve us.'

'It won't hurt me.'

'Phil had better do it,' I said.

She didn't argue and began to climb the slope. Nimmo stood staring after her, glancing at me occasionally, as though trying to weigh me up, then he turned away and sat down again. When Leach came down, Morena gave him food and tea without comment. He took it to the back of the lorry and sat down there to eat it, separated from the rest of us, and when he'd finished he cleaned his plate with sand and rolled over on to his back and closed his eyes, his face blank and expressionless and ugly. Nimmo was already asleep with the rifle cradled under him. Morena had immobilised the vehicles and was working on the leaking radiator, as tireless as usual.

I worked with him for a moment, talking desultorily, but I was restless and nervous and after a while I began to walk up the slope. Morena watched me go without comment, his face calm.

Phil was in a hollow at the top of the dune, where the wind had scooped out a little spoon-shaped dip. From where she was lying she could look out over the desert yet still be hidden from the two vehicles in the valley.

She looked up as I appeared, her face showing a fleeting anxiety, then it relaxed and she smiled her eyes startlingly blue in her brown face.

I flopped down into the sand alongside her and stared across the dun plain.

'How much longer?' she asked.

'Another five days,' I said. 'But we might be able to break back to the road before then. If we can get to the north of Ghad Ahmed he'll never catch us. He didn't get away with much petrol and he's using more than we are. It's my guess he has to keep sending one of the jeeps to Qalam to refuel. I'll bet he's hopping mad at losing us.'

'I shan't be sorry when it's over,' she said. 'Do you know what I'd like more than anything else? – to be able to pull the plug in a bath. Just to see the water actually running away to waste.'

She was silent for a while as we both stared out over the dunes, then she spoke softly.

'Was it always like this?' she said. 'During the war, I mean.'

'Most of the time.'

'I must look like the wrath of God.'

As I looked at her, I was surprised to see there were tears in her eyes.

'It's just that I'm scared and dirty and worried sick,' she said. 'I'm not the pioneering type, I guess.'

I took her in my arms and held her close to me, not moving while her lips moved in the hollow of my neck. She was warm and eager, her mouth searching desperately for mine, but I pushed her away gently and sat up.

'Later,' I said.

She stared at me in silence for a while, her lips parted, her eyes hot with an angry retort, then she sighed. 'Later. Always later.' She drew a deep breath that seemed to go down into the depths of her soul, and gave a little shudder.

'On that, I guess,' she went on, sitting up with a twisted smile that was full of frustration and a faint tinge of bitterness, 'I must expect to go from here to the North Pole.'

She drew another deep breath. 'I've gotten so I feel like one of your desert rats all the time, all dust and dirt and fear.'

I said nothing and she sighed. 'You've changed,' she said. 'You're different.'

'Am I?' I said, though I knew I was. I knew I'd become different the minute things had become difficult.

'You're remote. You're not the same man. There's no warmth to you suddenly.'

The note of bitterness seemed stronger in her voice and I took her hand. She pulled it away quickly.

'It's so long since anyone behaved like a human being towards me,' she said in a thin voice. 'Sloan, poor devil, was as dusty as his work, and David – well, you saw David.'

She looked at me and managed a smile, but it was twisted and still faintly bitter. 'I mustn't put you off your duties, Captain,' she said.

There was a brittle quality in her manner that worried me, but then her gaze grew warmer and the harshness went out of her voice again. 'Why did you give me first turn up here?' she asked.

'Because I think there's a blow coming and I thought it would be easier for you.'

Her expression seemed to stiffen. 'Not so you could follow me up here? Not because I was waiting for you to come?'

'Perhaps so. I don't know.'

She stared at me for a second, then she smiled unexpectedly and squeezed my hand. 'Anyway, I'm glad you came.'

For a second, neither of us moved, staring at each other. Her lips were parted and her eyes were shining, but suddenly, impulsively, I released her hand and got to my feet.

'I'd better be getting back down there,' I said.

The taut look returned to her face and her mouth drooped, and I hurried on.

'Ride with me when we leave,' I said.

195

She looked up slowly and her eyes were cool again and she was frowning.

'Thanks,' she said shortly.

When I got back to the vehicles Morena withdrew his head from the bonnet of the lorry and stared at me, but he didn't say anything.

'How's it going, Wop?' I asked, for something to say.

'It's losing too much water for comfort,' he said.

'Let's get going.'

He nodded and stirred Nimmo with his foot. The boy sat up, alert and alive at once. Leach's reactions were different. He lifted himself to his elbow slowly, and sat for a while staring glumly at the ground in front of him, grunting and scratching and yawning, his eyes narrow and puffed with sleep. Then he rubbed his knee and inevitably began to pick at the raw spot on his nose.

'On your feet,' I said. 'We're moving.'

He got to his feet reluctantly, staring resentfully at me and past me to the Land Rover.

I sent Nimmo to fetch Phil down and they came down together, holding hands and half sliding in the soft sand as he helped her to keep upright.

'Let's go,' I said.

Morena replaced the rotor arms and we began to move off. The hot sun had wheeled and the colour of the desert had changed from vermilion to rose and then to the empty greyness of ash. The morning wind fretted our faces and the glare was as bright as a looking glass, magnifying objects all round us and bringing out the surrounding desert in all its starkness. It was like a torch and everything metal about us burned the flesh, and the sweat on our shirts blackened the cloth and dried at once in the sapless atmosphere.

The sky grew as metallic as a brass gong, the air seeming to hum with the heat even above the dead beat of the engines, and the light appeared to crash to the ground in a dazing glare, glinting on the fragments of stone and grit that reflected it blindingly. All was emptiness around us, and loud silence, bound in a great glitter through the two colours of rust and silver-grey.

We stopped again at midday without a shadow, and Nimmo took the watch on top of the dunes. Phil sat next to me, close enough for her shoulder to rub against mine, but I noticed she made no attempt to allow it to do so. Nobody had much to say because it was too hot to talk. Once or twice I turned as I saw Phil's eyes on me, and though there was something unfathomable in their depths, I was grateful for the glances.

The wind was stirring more now, as I'd expected it would, and the moving sand and gravel scratched and pawed at the vehicles so that a piece of loose tent canvas sticking out of the Land Rover flapped softly against the metal. Occasionally, it came in strong fitful gusts, whipping low across the bare ridges to ruffle the summits so that it seemed as if they were smoking, or lifting the dust in the hollows into little whirling columns before sighing and dying away once more to resume its restless questing, while the sand sifted down again, secretly, obliterating our tracks.

The going was still poor and I decided to carry on until dusk and then stop for a long break, feeling that in the darkness we could all relax and rest more easily.

The vehicles lurched and rocked over the uneven ground in a powdery fog that swirled around us, covering us in grey-yellow dust that lay on eyebrows and lashes and banked up on the sweat marks. The hot rising wind flapped the tent canvas more loudly against the metal of the Land Rover now, and everywhere, every time the engines died, you could hear the gritty whispering of blown sand. Leach, on watch behind me on the lorry, grumbled constantly about it.

Towards dusk, with the wind blowing harder still in uneven gusts and the empty sky changing to an ugly saffron that grew darker all the time as the dust dimmed it to a yellow-brown haze in a warning of a coming storm, I heard the sound of a horn and became aware of Nimmo ahead swinging the Land Rover round in a wide fast curve and heading back the way we'd come. I stuck my head through the cab window and bawled to Leach and I could tell from the way he replied that he'd been asleep. Then I saw dust moving beyond the top of the next dune and realised that Ghad Ahmed had found us at last.

The two jeeps came rocketing over the summit like tanks with a tommy gun rattling from the leader. The men in them were the same tattered bunch I'd seen with Ghad Ahmed, but he'd obviously not trained them well, because if I'd been doing what they were trying to do I'd have brought them down one on each side of us to divide our fire. Instead, they came down together, clueless as Johnny Newcomes, close enough on each other's heels to make a target and far too fast for their firing to be effective, though I heard the whacker-whacker-whacker of bullets thumping against the rear of the lorry.

I heard Leach yelling with fright and Phil screamed, and I pushed her to the floor of the cab.

'We're going to look like mother's colander,' I shouted, suddenly wild with excitement, and I caught a glimpse of her staring up at me from the floor of the cab, her eyes full of bewilderment.

Morena was standing upright in the front of the Land Rover now, holding the tommy gun we'd captured in the Depression, one hand on the winsdcreen as Nimmo swung the vehicle round for him to get his sights on the jeeps. The windscreen flew into fragments and Nimmo ducked, but Morena stood there like a rock and I swear he never even flinched, though there was suddenly blood along his chest.

Phil was beating on my knee and screaming something I couldn't hear for the roar of the engine – as though she were pleading with me to provide some sort of protection, but I was too busy watching Nimmo and Morena to hear her and brushed her hand away irritably, trying to concentrate on what was going on. Momentarily, I saw the flicker of hurt astonishment in her eyes, then she turned away and buried her face in her hands and, as the two jeeps came closer, I saw Morena shout and Nimmo stood on the brakes.

Morena had only the magazine that had been on the gun when we'd captured it and if he wasted it the weapon was useless, but the Land Rover had stopped dead and Morena stood still, waiting, the blood on his shoulders and chest bright in the fading sunshine.

I had to watch, and I stopped the lorry in spite of Phil's pleadings to go faster, and reached for the rifle. The wind was making nervous querulous sounds around us now as it skirled round the dunes, setting the sand moving in giddy little zephyrs and flurries that carried the dry tang of dust, then, as the two vehicles swung past, I heard the abrupt rattle of Morena's gun and saw the ejected cartridges jumping out.

The driver of the first jeep fell forward over his wheel, grabbing at his shoulder, and the vehicle slewed round with a flung bow-wave of yellow sand, and came to a stop so that one of the men in the rear seat fell out. The other vehicle had to swerve abruptly to avoid it and rocked to a halt alongside it, and there were a few desultory bursts from their tommy gun as we revved our engines and got in motion again at once. The man sprawled in the sand scrambled to his feet and I saw him pushing the driver aside, then, as Nimmo brought the Land Rover past us into the lead, the two vehicles turned round and headed back the way they'd come.

'They always were a gutless lot,' Morena said flatly across the intervening space.

As we stopped again, I became aware of the turgid sky changing to a queer colour that was translucent yet metallic in the absence of sunshine, and of thickening clouds of flying dust that was as fine as baking powder. The first stars had come out, but they were obscured and the sky was only a blurred reflection of the land that stretched, dim and lonely, to the indeterminate darkness.

I stopped the lorry alongside the Land Rover just as Morena climbed out. As Leach jumped down after me and began his explanations, Morena walked straight up to him and hit him on the jaw so that he went flying into the sand.

'Next time, keep your bloody eyes open,' he snapped.

As Leach picked himself up, Morena fingered the blood on his chest and shoulders, his eyes narrow.

'I thought the bastards had got me at first,' he said. 'But it's only glass.'

There were sharp shining splinters sticking into his flesh and, as I turned, looking for something to bandage the wounds, I saw Phil still crouching on the floor of the lorry with the door open, her eyes wide and dilated.

'For God's sake get a move on,' I said sharply, hoping to shock her out of her fear. 'We need bandages and water.'

She came to life at once and without a word began to search among the remains of the first-aid kit. She found a piece of lint and bent over Morena's chest, trying not to grimace at the blood and probing at the wounds with her fingers.

'I can't get them,' she said, her voice high in a wail of despair.

'Let me do it,' I said.

I was about to push her aside impatiently, but Nimmo somehow got in front of me.

'Give her a chance, for Christ's sake,' he said quietly.

I stared at him, but his eyes didn't waver, and I nodded, and after a moment or two she seemed to pull herself together and found a pair of eyebrow tweezers among her kit and picked out as much of the glass as she could with them. When she lifted her head, however, there were still several tiny fragments deep inside the flesh.

Morena shrugged them off. 'They'll have to wait till tomorrow,' he said. 'The light's going.'

She managed to bandage the wounds after a fashion, but she was no expert and it didn't look very secure. It was all I could do to resist pulling it off and doing it again, but Morena moved away quickly, glancing at Phil.

'It'll do,' he said. 'It'll keep the dirt out.'

He looked up at the sky. 'And judging by what's coming it'll need to,' he ended.

Almost as he spoke, the wind grew stronger and the flying dust began to obscure the horizon, so that visibility fell to a few yards of unreal light.

'We'll stop here,' I said, and we began at once to prepare food before the dust grew too bad, stumbling around in the swirling dust-clouds like dim shadows seen through smoke.

Morena was crouching with his back to the wind, his eyes half closed, working over the tent, with the sullen Leach alongside him, their heads well down and huddled against the blast as they'd learned twenty years before. Nimmo was spitting out the grit that filled his mouth and nostrils and Phil was hopelessly trying to knock off the dust that gathered in the folds of her clothes, blinking and trying to wipe away the dirt that stuck to the tears streaming down her face.

'For God's sake,' I shouted to them, 'use your loaves! Turn your backs to it!'

As the leaden light decreased, we erected the tent and started to brew some tea, but, shuffling round inside to make room for Phil, Nimmo kicked the stove over and we had to start again.

'Sort yourself out this time,' I said sharply to him. 'This isn't the Ritz and we can't spare the water.'

Neither of them spoke, but I saw their eyes meet as
Morena got the stove going again. We drank the tea silently,
huddling together under the rippling canvas that smelled of
staleness and dust, to keep the flying grit from our food. It
was oppressively hot inside the tent, with the lamp swinging
like a corpse between us and the flap of the canvas in our ears
and the whispering of the sand outside. The night stirred
uneasily and I could see that the faces around me wore the
agonised concentration of weariness and strain.

'We'll be safe tonight,' I said, hoping to relieve them from
tension. 'Nobody'll come near us with this lot around. Least
of all the Arabs.'

The shadows flickered unnervingly under the swelling
shout of the wind, and beneath the thrumming whistling
square of canvas that flowed with restless movement the
gritty sand filled our plates and mugs, and the cigarette
smoke stirred and eddied and dispersed in gusts as the tent
swelled and collapsed and shuddered in the blasts.

The wind was increasing all the time and the sand that
came whirling through the opening was swift enough to sting
our faces, then we heard a tremendous rip as the sun-rotten
material tore across and the whole lot came down on us. We
scrambled for the outside, and instinctively I grabbed for Phil
and pulled her free of the whipping, maddening folds, then
we were lying face-downwards together out of the needle-
sharp bite of the sand in the lee of the lorry and the unloaded
cases that contained the rations. The others seemed to have
disappeared, though I guessed they couldn't be far away
from us, obliterated by the flying dust and lost in the
pounding of the wind.

The temper of the storm rose to an intermittent wailing
and then to a howl as the pall of dust swept over the bone-
dry plain, and you could hear above it the hissing sound as
the hard sand particles rubbed against each other and against
the floor of the desert in their headlong rush. As it struck us

like a blow, searing and blinding and parching with a thousand fiery tongues, I tried to make a shelter with my body for Phil, and she crouched against me, under my arm, so that I could feel the softness of her flesh with a hard yearning that longed for the storm to die away and leave us in the warm darkness of the desert. Her fingers touched my neck, then the silent, infiltrating dust came between us in a hot solid fog, creeping against the skin, beneath clothes, into eyes and throats with the hot air we breathed, even into the mind, until it was a case of merely hanging on until it stopped.

The stars had gone, rubbed out by the yellow clouds of storm-dust, and then a blanket, blown from somewhere, fell across us and, pulling it over us, we rolled in it together, gaining some blessed relief from the biting sand but tortured by sweat and the clammy heat of our own breathing.

'For God's sake, make it stop,' I heard Phil whimpering, and I pulled her closer to me and felt her fingers gripping mine.

The hours of darkness were agony as we lay filthy and exhausted, unable to sleep, fighting for breath, licking dry lips and swallowing with difficulty; and when dawn came daylight brought no relief from the misery of the night. The wind seemed to lose its ferocity at last, but the flying sand made it impossible to see more than a yard or two and impossible to contemplate movement or action of any kind. We could see with the coming of daylight, but the murk was unchanged, except for an incandescent glow where the sun was.

The atmosphere was darkened by a reddish haze and the intolerable air dried our tongues, matted our hair and burned our eyelids.

All perspiration seemed to have stopped, and our clothes all had an itching gritty coating. The light was grey and leaden like a glimpse of hell and occasionally a tuft of shrub, torn out by the storm, came bowling past, probably from miles away.

Later, when we were beginning to feel we were going mad, the wind dropped abruptly, but, as we lifted our heads, it changed direction almost at once and blew all the sand back again, coming brutally off the desert on the other side of us, the same dry burning wind, as though an eerie twilight had fallen across the world, a weird tawny half-light which rolled and eddied and blotted out the sky with a great curtain of dust that whirled into the heavens, thinned by the wind as it climbed into the upper air. Clutching the ground, it was as though a million men were marching over us, roaring with strange voices, tramping us into the depths of a pit that was full of darkness and reeking heat.

When we were goaded beyond endurance by the over-powering need to drink, the wind dropped at last and we were able to sit up. Feeling dehydrated and close to death, I saw the red sun briefly through the murk. My mouth was on fire and my tongue stuck to my palate as I dragged Phil to her feet, her face drawn and strained, her skin and hair grey-yellow under the coating of dust, her clothes layered with thick patches of it where it had collected in the folds. She looked at me, her lips muddy and her eyes big and full of tears.

We were still standing like that, weak with the relief from the nagging wind and the bite of the sand that seemed to have abraded every stone, when I heard the soft shuffle of hoots and I saw Morena approaching. He stopped in front of me and I swear I thought he was going to salute, so powerful was the feeling of it all having happened before.

'The Land Rover's gone,' he said shortly. 'That bastard Leach took it.'

PART THREE

Ancient Battlegrounds

o n e

So Leach had cracked at last. In the physical isolation the protective covering of courage had proved too thin and fragile, and there was now only a patch of oil where the Land Rover had stood.

At first I was dully angry, then I realised that perhaps we were better off without him. Now, at least, I could trust those of us who remained, and there would no longer be the necessity to watch our own party as well as look out for Ghad Ahmed.

I felt no grief for Leach's treachery. His greed had been greater than his sense of comradeship, which, in any case, had probably died, like mine, and like Morena's and everybody else's, once the crisis of war had passed. The influences of the present had been stronger than the influences of the past.

'It's my fault, I suppose,' Morena said heavily. 'I only removed the rotor arm last night. I could have done more, but I never thought anybody would be bloody fool enough to move off in that lot. He must have had a spare.'

He kept wincing as he moved, as though the fragments of glass in the cuts on his chest and shoulders were jabbing at his flesh, and the strips of shirt that were tied over the wounds were grimy and caked with dust which must have chafed and ground on the rawness. He seemed faintly depressed, too, as though he'd let us down, in the way he'd always seemed depressed whenever he'd felt there'd been the slightest neglect of duty on his part. Though, God knows, nobody could ever complain about Morena on that score.

'It doesn't matter,' I told him. 'We expected it, and he's got away with nothing except a box of rocks he thinks is money. He's still in short supply for petrol and water and rations. It'll do him no good, and he doesn't seem to have got away with any weapons.'

'God help him if Ghad Ahmed catches him,' Nimmo said in a flat voice, and I saw Phil give him a quick frightened look.

We stood in a tattered dusty group, staring round us at the empty desert, the small delicately shaped mounds at our feet showing the half-hidden items of equipment that had disappeared when the tent had blown over. Morena kicked at one of them and it turned out to be the lamp.

'He got the compass,' he said slowly. 'It was under the seat. The other one got smashed up the night of the fire.'

'We'll be all right,' I said. 'We can still steer a course by the stars and we've only got to keep going north to hit the sea.'

Though the wind had dropped it was still dry and burning and stirred up the sand and gravel to scratch at our skin, and eddies of yellow dust twirled and fell like collapsing tops.

We moved about with drooping heads and half-closed eyes, keeping our backs as much as possible to the dying wind, our eyes and ears and nostrils blocked by grit that grated between our teeth, then, as we searched for our equipment, the wind died completely and the dust fell so that the day became one of luminous clarity again, metallic and sharp with an immense hush that was terrifying after the storm.

Our eyes were sore and inflamed as we sat round the brew of tea, thankfully quenching our thirsts with the thick, sweet liquid, and munching grittily on biscuits and bully beef, while Morena painstakingly cleaned the sand from our weapons.

'We'll move off straight away,' I said. 'It'll be safer, and we might even run into Leach.'

Phil looked at me with a haggard appeal in her eyes. No more, she seemed to be saying. Let's, for God's sake, stay here and rest.

I ignored the look and we packed up slowly, but not easily. Nimmo and Phil, not realising the importance of meticulous care, kept dumping things down carelessly and we had to keep unpacking so that the things we would need first or quickly would be on top.

'I'm sorry, I'm sorry,' she kept saying in a low desperate voice as I changed things round again and again. 'I didn't realise.'

'Forget it,' I said. 'But we need the rifle on top, don't we? And it's no good putting the water under everything else.'

She nodded, not replying, stumbling around with weary limbs, trying to find the lost equipment while I was on edge all the time, wondering when Ghad Ahmed would appear.

'How about a drink?' Nimmo asked as we finished, but I shook my head, in spite of the appeal in Phil's eyes.

'Not now,' I said. 'Later.'

He glanced at Phil, his eyes concerned, and in the end I shoved the water bottle at her.

'Take it easy,' I warned. 'There isn't a tap just round the corner.'

The sun seemed to be hotter in the shining arch of the sky than on the previous day and we were all dirty and dry-throated, and none of us had washed since we'd left the camp in the Depression. Phil handed the water bottle back unwillingly and I knew she was longing to wet a handkerchief and rub it across her face, but I took it firmly and put it in the cab, because Morena hadn't been able to plug the leaking radiator completely and we had a long way to go. I was taking no chances. It was possible to be dehydrated in the wasted plains of the desert in a very short time.

Phil made no attempt to climb in the driver's cab with me. She walked silently to the back of the lorry and Nimmo put down a hand to pull her up, helping her over the equipment with his hands on her waist. I didn't say anything. Strangely, I was glad it was Morena's reassuring bulk alongside me in the cab, though he seemed in pain and a little depressed still.

'Makes you think, doesn't it?' he commented. 'It takes a war, with bloody murder and sudden death, for human beings to have any regard for each other. I never had a very high opinion of Tiny Leach but I never thought he'd do this to *us*.'

'You were lucky,' I said. 'I've been expecting something of the sort ever since we left.'

'What is it?' he asked. 'Why did he do it?'

'Because he isn't the same Tiny Leach,' I said. 'The other one was still young and hadn't been in clink and probably still found something to admire in the world.'

He nodded. 'I suppose so,' he agreed. 'I expect that's it.'

I started the engine, and we moved off, with Nimmo in the back keeping watch.

We pushed out of the valley, wondering all the time if we'd find Ghad Ahmed on the other side of the slope. Though the plain was clear, I didn't try to fool myself that he wasn't somewhere in the vicinity, waiting for his chance. There was plenty of time before we reached Breba.

I had decided now to head towards the road and chance it. We'd given a good enough account of ourselves the night before, thanks to Morena's steadiness, and Ghad Ahmed's men had been such rank amateurs I was prepared even to shoot it out with them if necessary.

I was still busy with my plans when the engine coughed and died and the lorry lurched to a stop.

'Oh Christ, no!' I said.

Morena glanced at me and began to climb out of the cab. As I joined him, Nimmo jumped down, too, and landed in a flat puff of dust.

'Better get back up there,' I said.

'He'll need some help,' he pointed out.

'I'll help him.'

'I can do it.'

'For God's sake,' I snapped. 'Just because *our* vehicle's packed up, it doesn't mean Ghad Ahmed's have, too. Get back up there and keep your bloody eyes skinned.'

As he stared at me, I caught a faint flicker of defiance in his gaze, then he climbed back into the lorry and I noticed that all the time he was sweeping the horizon he was talking quietly to Phil.

By the time I had joined Morena he had opened the bonnet and I caught a glimpse of the engine, caked with sand and oil and spattered rust, then he lifted his face to me, his eyes puzzled and red-rimmed after the storm.

'Petrol,' he said. 'Carburettor's empty. Pump's probably not working.'

There was something in his face that worried me.

'There was nothing wrong with the pump yesterday,' he said.

He walked round the lorry to where the petrol tank was situated, just under the chassis. The metal was coated with sand and dust which had stuck to the inevitable film of oil, but the hole in the tank was clear enough.

'Bullet,' he said, wiping away the sticky grit with his thumb. 'The bastards must have hit it yesterday afternoon.'

'Can we patch it?'

He shrugged. 'We can plug it,' he said. 'But it won't last long. Not on this sort of ground. Too bumpy. It's bound to leak.'

He got out one of the tent poles and cut a short length from it, and as he worked with his knife I opened the map

211

and stared round at the desert, tawny-grey and arid and littered with flinty stones.

'Changes things a bit,' I said. 'Doesn't it?'

Morena looked up from where he was pushing the rag-wrapped plug into the hole in the petrol tank. He pulled a face and, taking out his hammer, hit the plug hard. He gave it a few more taps then straightened up.

'Tell us the worst,' he said.

'I was going to head east to find the road,' I told him. 'But it also swings east about here and I reckon now we'd better press on due north. Shortest distance between two points. This way we go up near Karabub where the Jerries caught the Yeomanry on the way back to Benghazi.'

His eyes lit up. 'Any wrecks there?'

'Might be. Too far south for the scrap merchants to come collecting. Why?'

'Might find a petrol tank we can use.'

'After all these years?'

His face fell and he gave me a wry smile. 'Not very likely,' he admitted.

We found Leach with the sun like a brass eye in the heavens and without a scrap of shadow anywhere. He was lying face up on the sand, his arms and legs spread-eagled.

Morena, who was driving at the time, stopped the lorry short of the body, and walked forward. As I climbed down to follow him, I could see Nimmo's face, narrow-eyed and shocked, and Phil's, sick-looking and grey with horror.

The metal chest that had once contained the money lay on its side, the rope cut, the sand and stones with which it had been filled spilled out among the scattered equipment and the camping gear that had been on the Land Rover.

Nimmo stared at it, his eyes narrowed. 'Christ,' he breathed, 'there never *was* any money in it!' and I suddenly remembered I'd never told him what we'd done with it.

I jerked a thumb at the tin trunk he was sitting on. 'Don't let it get you down,' I said shortly. 'It's in there.'

He stared downwards at the trunk and then at Phil, and then at me again.

'You crafty bastards,' he said. 'You thought we'd run off with it.'

'Not you,' I said patiently. 'Only Leach.'

Morena was a little way ahead, bending over the corpse, and as I walked towards him, I stared round me at the empty illusive desert, with its tawny ridges, conscious again of eyes watching us. The silence was immense and threatening.

'The bastards must have got ahead of us,' I said.

'They'll not rush us again in a hurry, though,' Morena growled. 'We gave 'em something to think about last time.'

He straightened up and stared with me, aware like I was that any one of the folding dunes around us might hide men and vehicles.

For a long time we stood in silence, our eyes screwed up against the glare, then I heard Morena catch his breath with the pain of the cuts on his chest as he bent over the body again.

They'd obviously tortured Leach and he'd been unable to answer them because he'd been as surprised as they had to find the money they were looking for was not in the chest. I could just imagine his fury and then his horror that he couldn't escape his painful death because he knew only as much as they did about where it was. Ghad Ahmed would never have believed that he was not a decoy to lead him away from the rest of us.

Morena's eyes lifted to mine. His face was taut and grim under its coating of dust and half-grown beard.

'The bastards carved him up,' he said in a low voice.

'He asked for it,' I growled, trying to find a little sympathy in my soul for the treacherous Tiny.

213

'He was one of us,' Morena went on in a grieving, chiding voice, and I knew what was in his mind. First Bummer Ward and Gester, then Pike in Normandy, then Nimmo, senior, in his car accident. Then Houston, and now Leach.

He looked up at me.

'It only leaves me and you,' he said slowly.

two

Late in the afternoon we came down into the Plain of Karabub, a flat stony bowl where the Panzers had pounced in 1942 as the convoys had moved back to Egypt in a long detour to the south.

The lorry was dust-caked now and I knew the petrol wouldn't last much longer. Morena wasn't saying much, but I knew that he knew, too, and was worrying about it as much as I was. I'd almost forgotten the two in the back. They'd hardly spoken to us since the sandstorm and seemed withdrawn, talking quietly, as though my impatience with them in their inexperience had driven them together. I knew I had been unnecessarily sharp with them, but I was too tired with too much thinking to care much, and the knowledge of what could go wrong was constantly on my mind. They had no knowledge or experience to draw on and, though I knew they were trying to co-operate, their mistakes kept irritating me and I was unable to keep the asperity out of my voice. Somehow, it seemed now there was only Morena I could talk to, because I knew it was entirely up to the two of us if we were to escape alive.

We'd worked well together in tight spots before, however, but we were older now and probably didn't think and act as quickly as we once had. But Morena was Morena, and would always be Morena and that meant a lot, as I'd seen the night before. Nothing short of the last trump would touch Morena, and even then I suspected he'd be waiting for inspection before St Peter, properly shaved, his boots polished, his weapons clean, the everlasting sergeant, conscious of his own integrity and certain that whatever faults were to be held against him were well and truly overridden by his honesty.

We saw the relics of the battle lying in groups like old camel bones in the sun as soon as we topped the rise, shabby and unlovely intrusions in the impersonal grandeur of the desert. There was no sign of Ghad Ahmed, though I knew we had to contend now with three vehicles not two. Something had to be done about that, I knew, though I didn't know quite what. It was a thought that kept nagging at the back of my mind, but I was growing too tired by now to be able to concentrate sufficiently to produce anything intelligent to deal with it.

The wrecked tanks and soft-skinned vehicles dotted the plain in blackened dusty hummocks, half submerged in sand. I'd lost a good friend there and I couldn't speak at first with the choked feeling of memory as my stomach twisted at the thought of the Mark IVs rattling with squealing tracks down the slope, and the Schmeissers whistling off the ridges; and the frantic rush for drivers' cabs as the ambush was sprung and the Grants went rocking into action. I could see it all so clearly – the toppling figures and the mushrooming dust as the mortar bombs landed; and the unexploded shells and glancing shots hopping and spinning and whirring away in great leaps; and then the smoke and the sickening stench of burning rubber and roasted flesh.

'Must be just as it was left,' I said. 'Too far from the coast to make it worth salvaging anything.'

It was strangely moving looking over the scene of the battle, and eerie enough in the silence to be frightening.

'This is where Jimmy Bradshaw bought it,' Morena said quietly. 'Joined up with me. Him and that pal of his, Heck MacTavish. Jerry got 'em both.'

'For Christ's sake, Wop,' I said. 'Not now.'

He glanced at me, but he didn't say anything further and we stopped among the wrecks to brew up and have a meal. I don't know why I decided to stop there. Perhaps it was because I felt somehow safer among the ghosts of those Yeomanry boys and the blond young men of the Afrika Korps than I did in the lonely desert watched by Ghad Ahmed's tattered bandits.

There were half a dozen Grants, their rusted tracks curled round like dead caterpillars, one of them with its turret off and lying alongside it, and a lot of lorries huddled in the sand, the remains of their tyres sagging round the wheel-hubs. There were a few cars, too, twisted and torn as though they'd leapt into the air like wounded dogs and snapped at themselves as they'd been hit, and a litter of rusting petrol tins, coils of wire, discarded bottles and cans and helmets, and even a few broken weapons lying among the sand and shaly stones.

It was as we rounded the blackened shell of a two-and-a-half-tonner that we found the skeletons. There were two of them, stretched out in the sand, half buried, but the scrap of faded cloth sticking out of the sand with them was so old it was impossible to tell whether they'd been British or German. They lay together, almost side by side, one of them with one arm outflung, the bones still uncollapsed, as though it had been reaching for a weapon or for water or even for help, and I wondered if it could have been my friend and what thoughts had passed through the fading consciousness of the dying man as he lay there with his cracked lips and the smell of burning oil and rubber in his nostrils, staring at his own red blood staining the sand.

There were probably dozens of others somewhere nearby, shovelled into the sand and forgotten, because it had been a massacre that had quieted the messes in the Eighth Army for weeks afterwards, and neither I nor Morena had anything to say as we turned away.

Nimmo and Phil were preparing the meal as we returned, both of us silenced by memories, and I was aware of a growing feeling of resentment against us, that probably sprang from the knowledge that they were entirely dependent on us.

'We'll stop the night here,' I said, taking a slow swig of the metallic water from the container.

Morena looked round quickly. 'Here?' he asked.

'Why not? They'll never find one lorry among all these wrecks.'

He gave me a twisted grin. 'Might even surprise 'em,' he said. 'Might even knock off one of their vehicles. There are plenty of old bottles lying around and we've still got some spare petrol.'

I looked at him quickly.

'Molotov cocktail,' he explained. 'We've only got to bring 'em close enough. You could stop a tank with one. You ought to be able to stop a jeep.'

As I turned away from him, I saw that Phil's face wore a look of horror that was as far removed from her starry-eyed glances of the days before as hatred was from love. She had been bent over the food, her hair filled with sand and smears of dried mud across her face where she'd brushed away the tears and not been able to wash off the stains. She had been working clumsily over the stove, with Nimmo trying to help, but she had stopped now and was staring at me, with her lips slightly parted, a sick expression in her eyes.

'It's a good place,' Morena was saying. 'As good as we'll find.'

He glanced at the sloping sides of the shallow valley that lay like a bent dusty plate on the surface of the desert. I saw his eyes travel round him and I knew that he was thinking, as I was, that Ghad Ahmed was up there somewhere, out of sight, still waiting his chance.

Phil seemed to guess what was in our minds and she scrambled abruptly to her knees, her eyes suddenly angry.

'We can't stay here,' she said in a sharp high voice that sounded unlike her.

'Why not?'

'Jimmy says there are skeletons up there.'

I glanced at Nimmo standing near her, holding the water container, his face expressionless. 'Better tell Jimmy that they won't bite,' I said gently.

She stared at me and I realised there was no longer an atom of warmth in her glance.

'I think you're completely at home,' she said coldly. 'Thinking about it – all this death and destruction – just because you were part of it once, *hundreds of years ago.*'

I felt tired out, the tiredness coming heavy and urgent as the red ball of the sun fell lower, turning the dunes round the bowl of the plain into a fiery orange, but as soon as the glare had gone from the day and it was too dusky to see any distance I set Nimmo digging a slit trench at a point near the lorry where two wrecked vehicles formed an angle. We'd not discussed resistance again, but there'd been an unspoken acceptance between Morena and myself of the idea of surprising Ghad Ahmed's thugs. Suddenly our only hope seemed to be to draw them deliberately towards us, and we'd worked ever since with the idea un-outlined but clear in our minds. Nimmo had watched us, his eyes on our faces, and I could see he resented the fact that he didn't know what we were doing, because neither of us had said anything.

'What the hell's going on?' he asked.

'Nothing much,' I said.

I indicated the hole he'd scooped out of the ground. 'Better make that deeper,' I said.

'Why?'

'You couldn't hide a bloody rabbit in *that*,' I said, 'let alone a man. And make the sides more upright. That's no shelter.'

He pushed the spade forward. 'Why don't you have a go?' he said.

I ignored him and he returned to his original question. 'What the hell are you going to do?' he demanded.

Somehow his questions jarred on my nerves and I began to wish he'd get on with what he was doing without arguing all the time.

'They've got too many vehicles,' I said. 'Perhaps we can reduce the number.'

'Pity you didn't say so before,' he snapped. He jabbed angrily at the sand with the shovel. 'Are *you* going to get into this?'

'Yes.'

'You're going to fight? You're going to have a go at the bastards?'

'Yes.'

He started digging quickly, putting all his strength into the work, then he stopped again and looked up.

'You've a hope,' he growled. 'Fat chance we've got.'

'We've got a good chance,' I said. 'Because we know what to do, and they don't.'

He sneered. 'Old soldiers never die,' he said, and all the friendliness he'd begun to show had disappeared again.

Morena looked up from where he was filling bottles with the last of the petrol and stuffing their necks with long rag fuses, but he said nothing. I noticed that he moved stiffly as he worked, as though the cuts in his flesh were hurting more than he allowed to show, and there was a puffy look about his eyes that made me think he might have started a fever.

After a while he came across to us and laid his bottles down carefully in the slit trench, each one with its neck stuffed with rags torn from a shirt. Then he went back to the lorry and returned with the tommy gun.

'Ready?' he said.

I nodded at his row of home-made bombs. 'Will they work?' I asked.

He grinned. 'It's dicing with death,' he said. 'They'll probably blow *us* up instead, but it's worth trying. Anything's worth trying.'

He handed over the tommy gun, feeling its barrel lovingly with one hand.

'One good burp,' he said, 'then it's finished. You'll have to make it count.'

We emptied everything we didn't need from the lorry and, with scraps of anything combustible from among the littered wreckage around us, built it into a pile and, as the light died away, drained the last of the petrol from the tank and scattered it over it.

As we finished, I drew Nimmo to one side and pointed to the group of rusting Grants.

'See those?' I said.

'Sure, Captain,' he said, an edge of sarcasm in his voice. 'Tanks. I've read about 'em. In my *Illustrated History of the War.*'

'Get up there with Phil,' I said, ignoring the jeer. 'And get out of sight. You'll be safe there.'

He flared up at once. 'Do you think I'm made of bloody cotton wool or something?' he demanded. 'You know what they say: Young men make war. Old men just make bargains.'

'Oh God, man,' I said wearily. 'Don't argue. *We*'ve done it before. Together. You haven't. And she's got to have someone to look after her.'

He looked at me for a moment, then he nodded. 'OK,' he said.

They talked together for a while, then I saw them heading through the thin darkness towards the group of rusting tanks. I watched them longingly, my eyes on Phil's slender figure, then I turned back to where Morena was standing near the shallow trench.

'Now?' he said.

'Why not? Let t'battle commence.'

He carefully soaked the rag fuses of his bottles of petrol with paraffin from the primus stove, then he crossed to the bonfire we'd built and struck a match. There was a 'whoof' as it went up in a violent puff of flame like a rosy flower, illuminating the lorry.

'That ought to bring them down,' he said. 'They'll think it's us. They'll think they know where we are.'

Sure enough, we heard engines within a matter of minutes, and I could almost see the jeeps edging slowly forward among the wrecks, moving cautiously under the wispy light of the stars towards the dying fire, crossing obliquely down the slope as though they were determined not to be caught again by going too fast.

'They'll soon catch on it's just a bonfire,' Morena said softly.

'Sure,' I agreed. 'But after last time they'll be scared, and that's half the battle.'

We could hear the jeeps prowling closer now and it was clear there was more than one.

'I reckon we've got all three after us this time,' Morena commented, his head cocked and listening.

'Showdown,' I said. 'This is *it*.'

When I judged they were about fifty yards away I touched Morena's arm and we slipped into the shelter of the slit trench. Almost at once we heard shouts and the engines began to race.

'Stand by,' I said. 'They're coming. And they haven't a clue!'

Time dropped away in slow seconds as my eyes burned themselves out in my head. I could see enemies in every shadow, as the whole of my body ached with the need for movement. I knew the feeling only too well – the holding on to the nerves just that little bit longer than seemed possible, until the sounds in the darkness resolved themselves into nothing more than night noises, until the unseen became nothing more than shadows again.

Twenty years before, I'd sat on top of a ridge with Morena and a bunch of anti-tank gunners, watching the Germans probing blindly forward, my stomach knotted, my eyes narrowed, waiting in an agony of apprehension for them to come within range and almost sick with the need for action. Staring into the darkness, I'd felt then just as I felt now – the same curious hot tingling of fear down the spine and the same empty hollow in the stomach, an emotion that was compounded of excitement as the adrenaline was pumped through, and of nervous dread that you'd let the side down.

But I was surprisingly calm, much calmer than I'd expected, and I had no real fear that we'd fail. Morena and I had learned long since that, weapon for weapon, the man who was dug in always had the advantage of the man who was out in the open. All we needed was the nerve to wait.

'Let 'em get between us and the flames,' Morena whispered, standing alongside me, with one of his bottles in his hand. 'They'll be looking for us by the lorry.'

'Let's hope you're right.'

'I'll be right,' he said confidently. 'These blokes just haven't had the experience. They're going to make all the mistakes *we* made before we learned.'

Within a minute or two I saw the first of the vehicles prowling up towards the flames. It was the Land Rover they'd taken from Leach and they hadn't even had the sense to black out the buff paint, so that it stood out against the darkness like a target.

'A bit closer,' Morena breathed. 'We want at least two of 'em.' He patted his home-made fire-bomb and grinned in the ruddy light from the fire. 'Let's hope we set *them* alight, and not us,' he ended.

'Let's hope they come two in a bunch,' I whispered. 'Like they did last time.'

'They will. When you're new to it you don't like to be far from your pals.'

He was quite right, of course, but they had us worried for a while, because the Land Rover paused on the fringe of the light, its occupants watching the lorry, as though they were waiting for their companions, and we couldn't make out which way they were coming. Then it dawned on us that one of the jeeps was on the far side of the lorry, out of sight, and the other was behind us where we hadn't noticed it against the darkness.

'This chap's going to be nearest,' Morena whispered, twisting round and indicating the vehicle behind us. 'You take the Land Rover.'

The three vehicles were moving forward again now, their crews crouching low, obviously working to some prearranged plan that kept them separated, and obviously determined this time to winkle us out. But they were doing it wrong again, in spite of their care. Trained troops would have de-bussed long before this and moved forward on foot, but we'd banked on their inexperience of war and guessed they'd be nervous enough to stick to their seats.

I could see the Land Rover and one of the jeeps quite plainly now, and the second jeep in the glow beyond the lorry, too far away to be within range. They were growling forward in low gear and it was obvious they were more nervous than we were, even if twice as murderous.

They were close enough now for us to see the details and the Land Rover was silhouetted starkly against the flames. They obviously thought we were in the lorry by the fire, but clearly had no intention of taking a chance on their feet to look for us. I waited until they were almost past us, their heads still straining forward to see into the shadows by the lorry, then I touched Morena's arm.

'OK,' I said. 'Now.'

We rose slowly together while they were all staring away from us, wondering what to do next. I lifted the tommy gun, waiting for Morena to make the first move, and out of the corner of my eye I saw a match flare and then the quick burst of flame as the paraffin-soaked fuse of the bomb caught.

He hung on to it for what seemed an incredible amount of time, holding it low out of sight in the trench until the rag was well alight and I was expecting it to explode in his hand, then his arm swung back and I heard the fuse make a roaring sound as the bomb sailed through the darkness. Someone in the jeep saw it and shouted a warning, but before they could bring their weapons round I heard the crash of breaking glass, and the jeep seemed to be enveloped in flames and I saw a man running, shrieking, his clothes set on fire by the exploding petrol.

The Land Rover stopped dead as the crew panicked at the sight of the burning jeep and I let the tommy gun loose on it. The driver slumped forward against the wheel at once and a second man jumped up and rolled out and I saw his feet kicking as he fell to the ground, then a third and a fourth jumped out and started running away from the light. It was all over in a matter of seconds and they hadn't even fired a shot.

Morena was banging my shoulder with his hand. 'We did it!' he was shouting. 'One bomb and we did it!'

There were a few scattered shots from the second jeep beyond the lorry, and the thump of bullets hitting metal, and the sound of feet on the shaly surface of the plain, then I saw it come roaring round the back of the lorry with a load of men all firing together. We flung ourselves down and puffs of sand were kicked up in front of us, but they didn't really know where we were and, for the most part, the bullets went wildly over our heads.

As they rocketed past, I fired the tommy gun after them and thought I saw one of the men grab his shoulder, then the gun stopped firing and I realised it was empty. But it had done its work. They were gone and I guessed they wouldn't be coming back.

three

There were two bodies by the stopped Land Rover, one of them hanging half-out of the driving seat, the other about three yards away, but we ignored them for the time being and concentrated on making sure the vehicle was in sound working order.

It was covered with blood because I'd hit the driver in the throat and his life had drained out through the wound into a sticky puddle on the front seats and the floor, but otherwise it appeared to be sound. The jeep was a burnt-out wreck, sagging on melted tyres.

Working in the light of the flames, we dragged the dead man from behind the wheel, and as we drove it to the cluster of rusting Grants, Nimmo came slowly from their hiding place and walked towards us, trailing the rifle.

'We've got transport again,' I said, and I noticed my voice was brittle with excitement.

Phil appeared behind him, her face haunted and vacant-looking, deep lines of strain beginning to show about her eyes.

'We got another one, too,' Morena said sombrely. 'Burnt out.'

Nimmo's expression didn't alter, and it was neither triumphant nor sickened.

'We knocked out at least two of them,' Morena said.

'You mean, you *killed* them?' Phil's words came stiffly, dry as parched leaves.

JOHN HARRIS

'Reckon so. It looks like it.'

She seemed to draw away from us, her eyes narrow. 'It's just like it was twenty years ago, isn't it?' she breathed. 'Just like twenty years ago.'

There was such revulsion in her voice I stepped forward.

'For the love of God –' I began angrily, but Nimmo got between us.

'Leave her alone,' he said sharply.

As I stopped, Phil moved away quickly, stumbling as though she felt sick, and sat down on the sand. Nimmo stared at me for a second, and I could feel all the sense of triumph draining away, then he too turned away and went to her. Neither Morena nor I had moved.

'They don't realise,' I said slowly to Morena, staggered by her words. 'She just didn't understand.'

Morena was staring after them, his eyes slitted and unemotional. Then he swung on his heel.

'You can't expect her to,' he said. 'Women never understand men, any more than men understand women. The best ones try, but they never really succeed.'

The flames were dying now and there wasn't much more we could do in the dark. I was feeling exhausted now, partly from the dehydrating effect of travel in the sun and partly from the lassitude that comes after action. We parked the Land Rover close to the lorry and with the air full of the stink of burning rubber and hot metal I rolled up in my blanket nearby. Morena lay down near the lorry and Nimmo took his blanket and stretched out near the two wrecked cars where we'd dug our trench. I noticed that Phil was closer to him when she lay down than she was to me.

It was barely light when I woke next morning and in the grey half-wakening before sunrise the plain, with its scattered wrecks, looked depressingly lifeless and steeped in left-over

228

heat. Morena was already on his feet, peering into the engine of the lorry, tall in the vapours that draped themselves round the valley.

He turned round as I sat up and gave me a wry look. His dirty bearded face seemed strained and fatigued and I thought I saw sickness in his eyes. Then I noticed he was carrying his right arm stiffly away from his body, as though his wounds had gone wrong.

'We'll be in the Land Rover today,' he said. 'There's no petrol to spare for this.'

'How much have we got?'

'We'll be walking the last forty miles to Breba.'

He spoke bluntly, as he always had, hiding nothing, not trying to obscure the fact that it wasn't going to be easy.

'It won't kill us,' I said. 'It's only two days.'

'What about the girl?'

'I expect she'll do it if she has to.'

The glow of dayrise licked the slopes, and the sun burst above the horizon like a great red eye as Nimmo sat up, alert even in the moment of waking, and youthfully alive.

'Come on,' I said. 'Let's get cracking.'

He got to his feet without comment and I went across to where Phil was curled, small and frail looking and, with her tumbled fair hair and the smeared dust on her features, heartbreakingly young.

I knelt beside her. 'Phil,' I whispered my hand on her shoulder. 'Phil!'

Her eyes opened and she stared up at me, her eyes large and innocent as a child's as she wakened from sleep.

'We'll be off in a little while,' I said.

She made no comment and the silence became awkward.

'We've got to transfer everything to the Land Rover,' I explained. 'Perhaps you'll rustle up some grub for us.'

'You make it sound like a military operation,' she said.

Her voice was flat and dead sounding with dislike, and I stood up abruptly.

'That's what it's been ever since Ghad Ahmed burned that first lorry in the Depression,' I pointed out sharply. 'Only a military operation'll get us to safety.'

Her eyes were cold and unfriendly as she stared up at me. 'You can't fool me,' she said. 'I could see it in your face yesterday. I saw it the first day in the Depression when you buried those men. I think you're enjoying it.'

Deep down inside myself I knew there was an element of truth in what she said. There's always enough of the primitive in every man for him to enjoy besting another man and, way down out of sight, it was a sort of self-justification, a proof somehow to me that I was a better man, in spite of the extra years, than Nimmo. Because she'd touched on an uncomfortable truth and didn't see it the same way that I did, I took refuge in sharpness.

'Nobody ever enjoyed shooting at another man,' I said. 'Don't ever kid yourself on that score.'

She pushed aside the blanket and sat up. She'd unfastened her shirt and I could see the swelling of her breasts and the hollow between.

'Look, Phil,' I said. 'In a day or two we'll be where it's safe. Ghad Ahmed's not going to come back in a hurry. Not now. Not after last night.'

'No. Not after he's gotten two of his men shot to ribbons.'

'For Christ's sake' – the unreasonableness of it angered me – 'what would you have preferred? That we'd let them in so they could shoot *us* to ribbons and get you stretched out on the ground?'

Her eyes flashed with hatred. 'For God's sake leave me alone,' she said.

I straightened up. 'We'd be glad of food,' I said shortly. Morena was standing by the jeep when I got back. He looked at me strangely and, although he probably hadn't heard, he'd seen.

'It isn't worth it,' he said quietly.

I looked at him quickly. 'What the hell do you mean?' I snapped.

'Forget it,' he suggested.

'Mind your own bloody business!'

His eyes didn't flicker. 'You *are* my business,' he said. 'You were twenty years ago. And I'm *your* business. And getting everybody home's *both* our business. As it always was.'

I said nothing, and he nodded to where young Nimmo was just throwing his blankets down in a heap.

'You got in the wrong league by mistake,' he said. 'Look at her face. There isn't a line on it. Look at his. Then take a look at yours.'

'What's that got to do with it?'

'Haven't you seen 'em looking at each other?'

I stared at the two of them, angry and humiliated. They'd moved together now and were talking softly, their heads close.

'Christ,' I said bitterly. 'You make me sound like your grandfather.'

'I saw her when we first arrived,' he went on. 'She was dying for someone to take some notice of her. You did. That's all. It was a mistake and now it's finished. The future belongs to them. Give 'em a chance. It's bloody tough for kids like them. It's easier for us.'

I looked at the two youngsters, then at Morena, then I turned away. 'Let's have a look at those stiffs,' I said.

The callous way I said it made me realise how right he was. Young Nimmo and Phil hadn't ever been seared in war. It never stopped a man loving or feeling, but it put iron into his soul forever.

We walked across to where the bodies lay. One of them was a boy of about seventeen, and my throat went dry as I stared at him, thinking of the waste.

'Poor little bastard,' I said.

The man who'd been shot in the throat was an older man in a frayed baseball cap, leather-skinned and lined, the sort of man who with a bit of training would have made the sort of sergeant Morena had made.

For a second, neither Morena nor I spoke, then Morena pulled the lopsided cap down over the ruined face and straightened up.

'We'll bury them,' I said. 'We can't just leave 'em. We'll not ask the others. Let them stay where they are.'

Morena stared at me for a second, then he nodded and went to fetch the spade. I saw Phil and Nimmo looking at him, their faces puzzled and uncomprehending, not realising what we were sparing them.

We dug the holes right where the bodies lay and pushed them in and covered them up, with a few stones on top to keep the wild dogs out. Then we straightened up, sweating in the baking heat brought by the rising sun.

'The bastards are in better company than they deserve,' Morena said flatly, a brief weariness in his bloodshot eyes as he jerked a hand at the scattered skeletons of broken vehicles around us.

I nodded and we walked back to where the tea was waiting for us and we sat down in silence and began to eat.

After we'd finished we off-loaded everything from the lorry and put what we could into the Land Rover, first the money chest and then the flat boxes of drawings, and we stacked what we had left of water and food wherever we could get it. There wasn't much room for the passengers, let alone extra equipment, and it was going to be an uncomfortable, cramped ride.

Then Morena took the crowbar and smashed everything that was breakable in the engine of the lorry.

'At least those bastards can't use it against us now,' he observed.

I nodded and jerked my head at the others. 'OK,' I said. 'Let's go!'

They moved forward together, then Phil stopped, staring with horrified eyes at the Land Rover. At first it didn't occur to me what was troubling her, then I realised it was the dried blood on the seats and on the floor of the vehicle. We'd got rid of as much of it as we could, and I'd been too tired to care much about the rest of it, and I jerked my hand angrily, still humiliated by her attitude towards me the night before.

'Take your pick,' I said. 'You can walk if you prefer it.'

She stared at me for a second, then she swallowed quickly and, without looking at me again, she climbed gingerly into the rear seat. Nimmo got in with her, and they huddled together among the equipment. Morena started up the engine and let in the clutch and we moved away, our eyes squinting against the glare that came up in hammer blows off the sand.

The lorry and the burned-out jeep and the turned earth where we'd buried the dead men dwindled in size as we drew away, two more wrecks in a plain full of wrecks, two more ghosts in a plain full of ghosts.

We saw nothing of Ghad Ahmed's men that day. They'd had enough and they were probably even then in one of their villages fighting over the ownership of the remaining undamaged jeep.

Nobody spoke and the noise of the engine didn't encourage it. There was nothing else but the brassy sky and the ever-increasing sun. I was conscious of a raging thirst, but I kept the water well tucked away between my fret so that nobody could get at it. I didn't expect for a minute that Morena would ask for it, but the other two might not understand its importance, especially for that last stretch when we were going to have to walk. There was no desire for food under the weight of the sun, and even the breeze of our own passage was hot and parched the throat as we progressed mile after uncomfortable mile, with first Morena and then me hunched over the wheel, hands slipping in their own sweat, watching the mirage bobbing and swaying in front.

Just before dusk we ran into a patch of soft sand and, as the Land Rover lurched in a hole dug by the spinning wheels that ground the earth to the consistency of snuff, the petrol ran out and the engine dried up. In front of us there was a high dune, long and low like a crouching animal.

'That's it,' Morena said, strained-looking through his beard and the mask of dust on his face.

For a moment nobody moved. At first I was unable to absorb that this was as far as we could ride, and that from now on it depended on our own limbs and strength and guts. Then Morena climbed down slowly, and I noticed he moved awkwardly as though he were dizzy, and I followed him, stiff-legged with sitting.

'From now on,' I said, 'we walk.'

Phil's jaw fell and I could see this was something she couldn't really believe, even though she'd known at the back of her mind like all of us that it was inevitable eventually.

'Walk?' she repeated. 'It must be forty miles to the road from here.'

'All of that,' I said.

'We can't do it,' Nimmo burst out wearily.

'You've got to. Nothing's going to carry you.'

They began to protest and as I pushed them away young Nimmo's temper flared and he lifted his hand. Immediately Morena's thick arm was round his throat and he was gagging on his own words.

He glared as he was released, knowing that for all his youth, he was no match for Morena and me. 'Christ,' he said slowly. 'You old soldiers! You don't half stick together! It's like a club that nobody else can join! What about the money?'

'We can't take it with us,' I said. 'That's for sure.'

'We could manage it between us.

'Son,' I said, trying hard not to sound too much like Big Brother. 'Half an hour from now, you'll be sorry you've even got a water bottle and a packet of sandwiches.'

He looked at Morena, who nodded slowly.

'What can we do with it?'

'Bury it.'

'We'll never find it again.'

'We will if we push the jeep over it and burn it. There'll be enough petrol in the tank to start it off and we've got a drop in the can.'

'Christ!' He spoke bitterly. 'If we've got more petrol, why the hell don't we push on?'

'Take your pick,' I said. 'If we push on, we can't burn the jeep. If we don't push on, we can mark where the dough is and come back and pick it up.'

'What about the drawings?' Phil asked.

'We can bury them.'

'They'll be ruined.' Her voice was full of anger and dislike.

'Not here under the sand,' I pointed out. 'We'll be in safety inside a couple of days. Three days from now you can pick them up again.'

Nimmo gestured at the glaring arc of the sky. 'Are you proposing to walk in this lot?' he asked.

'Not much choice,' I said.

'But, Christ, man, the sun! Why can't we walk at night?'

'Because we can't afford to wait. What food we can carry won't last us long. We can't even afford long rests. We'll walk tomorrow, rest in the evening and carry on after the moon's up. That way we'll cover a lot of ground before the food gives out. We can't dawdle, and that's a fact.'

Phil gave me a bitter look, as though she held me responsible for all the disasters, then she turned away abruptly and flung herself down in the sand. Morena spoke to her as he always did, like a father.

'We've still got food and water,' he pointed out slowly. 'And we're all sound in wind and limb.'

We drained the radiator, but the water was warm and too evil-tasting to drink, so, because we had more water now than we could hope to carry, we used it to cool and clean our bodies, trying to get rid of the stink of the sweat and the feel of the dust that we'd begun to wear like hair shirts.

Nobody worried much about nakedness, and I saw Phil strip off her clothes unconcernedly at the other side of the Land Rover, her face taut and angry, and the sheen of luke-warm water trickling across the dusty skin of her neck and the curve of her spine and hips as she scrubbed away the sand with the soggy ball of a dirty handkerchief.

When we'd finished we ate our evening meal in silence. It was only the usual bully beef and biscuit and water that had been too long in the container, and afterwards Morena sat with his back against the wheel of the jeep, silently staring across the desert. We'd tried once more to dress his wounds, but they were puffy and ugly looking now and obviously in need of proper attention. From his sluggish manner I could see the poison from the infection in them was affecting him, but he seemed unworried and after a while took out his mouth organ and began to play it softly.

Nimmo growled something in protest and Morena put the instrument away at once without a word. I offered him a cigarette and sat down alongside him.

As the darkness began to spread across the desert, he held the cigarette up. 'I've one more after this,' he said. 'How many have you got?'

'Three.'

'Wish I were like those two.'

'Kids have a lot more sense these days,' I said. 'More intelligent and better looking. They don't smoke much now.'

His eyes crinkled at the corners. 'Drink milk instead of beer,' he said.

I managed a laugh, a mere shaking of the shoulders.

'That's it. Milk instead of beer.'

'And worry about the bomb.'

'And worry about the bomb.'

He looked at me. 'Do *you* ever worry about the bomb?' he asked.

I shook my head.

'Nor me.' He paused. 'I never met an old soldier who *was* scared of the bomb.'

He threw away his fag end, and as it curved in an arc to the sand and fell in a shower of sparks, I lay down in my blanket, thinking I'd have to abandon that, too, tomorrow. The prospect scared me, because the desert was so immense and I was full of sick anxiety and overpowering weariness that struck at the depths of my soul, full of all the apprehensions and misgivings that were never far below the veneer of civilisation. It was the old Adam that lurks in all of us, the old instinctive prehistoric fears that hide in the disused chambers of a civilised mind, and I couldn't sleep for it. Disaster had made a tangle of my nerves and I was restless under the numberless stars. I needed comfort and kept thinking dumbly of Phil and, finally, I sat up and lit one of my last cigarettes.

It was pitch dark and I couldn't see her. She'd taken her blanket away from the rest of us and lain down quietly after the meal, and in the end, in desperation, I walked across to where I'd last seen her.

As I approached, I heard whispering and knew that Nimmo was with her, and I dropped to the sand at once, frightened of being seen, and lay still, not wishing to hear them but afraid they'd think I was spying on them.

I could hear them breathing and knew they'd come together with infinite understanding and the tenderness of youth, and I heard her shuddering moan of ecstasy and felt my fingernails bite at the palms of my hands as I realised it was Nimmo, not me, who was close enough to her now to hear the thud of her heart and feel the beating of her pulsing blood. Then I heard her voice, thick with passion and choked with tears.

'Oh, Jimmy, Jimmy!'

I lay there for a long time, my fingers curling in the sand, trying to scour myself of the jealousy I felt inside myself, while the shuddering sighs ceased. Then they became silent and I guessed he was kissing her wet flushed face as they sprawled on the disturbed sand, and I crept away, humiliated and feeling as old as the desert itself.

As I curled up in my blanket, I realised Morena was awake. Without a word, he lit a cigarette and drew a couple of deep puffs at it. Then he jabbed my shoulder with his fist and, as I sat up, he passed it to me without a word in a gesture full of gentleness and sympathy and understanding.

It was only when I'd finished it and thrown it away that I remembered it was the last one he had.

four

It was still dark when Morena woke me next morning. We sat up together and, guiltily, I lit a cigarette and offered it to him.

He grinned and took it from me, but after a couple of drags at it he pushed it back towards me with a 'Thy-need-is-greater-than-mine' look.

I could see the other two a little way away, huddled together under their blankets, unashamedly close, their bodies entwined for warmth and reassurance in the empty desert.

Morena and I did the digging, going down deep to sink the tin chest. Then we piled stones on top of it and filled the hole up with sand again and dug another hole, twenty yards away due east, towards the sun, to bury the drawings. We marked the spot with a few carefully arranged stones that looked as though they might just have happened to be there, and left it to the sun to reduce the new smoothed sand to the same texture as the baking surface of the desert.

Finally, we pushed the Land Rover over the spot where we'd put the money, and Morena lifted out the can with the remains of the petrol in it and began to scatter it over the seats and the pile of discarded equipment against the wheels. When it had burned, Ghad Ahmed would never guess what was underneath it. There wasn't much in the petrol tank to help out, however, and the vehicle burned badly until the tyres caught and the air began to shimmer with the heat. The minute it was alight, the enormity of what we'd done struck me with full force and I began to wonder if we were right. Only Morena's confident movements reassured me.

As we turned away, picking up what scattered equipment we felt we needed, I saw the other two standing close together, watching us and faintly defiant.

Morena began to empty his pockets of money and the old photographs we'd all brought with us and, as they lay on the sand, staring up at us, the faces looked faded and long-vanished. They were all of them gone now, except me and Morena, and I felt I wanted to cry with lost illusions.

Morena saw the expression on my face. 'They weren't the same men,' he reminded me. He took the mouth organ out of his back pocket, stared at it then, giving me a sheepish grin, pushed it back again.

'Had it a long time,' he said.

None of us said anything and it was Morena who opened the bully beef and handed round the biscuits. We sat on the sand in a little circle, almost in two groups, Morena and myself in one, Nimmo and Phil in the other.

Then we began to put our belongings into containers and stood up ready to move off.

I knew I'd lost Phil for ever now, but because I still wanted to show her she was wrong there was a sudden senseless urge in me to prove that I was a better man than Nimmo, a nagging foolish drive that made me want to demonstrate how much better I understood the desert, how much more I could endure in spite of my age.

Morena had saved one or two rags of clothing, which we wound, round our heads like turbans, and he poured the remains of the spare water over them to keep the temperature of our heads low.

'It'll help,' he said shortly.

I had a jerrican half full of clear water that I knew would taste of petrol and would feel as though it weighed a ton before I'd gone a mile. Nimmo had a side-pack containing the biscuits. Morena had another pack with a few tins of bully beef in it. We also had a water bottle and the rifles and the revolver.

'Right,' I said. 'Move off, Wop. Due north. I'll be back marker.'

We set off in Indian file, moving away from the curving sun as we shuffled through the shaly sand. Nimmo had rolled up a blanket and put it round his shoulder, probably for Phil to lie on, but I noticed that when we stopped at midday it had vanished.

The sun was already high, raging above us, so that as we plodded northwards the sweat burst out of me and ran down my body and legs, and the heat caused my face to blister and my lips to crack. The low hills in front of us shimmered and receded, and when we called a halt the shaly rock was too hot to lie on and we sat with our heads down, our faces raw, in a stupor of exhaustion. Only Morena stayed on his feet because he knew, as I did, that it became harder after every stop to get going again. As we started off once more, my body felt as though it weren't flesh and blood any longer but a construction of wants and aches and pains, and my stomach was knotted with hunger. My tongue, nostrils and eyes were sore and the skin of hands and arms crawled with burns so that I felt I'd been grilled like a steak by the flaring sun.

The afternoon was worse than the morning. The sun bored into us like a gimlet, jabbing us along in the shadeless dust, the sweat running down our faces like water from a guttering. The light took away my sense of perspective and the plain seemed endless and without horizon, like a brassy bowl curving away from us up into the heavens, blank in the insufferable afternoon light. The dust on my face, mixed with the sweat, became a thin film of mud that was smeared across my features as I wiped it away.

The figures in front of me seemed to weave and stagger in the heat, first Morena, plodding onwards, one heavy step after another, head low, eyes slitted against the dust he kicked up, and then Phil and Nimmo, and then me, afraid of falling and being left behind in the awful loneliness of the vast plain.

We stopped again as the sun began to sink, in the fiercest heat of the afternoon, the tiredness coming back with a heavy urgency that begged for relief in rest, and the figures in front of me merely crumpled up as I called out the time, and stretched flat on the sand, hands shielding their eyes. Only Morena stayed splendidly upright, solid as a rock and immovable. His arm was red and inflamed and stiff now and his face was drawn and strained, but there was no anger or resentment in his expression. In Phil's face there was blind bewilderment and in Nimmo's sheer unadulterated hate.

In my bitterness there was a childish fear that he looked better than I did after the gruelling journey and that I was going to weaken, after all, before he did, and though I knew it would never make any difference now, it was terribly important that I shouldn't. Somehow it had become urgent that I should show Phil that in spite of twenty extra years I was still young and strong and that she'd been wrong in rejecting me, but even as I needed the proof for myself, I knew it meant nothing to her. It never would now, and she was too far gone with exhaustion to notice, anyway.

As she stared at me with her weary stony gaze, her face seemed to have grown smaller and there was an excited feverish light in her eyes so that I seemed to be looking at an aged child. She had made no attempt to keep herself tidy in the awful heat, and her hair, like mine, was plastered with a thin-caked film of yellow mud compounded of matted dust and sweat.

The sun was beginning to drop fiercely towards the horizon, and the rolling shapes of the desert were changing colour. For the first time since we'd started that morning I could see shadows, pale, purple-orange shadows that were really hardly shadows at all, and the sky seemed to be on fire with the flames leaping upwards as the sun sank lower, turning the white glare of the day into the dulled salmon of evening. Soon it would be dark and if Ghad Ahmed was going to make a last attempt at us this would be his opportunity. By tomorrow I hoped we'd be near enough to Breba for him to be frightened away.

The sun was still strong but with the glow of old copper, and the sand was a thunderous orange below it. Morena stopped, guessing somehow what was on my mind, and we shuffled together into a group. There were a few muttered words of advice, but neither Phil nor Nimmo seemed to be listening or to care, and when we shuffled off again, in the same order, in no time we were strung out once more, Morena leading and trying to set a pace because we knew we had to keep moving steadily; then Phil and Nimmo, both of them dawdling as her strength gave out; and finally me, determined to remain rearguard, yet not wishing to push her more than necessary.

Every now and then as I saw Nimmo stumble I felt a swift surge of pleasure, as I imagined him having to accept help from me. But then it died immediately as he recovered and, every time, the old fear started in me again that he was standing straighter than I was, that his breathing was more easy. We were all flagging now and I was wondering, in fact, if I hadn't possibly driven us all too hard.

Phil was staggering now with exhaustion, but in the distance I could see the sand in soft blown ridges where a vehicle couldn't manoeuvre and felt we'd be safer there, and wouldn't allow her to relax.

'Please,' she begged, her face haunted, her eyes moving hopelessly, her hands knuckled and rigid by her sides. 'Can't we stop?'

'Another hour,' I said my mouth tight.

'For Christ's sake,' Nimmo said, 'can't you see she's had it?'

'One hour,' I repeated. 'Then we'll all stop.'

'You bastard,' Nimmo growled. 'I ought to blow your bloody head off with this rifle.'

It was cruel, but I had no alternative. My own legs were as sloppy as sponges, but I could see Morena standing on the slope of a dune, his feet up to the ankles in soft sand, the rifle trailing from his fingers, waiting for us.

Nimmo glared at me, then he took the revolver from Phil's waist and buckled it round his own, and we set off again.

The air was cooler now and I felt a little better, but I knew that Phil couldn't keep going much longer, and I had to decide the dividing line between safety and over-exhaustion, because she had to be on her feet for the next day.

'Give her a drink,' I suggested to Nimmo, but he shook his head.

'It's finished,' he said. 'It's all gone. We drank it this afternoon.'

'You prize bloody fool!' I felt choked with anger. 'You deserve everything you've got. All we have now is what I'm carrying. Without water you can end up as dry as a prune.'

'She needed it,' he said fiercely.

'She'll need it a lot more tomorrow.'

'I think you're a prize bastard,' he said in a low grating voice and he seemed very young as he spoke.

He turned away quickly and took her arm. For a while they walked together, then she seemed to push him away, as though she were determined that I shouldn't have the satisfaction of seeing her in need of help, and we began to walk in a single file again that gradually grew more and more strung out.

It was just when we were at our lowest ebb, with our heads down and dull with misery, strung out across the side of a dune, that I heard the sound of the jeep's engine.

Straightening up, I saw it come roaring over the crest towards us, with Ghad Ahmed himself by the driver.

Immediately Phil's head rose and she started to run, staggering to her left out of the line, her feet kicking up the sand – blindly, in a state of panic and half dizzy with exhaustion, knowing only that the jeep was an enemy.

The light was bad and as I stumbled after her the jeep came between us. For a moment I wondered what the hell they were doing, then I realised they'd seen we'd not got the money with us and that if they could grab her they could force us to tell them where we'd buried it. They were trying to cut her out, just as you'd cut out a wild animal from a herd, just as the tanks had tried to get into the columns of soft-skinned vehicles during the war and cut out bunches of them for slaughter.

I fired the rifle at the racing jeep, but the light was bad and my eyes seemed to be whirling in my head and I couldn't see it properly. Morena was on top of the dune, looking down, but he was shooting into the shadows and hadn't a cat in hell's chance of hitting anything.

'Phil,' I croaked, trying to warn her, but my throat was so dry I couldn't make my voice come.

The jeep had almost caught up with her by this time, and Ghad Ahmed was standing up by the driver. This was his last chance, he knew, and it looked as though he was going to pull it off.

I saw Phil look over her shoulder and, trying to keep an eye on the jeep, collapse as the dragging sand gripped her tired feet. Then, as the vehicle roared up towards her, I saw Nimmo lift the rifle to his shoulder in a swift movement and pull the trigger.

The jeep was just slewing round as the rifle fired, with the sand spraying from the front wheels like a bow wave, and it looked at first as though Ghad Ahmed had been thrown out by the swift turn, then I saw from the way his body fell that there were no longer any living muscles and no living brain to warn him, no living instinct to help him save himself. He fell like a limp sack full of wet straw, and I saw his body hit the sand in a puff of dust and bounce in a flat leap, then it rolled over, all arms and legs, and came to a stop right in front of Phil.

As she sat up, her hand over her mouth, a thin scream escaping her, the jeep stopped and I heard Morena's rifle crack, and the windscreen shattered. The men in the jeep stared backwards to where Ghad Ahmed's body lay, then I heard the engine race, and the wheels kicked the sand as it shot off, rocketing and lurching over the dune.

I was the first to reach her as she sat up, her face grey-yellow with caked dust, her eyes dilated as she stared at Ghad Ahmed.

I stopped in front of her as she scrambled to her knees. She had unfastened her shirt to let what air there was cool her body, and I could see she was wearing nothing underneath. It was open to her waist and barely concealed her breasts, and as I stopped in front of her she pulled it across and tucked it into the waistband of her trousers, her eyes blank with dislike.

'Keep away from me,' she said in a flat dry voice.

I stared at her for a second, then I turned towards Ghad Ahmed. Nimmo's bullet had hit him straight between the eyes, smashing in the bridge of his nose. He was as devoid of feeling and emotion now as the sand he lay on.

As I straightened up, Nimmo ran up and caught Phil in his arms, and she clung to him like a frightened child, sobbing, her face in the curve of his neck, while his hands moved gently along her spine.

Morena came slowly towards me, and stopped by Ghad Ahmed.

'There'll be no more trouble now,' he commented. 'Not without him. They hadn't the guts.'

'We'll stop here,' I said. 'We'll rest. We'll try to make up a bit of ground during the night when it's cool.'

We left Ghad Ahmed where he was lying and moved over the dune into the next valley. I opened a couple of tins of bully beef and shared out the water. Only Morena bothered to thank me, and as we finished we sat in two groups again, representatives of two generations.

I could just make out Phil and Nimmo sitting together, her head against his shoulder, and could hear them muttering. Nimmo was the hero of the hour. Without doubt, his shot had saved her, had saved us all probably, and there was a taste of bitterness in my mouth at the thought that it hadn't been mine.

Morena seemed to guess my thoughts. 'It's only youth running to youth,' he said gently. 'Their generation'll never understand ours, any more than the next one will understand theirs.'

After a while they stretched out together, while I sat unsleeping, hearing little sighs and shuffles and movements like a bird fluttering its wings, and I knew that even in their exhaustion they were reaching out for each other, as a panacea against injustice, loneliness and weariness.

Nothing had made much difference. Strength had had nothing to do with it and never would have, nor had courage and endurance. Dumbly, I wondered how I could have been so blind as to think they mattered and, curiously, as the realisation came, I felt easier in the acceptance that Phil was beyond reach forever.

The glow of the old moon was just appearing when I woke them. There was just enough light to see by, and I could tell their bodies were close together, and Nimmo's arm was round her. They didn't move apart as I stirred them, but merely turned their heads and stared at me unashamedly, as though defying me to comment. I said nothing and moved on to Morena, and we all had a sip of water and began to move off almost as the last sliver of the moon came over the lip of the dune.

After a while the sand gave way to a thin rock strata with the stone lying in flaked stripes of blackish brown. The dying moon was full in our faces as we walked and it glinted on the grains of quartz and porphyry that made up the desert, and the black shadows of the dunes lay athwart our path like great bottomless ditches that had to be bridged, so that as we descended into them the moon disappeared and we were in darkness, and as we climbed the other side, struggling against the soft sand, we seemed to emerge into life from the pit of hell. The silence was terrifying and my head felt vacuous and large and it was agony to stay awake.

We stopped again just before daylight. Inevitably, Phil and Nimmo lay down together, holding each other close and sinking into sleep with the sure knowledge of the young that someone older was being responsible.

We allowed ourselves a swallow of water each before we moved on. There was only a little left in the canteen now, but I knew we were within striking distance of safety at last.

The sun was just rising and the plain was absorbing the colour of the approaching day as we set off, Morena first, as before, myself bringing up the rear. Nimmo and Phil no longer made any attempt to keep in single file and they walked alongside each other, almost within touching distance, so that Nimmo could help her when the dragging sand made her stumble.

We moved like cripples now, even Morena walking stiff-legged, his head hanging, the rifle trailing through the sand. I guessed we must be within reach of Breba by this time and ought to see it some time after the sun had reached its height, and I was spurred on by a feeling that we shouldn't die. I knew we deserved to get through and I felt we would.

The sun came up behind the purple distances in masses of pink fire that feathered off in great rays against the misty blueness of the sky. Then the naked scarlet ball of the sun appeared, and I knew that in two or three hours it would be there behind us and to our right, blistering our brains, addling every thought we tried to make.

We all looked like clowns now, with brown-black faces with staring eyeballs, and pinky-white mouths where our dry tongues had licked the salt from our lips. We walked with our shirts open and I could see the white shape of Phil's body and the slenderness of her waist with a maddening clarity.

The sun was clear of the desert floor now, and its reddish fire was changing to copper that would change again to molten brass and then to a white-hot glare. The heat haze that had lain in the valleys began to disperse and the long torment began again, drying the sweat on our flesh even as it started through the pores.

Once Phil stumbled and fell, sprawling on her side and rolling over on to her back, her eyes closed against the sun. As we gathered round her, Nimmo gently drew the open shirt across her body, his eyes angry as he looked up at me and Morena, then he lifted her against his knee and forced a little water between her cracked lips.

I knelt in front of her. 'Only a few more hours,' I said. 'Then you can rest. We'll go on and fetch help.'

We got her to her feet and stumbled on, rising like ghosts from the ground, but within half an hour she was on her knees again, half sitting in the sand, her head hanging, her hands at her sides. Nimmo helped her to turn and sit, her legs sprawled in front of her.

'You bastards!' he muttered as we approached. 'You heartless bastards!'

Morena stared at me, his eyes red-rimmed with lack of sleep, and jerked his head in the direction of the north. Then he peeled off his shirt and I saw the flesh of his shoulder was puffed and ugly and I wondered how he'd endured the pain.

'Here,' he said to Nimmo. 'You can make a bit of shade with that. Just enough to get her face out of the sun. It'll be some sort of relief. We'll leave the canteen. We'll be back by tonight.'

Neither of them thanked us as we moved away. From the top of the dune I saw Nimmo had his shirt off, too, and had made a three-sided tent with the rifle to support it, so that the sun was kept from her head and shoulders, and he had the water bottle in his hand and was sponging her body with his handkerchief to bring a little relief.

Morena and I kept going all the rest of the morning. We didn't even stop for rests, just plodding steadily on towards the north, staggering a little now, heads down, aware of blinding headaches as the glare split our eyeballs. Walking in the increasing heat, I began to wonder if it were all a dream, and as the moisture evaporated from my body I even began to think I was twenty years back. I'd walked once before, and, as I grew weaker, the two incidents seemed to merge together and I found myself constantly jerking my head up in alarm as I started from a half-sleep of exhaustion, staring at the horizon on the look-out for the Germans.

I was almost done now and because Nimmo had stayed behind I'd never find out now who could endure most. It had been a stupid childish whim that had sprung from bitter jealousy, but now, weakened and half demented by the sun, the fact that it was not answered – one way or the other – nagged at me in a way that seemed to exhaust me as much as the walking.

The light came off the empty flatness with a white and murderous brilliance, in long waves that drove sharp stabbing knives through the retinas to the brain, so that from time to time the glare became ash-grey and I felt I'd gone blind. There was no green anywhere that meant water, no human or animal trail in that vast emptiness.

I could tell without looking when we'd reached the afternoon, because the sun started to take on a beating hammer-stroke that banged against the skull, and I walked with my eyes shut, muttering to myself to keep myself going, nostrils dried, tongue swollen, the sun raging at us like a wild animal.

It was Morena who stopped first. He was walking just in front of me, plodding heavily forward, almost as though, in spite of his injuries, he were untouched by the ordeal, so that I envied him his endurance, then suddenly he weaved a little, stopped, and fell flat on his face.

I got down beside him with blurring eyes and creaking knees, feeling my joints would never move properly again. He opened his eyes as I rolled him over and I saw the sand was stuck round his mouth and on his tongue. The bandages had come loose and were hanging limply round his shoulder and the lips of the wounds were scarlet and inflamed.

At first I thought he was dead, then his eyes opened.

'Go on,' he said in a steady voice. 'You go on.'

'Don't be a bloody fool. Got to stay with you.'

'Go on. Go on.'

I took off my shirt and stuck the rifle into the sand by his head. Then, hanging the shirt on it, I pinned it down with piles of sand at the corners, so that there was the faintest scrap of shade for his face.

I had to go faster now, because they'd all be dehydrated soon unless I found help.

He was sleeping or unconscious when I stood up and faced north again. Once or twice I glanced back and could see the blurred dot on the sand that was Morena growing smaller with every step. Then I topped a rise, and as I descended to the other side I was alone and terrified at the emptiness.

The heat leapt out like an assassin, knocking me off-balance, the glittering vicious waves of light skimming off the surface of the desert with unutterable cruelty, so that I couldn't escape the pain of the dazzle as it shimmered in front of my eyes. My tongue felt like a leather ball in my mouth and every step forward was an exertion so that I kept saying to myself I'd never get back the energy I was using. It was like sleep, I kept thinking. A night out of bed was a night lost out of your life. A year in the desert without laughter and happiness and lovemaking was a year out of your life. This was the same. Not one ounce of the energy I spent would ever be returned.

I was a dumb, blind, anonymous figure now with screwed-up eyes, struggling northwards because it was the only thing left to do. Once I fell and lay there, clutching the hot sand, thankful for rest, then I realised I wasn't supposed to be resting at all, and struggled to my feet, lurching and staggering, the merciless sun resting on me like a leaden weight. Then I saw patches of scrub and suddenly, unexpectedly, birds – little brown birds fluttering out of a grey-green patch – and I realised they were the first signs of life I'd seen. For a moment I thought I was going mad because the light seemed brighter than ever and my body felt shrivelled to mere skin and bone and stringy muscle, then I heard one of the birds call out, jarring and remote, and I knew it was real and that I'd made it.

I passed a patch of acacia-like trees and a deep ditch, then I noticed an eruption on the face of the desert ahead of me and found myself wondering what it was, before I realised it was palm trees and small empty-eyed white houses. The glittering light lay everywhere and I couldn't believe I was looking on civilisation again after so long. Then, just over to my right, I saw what looked like a stone bridge, and I remembered there'd been a bridge at Breba, built over a dyke that had been run across the fields.

I saw thin wobbling rods through the blur that I realised were telegraph poles, and then a blue lorry rushing past in the distance on a road beyond the bridge, moving with the speed and freedom of spirit of a wild bird, and it seemed wonderful that it was so much alive. Then I was stumbling along a corrugated dusty road which kept bringing me to my knees with shattering jolts that jarred on every nerve in my body, and struggling through shallow sand-drifts that had left bare the roots of trees. I saw a man on an ass that tottered along on its toes like a ballet dancer, and a woman kneading fuel cakes of dung with long thin hands, and a camel walking in circles round a length of carved wood that I knew belonged to a well.

Two girls standing in the still-shimmering heat of the afternoon, old petrol tins on their heads, stared at me, and, though I knew they were carrying water, I felt I daren't stop to drink. I plodded on until I came to houses where the wind had drifted the sand against the walls, and people came out to watch me as though they didn't know what to do to help.

I must have looked like a dusty scarecrow as I stumbled past them towards the open space ahead where there was a flat-roofed police post with a flag flying. All the way across the square, doors opened one after the other and people emerged to watch me, a few children following me at a discreet distance, as though I were a monster out of the desert.

The sun caught the side of a minaret by a snow-white mosque and glinted like gold on a brass drinking pot in a girl's arms. I saw trees and the feathery tops of palms, and even oranges, and then a man came out of a black square that was a door and, as he hurried towards me, I saw with relief that he was in uniform and, because of it, I felt I could trust him to take over from me and sank to my knees at last, pointing backwards the way I'd come.

Dimly I heard shouts and saw a big sand-coloured vehicle with a high body appear from behind a building. It stopped alongside, throwing the blessed relief of a shadow across me, and the man in uniform climbed aboard, talking loudly to the driver. Two more men came up alongside me, and I seemed to be giving them instructions and directions.

'South,' I kept saying, struggling against the dryness of my mouth to get the words out at all. 'Due south. First one of them. Then two together.'

'Are you sure?' The man in uniform was bending over me. 'Are you sure?'

'Yes. Due south. We never went off course at all. North all the way. For Christ's sake – !'

I tried to struggle up, with some idea in my mind of going with them, but the man in uniform smiled and patted my shoulder, then the lorry roared off, and as I felt the dust on my face, choking me, the village of Breba seemed to whirl and grow red and I sank out of sight in a blissful sleep.

epilogue

When I woke up I was in bed in what appeared to be a hospital but what I learned later was the back room of the police post. It was cool, with a fan in the ceiling, and over-looked a deserted courtyard full of geraniums and Ali Baba jars. Bougainvillaea grew in at the window under a striped blind that was faded with the sun, and it was glitteringly bright outside and the flies were making the room loud with their buzzing.

They'd set up beds in there, and Morena was alongside me, smiling weakly, fresh bandages on his body, looking as though all the moisture had been dried out of him by the sun. There was another bed just beyond, but it was empty.

A policeman came in later and told me I'd slept for forty-eight hours. He was a Libyan, with a dark skin and a mouthful of teeth like gravestones, and it was a joy just to see his smile. He told me in halting English that the others had been found. They were all well, he said, and gave me water that was cool and tasted like wine. I could see my reflection in a glass-fronted case that looked absurd against the bare white wall because it was the sort of thing my mother had used to hold her china, and was probably some sort of loot from the desert war where Italian generals had always carried around everything but the kitchen sink.

I seemed to have lost stones in weight and was starting a lovely beard, but my eyes were hollow and the lines that had long been forming on my face seemed to have been etched deeper by the sun.

After a meal of tough old mutton and cups of intolerably sweet mint tea the man in uniform whom I'd met when I'd first staggered into Breba appeared again. He seemed to be some sort of official and for an hour or more he badgered us with questions.

'What happened?' he kept asking with desperate earnestness, as though he sensed some tragedy. 'What happened to your transport? Why were you off the road?'

'Because it was safer,' I said, shaking my head with weariness at the nagging questions. 'If we hadn't got off the road none of us would have reached here.'

'Why not?'

'Because of Ghad Ahmed.'

'Ghad Ahmed?' His brows came down. 'Who is this Ghad Ahmed?'

It took a little doing to remember all that had happened, but slowly, prompted by the police, we went through the whole story, right from the beginning, right from the moment we'd first reached the Depression and seen Crabourne's party there in front of us and caught the first scent of something wrong. It took me all my time to give them instructions where to find Houston and Leach and Selinski and all the others we'd left behind on the way, and, as I spoke, the uniformed man's face grew horrified.

'There will have to be an enquiry,' he kept saying. 'There will need to be an investigation. This is serious.'

'You're damn right it was serious.'

'But all this shooting! All these lives lost! This isn't wartime!'

'You'd never have noticed the difference,' Morena commented dryly.

The man in uniform straightened up. 'I shall have to inform higher authority,' he said. 'I think this is too important for me to handle.'

After that they left us alone for a while and I was able to sleep some more, and when I woke up again Nimmo appeared. He looked well while I knew I looked like hell, and I experienced a moment of childish disappointment at the knowledge. After all my worries I'd proved nothing except that he could recover faster than I could.

He was in borrowed clothes and seemed a little embarrassed and shy with us, but there seemed no enmity as he asked how we were – as though, as his exhaustion had dropped away from him, so had his bitterness.

'They've been in touch with the coast,' he said. 'The Embassy's sending someone down to go into it. The old boy out there's worried silly by what's been going on.'

After a while he went away and came back with Phil. She, too, was wearing borrowed clothes, but, apart from the dark rings under her eyes, she looked as though she'd never been out in the desert.

She also seemed embarrassed and shy, and stood near Nimmo all the time. She told us that the American Ambassador had got permission for them to leave before any enquiry was held and had even advised them to go. They'd been offered a lift in a police car to the coast and they'd decided they might as well accept.

She stood by the bed for a moment, staring at the glittering brightness outside. The afternoon sun seemed to have para-lysed all activity, regulating life like an unwritten law as it always had, driving everyone indoors until it sank towards the horizon and the doors opened at last and the shops woke up and the veiled women appeared in the streets. For a long time she said nothing, standing awkwardly, devoid of friendship *or* dislike, but merely depressingly neutral, then she thanked us haltingly.

'We owe a lot to you both,' she said slowly. 'The drawings are undamaged. They've gotten them out. We shan't have to do them again.'

When they left, moving out together, her hand in Nimmo's, they looked so heartbreakingly young I felt as old as God and probably just as weary.

'The drawings are undamaged,' I repeated slowly. 'We shan't have to do them again. That's a bloody relief I must say.'

After that, Migliorini and the newspapermen came down from the coast, and we were photographed together. Later we saw pictures of the drawings Crabourne had done and the headline said 'TREASURE FROM THE DESERT'. Then an Englishman came to see us who, it seemed, was on the staff of the British Ambassador. He was a languid young man, not much older than Nimmo, with dark glasses and a lazy manner and a limp handshake like a warm wet fish.

He was bored with the whole affair, and it was obviously a bloody nuisance to have to drive all the way from the coast to Breba on a hot day. He reminded me of some of the specialist half-colonels who used to come up from Cairo to give us pep-talks before operations and got medals for sitting at desks – smooth young men with good connections who were always too intelligent to risk their own necks and preferred to do the talking to dimmer people like me and Morena, while they stayed themselves where it was cool and there was plenty of pink gin.

'It's all right,' he said. 'It's going to be all right. They've picked up the last of the jeeps. They've found the men who stole it. They've got the whole story. Confirms what you said. No trouble now. This chap Ghad Ahmed's known to the police at Qahait and Qalam as a bit of a troublemaker.'

'A bit of a trouble-maker,' Morena said. 'Christ, they should have seen them in action!'

'Yes, well' – the young man shrugged – 'you know how it is. Anyway, it's all over now and we got the money all right. Hell of a long way to go, though. Pity you couldn't have brought it with you.'

Morena glared. 'Pity we didn't let that bastard Ghad Ahmed have it in the beginning,' he said bitterly. 'It might have saved us all a lot of trouble. I don't suppose anybody gives a damn, anyway.'

' 'Fraid that's true,' the young man said easily. 'HM Government won't miss it when you consider what a penny duty on cigarettes brings in, in the course of a year.'

We got a lift to the coast in a car belonging to a couple of oil men, both of them so young they seemed to be children, and the aircraft we caught at the coast was full of more of them coming out, so full of hope and youth and energy they made me feel ancient.

We got a letter of thanks from the Ambassador and another from some vague department in London who said there'd eventually be a reward. But the department that had rustled up the money in 1942 had long since disappeared, they said, and the file had been passed around so much in the years between they'd almost forgotten about it, and it would take some time.

I never saw Phil again, though later I saw a picture in the paper of her, dressed in virgin white, getting married to Nimmo. 'EXPEDITION HERO MARRIES', the paper said. 'DESERT BROUGHT THEM TOGETHER'. Not half it didn't. So bloody close you couldn't have got a fig leaf between them.

Nimmo wasn't so different from his father, I thought. In fact, we'd all acted according to character in the end. Houston hadn't got what it took, and probably never had had, and Leach, the prize scrounger, had gone on scrounging to the limit and couldn't stop. Morena was still Morena and

I was still me, in just the same way, only more so. Nimmo had come out expecting to get a share of the loot and because he hadn't managed it he'd done just what his father would have done in the same circumstances and run off with somebody's girl instead.

As Morena said with a smile over the last beer at London Airport before we parted, me for Fleet Street again, him for his garage in Reading: 'It was always the same poor bastards who copped it and always the same clever sods who got all the credit.'

Which, when you come to think of it, was right all down the line.

Nothing had changed. We'd been arrogant enough to think we might be as good as we'd been twenty years before. But we weren't. We weren't. Only in the desert had time stood still. Only the desert remained the same, hiding everything, shrouding the good and the bad alike with its advancing sand, covering Crabourne and Selinski as it had the Paymaster and Houston and Leach, and Ghad Ahmed with his fervent ambition.

As we'd moved, the desert had closed behind us, the lonely wind obliterating the marks we'd made with our tyres, the sparse trampled grass taking fresh root, the shifting sand covering the ashes of the fires we'd built, so that anyone coming afterwards could never tell who'd gone before – so that there was nothing left except the limitless spaces and the timeless quality of the nights and mornings.

Only the young men with their instruments and energy knew how to deal with it. For men like us, working by the old methods, using wheels instead of wings and navigating by the seat of our pants, for us there was no going back, after all.

JOHN HARRIS

CHINA SEAS

In this action-packed adventure, Willie Sarth becomes a
survivor. Forced to fight pirates on the East China Seas,
wrestle for his life on the South China Seas and cross the Sea
of Japan ravaged by typhus, Sarth is determined to come out
alive. Dealing with human tragedy, war and revolution,
Harris presents a novel which packs an awesome punch.

A FUNNY PLACE TO HOLD A WAR

Ginger Donnelly is on the trail of Nazi saboteurs in Sierra
Leone. Whilst taking a midnight paddle, with a willing
woman, in a canoe cajoled from a local fisherman, Donnelly
sees an enormous seaplane thunder across the sky only to
crash in a ball of brilliant flame. It seems like an accident...
at least until a second plane explodes in a blistering shower
along the same flight path.

JOHN HARRIS

LIVE FREE OR DIE!

Charles Walter Scully, cut off from his unit and running on empty, is trapped. It's 1944 and, though the Allied invasion of France has finally begun, for Scully the war isn't going well. That is, until he meets a French boy trying to get home to Paris. What begins is a hair-raising journey into the heart of France, an involvement with the French Liberation Front and one of the most monumental events of the war. Harris vividly portrays wartime France in a panorama of scenes that enthral and entertain the reader.

THE SEA SHALL NOT HAVE THEM

This is John Harris' classic war novel of espionage in the most extreme of situations. An essential flight from France leaves the crew of RAF *Hudson* missing, and somewhere in the North Sea four men cling to a dinghy, praying for rescue before exposure kills them or the enemy finds them. One man is critically injured; another (a rocket expert) is carrying a briefcase stuffed with vital secrets. As time begins to run out each man yearns to evade capture. This story charts the daring and courage of these men, and the men who rescued them, in a breathtaking mission with the most awesome of consequences.

JOHN HARRIS

TAKE OR DESTROY!

Lieutenant-Colonel George Hockold must destroy Rommel's vast fuel reserves stored at the port of Qaba if the Eighth Army is to succeed in the Alamein offensive. Time is desperately running out, resources are scant and the commando unit Hockold must lead is a ragtag band of misfits scraped from the dregs of the British Army. They must attack Qaba. The orders? Take or destroy.

'One of the finest war novels of the year'
– *Evening News*

THE UNFORGIVING WIND

Charting the disastrous expedition of Commander Adams, this novel follows the misfortunes of his men across the Arctic after his sudden death. Whatever can go wrong does go wrong as transport, instruments, health and sanity begin to fail. The team seems irretrievably lost in the dark Arctic winter, frightened and half-starving even when it finds a base. Only one man can rescue them, the truculent Tom Fife who must respond to the faint radio signals coming from the Arctic shores. A powerful and disturbing novel, this story aims to take your breath away.

TITLES BY JOHN HARRIS AVAILABLE DIRECT
FROM HOUSE OF STRATUS

Quantity		£	$(US)	$(CAN)	€
☐	ARMY OF SHADOWS	6.99	12.95	19.95	13.50
☐	CHINA SEAS	6.99	12.95	19.95	13.50
☐	THE CLAWS OF MERCY	6.99	12.95	19.95	13.50
☐	CORPORAL COTTON'S LITTLE WAR	6.99	12.95	19.95	13.50
☐	THE CROSS OF LAZZARO	6.99	12.95	19.95	13.50
☐	FLAWED BANNER	6.99	12.95	19.95	13.50
☐	THE FOX FROM HIS LAIR	6.99	12.95	19.95	13.50
☐	A FUNNY PLACE TO HOLD A WAR	6.99	12.95	19.95	13.50
☐	GETAWAY	6.99	12.95	19.95	13.50
☐	HARKAWAY'S SIXTH COLUMN	6.99	12.95	19.95	13.50
☐	A KIND OF COURAGE	6.99	12.95	19.95	13.50
☐	LIVE FREE OR DIE!	6.99	12.95	19.95	13.50
☐	THE LONELY VOYAGE	6.99	12.95	19.95	13.50
☐	THE MERCENARIES	6.99	12.95	19.95	13.50
☐	NORTH STRIKE	6.99	12.95	19.95	13.50

ALL HOUSE OF STRATUS BOOKS ARE AVAILABLE FROM GOOD BOOKSHOPS
OR DIRECT FROM THE PUBLISHER:

Internet: www.houseofstratus.com including synopses and features.

Email: sales@houseofstratus.com
info@houseofstratus.com
(please quote author, title and credit card details.)

TITLES BY JOHN HARRIS AVAILABLE DIRECT
FROM HOUSE OF STRATUS

Quantity		£	$(US)	$(CAN)	€
	PICTURE OF DEFEAT	6.99	12.95	19.95	13.50
	THE QUICK BOAT MEN	6.99	12.95	19.95	13.50
	RIDE OUT THE STORM	6.99	12.95	19.95	13.50
	RIGHT OF REPLY	6.99	12.95	19.95	13.50
	ROAD TO THE COAST	6.99	12.95	19.95	13.50
	THE SEA SHALL NOT HAVE THEM	6.99	12.95	19.95	13.50
	THE SLEEPING MOUNTAIN	6.99	12.95	19.95	13.50
	SMILING WILLIE AND THE TIGER	6.99	12.95	19.95	13.50
	SO FAR FROM GOD	6.99	12.95	19.95	13.50
	THE SPRING OF MALICE	6.99	12.95	19.95	13.50
	SUNSET AT SHEBA	6.99	12.95	19.95	13.50
	SWORDPOINT	6.99	12.95	19.95	13.50
	TAKE OR DESTROY!	6.99	12.95	19.95	13.50
	THE THIRTY DAYS WAR	6.99	12.95	19.95	13.50
	THE UNFORGIVING WIND	6.99	12.95	19.95	13.50
	UP FOR GRABS	6.99	12.95	19.95	13.50
	VARDY	6.99	12.95	19.95	13.50

ALL HOUSE OF STRATUS BOOKS ARE AVAILABLE FROM GOOD BOOKSHOPS
OR DIRECT FROM THE PUBLISHER:

Tel:	Order Line
	0800 169 1780 (UK)
	1 800 724 1100 (USA)
	International
	+44 (0) 1845 527700 (UK)
	+01 845 463 1100 (USA)
Fax:	+44 (0) 1845 527711 (UK)
	+01 845 463 0018 (USA)
	(please quote author, title and credit card details.)

Send to:

House of Stratus Sales Department
Thirsk Industrial Park
York Road, Thirsk
North Yorkshire, YO7 3BX
UK

House of Stratus Inc.
2 Neptune Road
Poughkeepsie
NY 12601
USA

PAYMENT

Please tick currency you wish to use:

09/04

☐ £ (Sterling)   ☐ $ (US)   ☐ $ (CAN)   ☐ € (Euros)

Allow for shipping costs charged per order plus an amount per book as set out in the tables below:

CURRENCY/DESTINATION

	£(Sterling)	$(US)	$(CAN)	€(Euros)
Cost per order				
UK	1.50	2.25	3.50	2.50
Europe	3.00	4.50	6.75	5.00
North America	3.00	3.50	5.25	5.00
Rest of World	3.00	4.50	6.75	5.00
Additional cost per book				
UK	0.50	0.75	1.15	0.85
Europe	1.00	1.50	2.25	1.70
North America	1.00	1.00	1.50	1.70
Rest of World	1.50	2.25	3.50	3.00

PLEASE SEND CHEQUE OR INTERNATIONAL MONEY ORDER
payable to: HOUSE OF STRATUS LTD or HOUSE OF STRATUS INC. or card payment as indicated

STERLING EXAMPLE

Cost of book(s):..................... Example: 3 x books at £6.99 each: £20.97

Cost of order: .... Example: £1.50 (Delivery to UK address)

Additional cost per book:............. Example: 3 x £0.50: £1.50

Order total including shipping:.......... Example: £23.97

VISA, MASTERCARD, SWITCH, AMEX:

☐ ☐ ☐ ☐ ☐ ☐ ☐ ☐ ☐ ☐ ☐ ☐ ☐ ☐ ☐ ☐ ☐ ☐ ☐ ☐

Issue number (Switch only):

☐ ☐ ☐

Start Date: Expiry Date:

☐ ☐ / ☐ ☐   ☐ ☐ / ☐ ☐

Signature: _____

NAME: _____

ADDRESS: _____

COUNTRY: _____

ZIP/POSTCODE: _____

Please allow 28 days for delivery. Despatch normally within 48 hours.

Prices subject to change without notice.
Please tick box if you do not wish to receive any additional information. ☐

House of Stratus publishes many other titles in this genre; please check our website (www.houseofstratus.com) for more details.